CONFLICT CONTRACT

Jonathan Miller

D1368405

COOL
TITLES

T I T L E S

Published by
Cool Titles
439 N. Canon Dr., Suite 200
Beverly Hills, CA 90210
www.cooltitles.com

The Library of Congress Cataloging-in-Publication Data Applied For

Jonathan Miller—
Conflict Contract

p.   cm
ISBN 978-1935270027
1. Mystery   2. American Southwest   3. Legal Thriller   I. Title
2010

Printed in the United States of America

1 3 5 7 9 10 8 6 4 2

Book editing and design by Lisa Wysocky, White Horse Enterprises, Inc.

For interviews or information regarding special discounts for bulk purchases,
please contact us at
njohnson@jjllplaw.com

Distribution to the Trade: Pathway, Book Service,
www.pathwaybook.com, pbs@pathwaybook.com, 1-800-345-6665

Also by Jonathan Miller

Rattlesnake Lawyer
Crater County
Amarillo in August
Volcano Verdict
LaBajada Lawyer

To Ned Miller

Part I

FRIDAY
SONG: "Albuquerque" by Trevor McShane

G-SPOT

IT WAS THE WORST POSSIBLE time for the phone to ring.

Four-fifty in the afternoon marked the end of visiting hours in Albuquerque's Metropolitan Detention Center. I hoped to finish my last minute trip to G7 Pod—the "G-Spot," as the aggravated-battery and armed-robbery residents called it—by five. I hated going all the way out to MDC, way out in the high desert. Unfortunately, my clients all begged me to save them before the weekend rush.

They expected me to be Moses and let my people go.

Moses never had a cell phone. I ignored the first ring and scanned the inmates' angry faces. This pod held sixty residents stacked in two layers of cells surrounding the concrete courtyard. I sat at a plastic table under the single skylight, talking with a client named Alejandro, who was a rather petite armed robber.

I just explained why a deferred sentence was better than a suspended sentence, but not quite as good as a conditional discharge, and then explained it again, and again. Alejandro kept asking me hypothetical questions: the Socratic method on speed.

"Maybe you should study physics in the jail library, and then you can invent a time machine so you can go back and get rid of your prior felonies," was my last sentence before the phone rang.

Ten other inmates huddled around our plastic table, staring at me like a coach who just called the wrong play. On the second ring, their expression abruptly changed. I was the loose football and they wanted to pounce. Would I be stupid enough to answer my phone in the middle of the G-Spot?

Alejandro had a tattoo of a beautiful naked brunette on his forearm. "Maybe it's my girlfriend calling," he said, pointing to the tattoo. "I gave her your number."

"Yo. Clark Kent," another inmate said, commenting on my resemblance to Superman's mild-mannered alter ego: horn-rimmed glasses and a dark suit. "You better turn that shit off before the guard goes kryptonite on your ass."

I had five rings before the phone shifted the call to voicemail. Hopefully the Correctional Officer (CO) wouldn't notice. The metal detector didn't pick it up during my entrance to the facility. What else did that metal detector miss?

On the third ring, the CO awoke from her reverie. "You're not supposed to have a phone in here." Virginia Villalobos, aka Double V, was a stickler for the rules. Hispanic, she bleached her Marine buzz-cut with God knows what. I had represented her on a juvenile domestic-violence charge years ago, but she pretended to forget my assistance. Once a wiry woman, now her pregnant belly could easily hold octuplets.

Did the ink from the tattooed devils on her arms seep into her womb with all the other bad influences from the jail? Pregnancy made her even moodier, but every visit she constantly complained about sticking with the job for the pre-natal health-care benefits.

Her control desk offered little protection from the elements or the inmates—no bullet -proof screen, just empty air. She pressed a button on her control panel with her long metallic fingernail.

"I said, aren't you going to get that?" Double V shouted, pressing another button. "Don't you wanna know who's responsible for ruining your visiting privileges forever?"

"Dude, you better pick it up," Alejandro said. "If you piss her off, she'll take it out on the whole pod."

I squeezed my obsolete cell phone, a gift from a client who supplied half the pimps and drug dealers in town. He swore he'd get me a better one with all the bells and whistles the next time he got popped. How do you get this damn thing to "vibrate" mode?

Private Number.

It could be a potential client, hopefully one with money. It might be the magic phone call from Hollywood. It could even be Alejandro's girlfriend, who said she'd call me with the number of a character witness.

"Dude, pick it up." Alejandro urged. "Before it's too late."

A buzzer echoed throughout the unit. Not just a lockdown buzzer, this was louder, faster, like the two-minute warning for the Apocalypse. Double V looked at the control panel anxiously, then at me. Had I caused Armageddon at the end of the shift?

"Hello?" I shouted into the phone.

Nothing came from the other end. The inmate huddle laughed harder. Alejandro might have muttered another "dude."

"Hello?"

The buzzing stopped abruptly.

My last "hello" echoed throughout the concrete walls of the G-Spot, bouncing off the heads of the inmates along the way.

"This is Dan Shepard, Attorney at Law," I said. "Shepard with an 'a,'" I added out of habit.

"Dan," she said, her slight Spanish lilt rolled like piñon-covered hills. "It's me, Luna."

Luna Cruz, lawyer turned judge. Our history together could

fill a book. The huddle tightened around me, straining to catch every word.

"Do you mind?" I asked.

They didn't retreat an inch. They could easily gang tackle me before Double V threw a flag or pressed a button. Another semicircle blocked any scramble to the rear.

"Sorry, you're catching me at a really bad time. I'm in jail."

"Jail?"

"I'm not a resident. I'm visiting clients, but I don't have much time."

She took a deep breath. "My daughter's been kidnapped."

"Kidnapped?" I asked. "Judge, ah, Luna, did you say your child was kidnapped?"

Instantly I realized my fatal error: saying Luna's name and the word "judge" out loud in the pod.

"Serves that bitch right," an inmate mumbled. Everybody in MDC knew Luna Cruz, aka "Judge Looney Toons."

Several inmates hurried to the G-Spot's three house phones, playing a massive game of Jailhouse Telegraph. Even Double V got into the act, whispering into the intercom. The entire state would know before nightfall. A kidnapped daughter of an unpopular judge was big news in the underworld.

"Is there anything I can do?" I asked, trying to talk as softly as possible.

"Just come to my loft as soon as you can," she said. "Everybody's here. I just need all my friends right now."

"I'll get there as soon as I can."

"One more thing," she said. "Jen's back."

I sat down suddenly after a rush of blood drained out of my brain. "She's back?" Jen and I had once been engaged to be engaged. We then disengaged. We had not talked in months. Jen was Luna's half-sister, even though Jen was Korean while Luna was Hispanic. Same father, different mother.

"She hasn't called you yet?" Luna sounded surprised. "She's been back for a couple of weeks."

"No. She hasn't called me."

"I'm sorry that you two stopped talking. But really, I never thought you were right for each other. I still can't believe that after I dumped you, you went for my sister."

"Half-sister," I said. "Jesus, she looks Korean, how was I supposed to know?"

"There's something else," she said. "I'm worried that Jen might be in real danger."

The inmates closed their huddle tighter. "Get here as soon as you can," Luna said. "If you hear from Jen, bring her right over where it's safe."

"I'll try." I hung up, and put the phone guiltily into my shirt pocket. The murmuring in the G-Spot increased. As the newest judge, Luna had handled the bond arraignments for most of these men. They met her under the worst possible circumstances.

"That bitch is holding me with no evidence!" an inmate shouted. "My bond is a million dollars on a shoplifting."

"You know Judge Looney Toons, *ese?*" Alejandro asked. "You ever tap that ass?"

"None of your damn business," I said.

The buzzers began again. The jail lights blinked a few times, then went dark. A single beam from the dying sun peeked through the small skylight.

The G-Spot's three wall phones still worked—for the moment. Three inmates simultaneously whispered through the ancient black receivers to their homies on the outside. I distinctly heard the words "Judge" "Looney" and "toons" between the buzzes.

The lights flashed again, an angry strobe light.

"Oh shit," Double V said as she stared at a blinking light on her control panel. She rubbed her belly, and then appeared to pray silently to the angel tattooed on her arm. She took a deep breath, and then took another.

"Lock down!" Double V shouted. "Everyone get back to your cells!"

The inmates hurried back to the edge of their cells. Without power, the doors wouldn't close. The inmates stayed out in the pod.

"Don't you go anywhere!" Double V yelled to me. She looked at me with the eyes of a seventeen-year-old drunk driver right before her disposition. She was even more afraid than I was. I knew I should do something, but what?

An inmate walked toward the door to the outside world, and pulled. Unfortunately for him that door stayed very much locked.

"I said, don't anybody go anywhere. All of you!" Double V enunciated the words "I said," as if practicing to be a mother.

"I don't think there's anywhere we can go," I said.

FIVE O'CLOCK LOCKDOWN

I'M NOT SUPPOSED TO BE here.

Five o'clock sharp, the sun hurtled toward a head-on collision with the desert horizon. I hated coming here so late in the afternoon, but if you missed the mornings, you couldn't get in until four because they were locked down for count. Inside the pod, the inmates kept chattering about "Judge Looney Toons."

"Who did she have to blow to get her job?" An inmate shouted from the second floor.

"Show some respect," I said. "She is a judge after all."

"Remember what happened to Judge O'Hare," a first floor inmate said. "He got arrested on drunk driving and ended up here over in Seg Nine."

"I shanked him," a voice shouted from the shadows.

A hand-made knife was a shank, right? Or was that a shiv?

"I don't care whether you like Judge Looney Toons or not, but her child has been kidnapped! You guys hate people who fuck with kids!"

The jail locked sex offenders in "Chester units" after some notorious criminal called "Chester the Molester." One of my sex offender clients was killed by a mop handle when mistakenly put in this very unit. The mop handle exited through the top of my client's skull. I didn't want to imagine its point of entry.

The sheer emotion of my words shut them up for the moment. I stood up for Luna's honor a lot, although she could be arbitrary and capricious. The woman inspired intense emotion, pro and con, sometimes at the same moment.

"Whatever." Double V shrugged her shoulders. "It's lock down, lawyer. No one goes in or out. We don't got no power, so I can't open their cells or close them. Just be cool. Be cool."

Had I ever been cool? A few months ago a powerful producer was "considering" my self-published public defender diary, *Legal Coyote*, as a potential TV series. I truly felt cool as the coolest cucumber for the first time in my life, but coolness had a half-life of three weeks. I soon reverted to my Clark Kent persona.

Cool certainly wasn't the word to describe me right now, "super" didn't apply either. Men of steel didn't spontaneously combust in sweat and start rusting.

"You be cool too, V," I said. "Let's both be cool."

She nodded at me. We were both in this together. She expected me to protect her, and her unborn children if things got ugly. She had one can of mace at best, and maybe a billy club. She probably wouldn't be able to swing very hard.

I was the white boy among the Na'vi in the film *Avatar*, and the Na'vi were pissed.

I moved to the one empty table closest to Double V's desk. The inmates stared at me like a day-old bologna lunch, not something they wanted, but something they would devour if need be.

"Stay the fuck in your cells," she told the inmates. They kept one foot in and one foot out, doing the hokey pokey from hell.

"We've still got a few moments of sunlight left," I said. "Remember, the video cameras are still rolling."

Then my phone rang again. Damn!

"It's for me!" Alejandro shouted. "I told you it's my girl. Tell her I'm all right."

Double V shrugged. "Let the outside world know what's going on."

The phone rang again — a number with a 310 area code. Beverly Hills. I answered immediately.

"Dan, it's Jen Song," she said. Jen used her last name as if I could possibly forget it. "Sorry I didn't call you sooner. I've been back for a while."

No time to catch up. "Have you heard about Luna and her daughter?"

"She left me a message about a kidnapping. I tried and tried, but I couldn't get through to her."

"Yeah," I said. "Luna called me too. That's all I know so far. Are you all right? She was worried about you."

"I'm fine. I guess."

"Why the hell didn't you call me when you got back?" I asked. "How long have you been in Albuquerque?"

"I can't really talk right now," she said. "Let's just say my whole life has gone into the toilet. And I didn't want to burden you. I'm stuck at the airport and the airport is closed because of the sand storm."

"Are you coming in?"

"No, I told you, I've been here. I'm leaving. I had to get the hell of out of dodge, like right now."

"I'm kinda tied up right now, too," I said, trying not to betray any emotion, and failing. Why was Jen in town? What had she been doing the past few weeks? Why was she leaving?

An inmate flushed, and I jumped.

"There's something jamming the toilet," he called loudly to Double V.

Perhaps it was my heart.

"Dan," she said. Somehow she stretched the one syllable of my name into three. "I really, really need a ride to Luna's house. The airport is totally closed because there's like no visibility at all. They sent everybody home."

"Jen, I'm stuck in jail during a lockdown and I think the natives are getting restless," I whispered a little too loudly.

A big Navajo heard me and shot me a glance. "Who you calling a Native, asshole?" Some other inmates laughed. Their hokey got way more pokey. They left their cells behind and stood in a ring around the pod.

"Dan, I'm sure you'll be fine," Jen said. "But I feel that somehow the kidnapping has something to do with me."

"I don't know, Jen. I think a lot of people hated Judge Looney Toons."

"Don't call her that!" Jen was mad. "No one hates her! Everybody loves her!"

At least sixty residents of this pod disagreed, but I certainly didn't want to bring that up now. More inmates whispered in each others' ears.

"It's my fault," she said.

"Jen, I'm sure it's not your fault."

"Well, if you can make it to the airport soon, please pick me up and take me to Luna's. I can't get through to her and I'm so worried."

"I don't know," I said. The inmates moved another inch from their cells. "I just don't know. You totally broke my heart, Jen. I don't know if I want to see you again."

"Come by if you change your mind. Please, I need you. I really, really need you."

"You never needed me." I could fill a whole pod with the men Jen had while she was supposedly with me. Hell, some of them might be in here right now. "You never loved me! Why don't you call one of the twenty other million dudes you fucked in L.A.? Hell, who knows how many dudes you fucked when you were *allegedly* with me?"

I hung up and instantly regretted it. What had I just done?

"You're harsh, dude," Alejandro said. "You know what the difference is between you and me?"

"What's that?"

"My girl calls back after I pull that shit," he said. "And I won't back down. But you're you, and I'm me. You'll have to totally kiss your girl's ass."

"I don't know if she was ever my girl."

The speakers buzzed again, louder this time, and faster, like an air raid. The F-16s from Kirtland Air Force Base were only twenty miles away, perhaps the powers that be just wanted to cut their losses and destroy the facility in order to save it.

Heavy footsteps echoed down the G hallway. They passed us, past G2, G3, all the way to G4 at the end of the Pod. The sounds of batons cracking on flesh lingered in the air. Inmates on the top row tapped messages to the cells behind them; the riot spread like a virus.

"Is anybody out there?" Double V spoke into the mike, anxious. She glanced up at the sun and then at the inmates. "I said . . . anybody?"

She rubbed her belly, and then touched her angel tattoo as if it was some kind of ritual.

I shivered. I barely survived my single night here in solitary. Sometimes what you *don't* hear scares you the most.

The last slivers of sunlight lit the pod in an unearthly pinkish glow. This felt like prison on Mars. In the Santa Fe prison riots, an hour from here, inmates had played volleyball with people's heads, soccer too. The State turned the facility into a movie set, but hadn't bleached out the blood because the directors liked the authenticity.

Authenticity? It didn't get more authentic than this.

"I said, everybody stay calm and in your god damn cells!" Double V shouted. "All the way in!"

Who was in worse danger, her or me? Whose head would make the better volleyball?

I had earned a smidgen of respect from the inmates in this facility to be sure, but how much? They wouldn't rape a pregnant woman, would they? I didn't know. Criminals were capable of anything.

"I'm here for you, V," I said.

"What does that mean, exactly?" she said.

"I don't know."

"Did you happen to smuggle a gun in with that phone?"

"Not exactly."

Several inmates left their cells and gathered at the furthest table, like the defense huddling to diagram a quarterback blitz.

"I heard this was going down a couple weeks ago," someone said. "The whole Judge Looney Toons thing. The guys in F pod were always talking that she was going to 'get hers someday.'"

"I heard about it from someone over in Crater County."

"I heard about it when I was down in the Cruces jail."

"The hit was on!"

The camera lights no longer flashed red. The outside world didn't care about us anymore. A few inmates sported hoods fashioned out of pillowcases. They could pass for sloppy Klansman as they shuffled down to join the others at the far table. Some used towels; others used t-shirts. One even used his dirty underwear. The inmates from the upper level walked slowly down the stairs.

"Bitch. Bitch. Bitch." They chanted. That couldn't be a good thing.

Every inmate had made it as far as three feet out of his cell. "Bitch, bitch, bitch."

Were they referring to me, or Double V? Were they using the word as a noun, or even scarier, as a *verb*?

"You ever been a bitch, *ese*?" A hooded figure asked. I couldn't make out the directions of the voices in the echoes.

"He's my lawyer," Alejandro said. He didn't have his hood on yet, but he did have a pillowcase in his hands. "He can be good. Sometimes."

"Remember how he got that Jesús dude off down in Aguilar," someone else shouted.

"And that crazy bitch, too," another said. "The dude's got *skillz*."

"He's all right," someone said from upstairs.

"Thank you, whoever you are," I whispered.

"But remember what happened to my brother," another shouted from the gaggle of hooded inmates that were now only ten feet away from me. "He fucked up the order and commitment and the guy did an extra five months." Was that the Navajo who had snapped at me? How many inmates in here had brothers whose cases I'd lost?

I didn't win all my cases. No lawyer did. Sometimes I took deals that sounded good, only to watch a co-defendant take it to trial and triumph. I had rejected pleas for probation and then gone down swinging. My entire caseload flashed before my eyes.

"Just remember I'm the only lawyer here right now," I said. "With times so tough, no other lawyer comes out here to see you guys as much as I do. I come once a week."

"Once a week?" Was that Alejandro's voice behind a hood?

"Well at least twice a month," I said. "I work my ass for you!"

"Nice ass, *ese.*"

One of the side effects of being a lawyer was that you actually gave a shit about people nobody cared about. Did I still give a shit?

Why did I keep coming here for these fuckers?

Alejandro had smiled when I entered the pod just fifteen

minutes earlier. When I came here, more often than not, people were glad to see me.

Jail made sense. It was simple. Bad people were locked up. If I did my job, they got out in less time. Not too hard to understand. The rest of my life was messed up. I didn't have that many friends who weren't lawyers or criminals, and most of my lawyer friends were busy.

My criminals called me all the time, so did their mothers, fathers and sometimes two or three baby mamas.

The phone rang again. Jen's number flashed on the tiny screen. "I told you I don't want to hear from you right now! Maybe ever!" I said, before hanging up.

More guards passed through the outside corridors. Everyone inside tensed until the footsteps kept going, down to G-1. Six more pods to go before they came to us.

"How much time you think we got?" one asked.

"Plenty," another responded.

"Used, abused and losed," a hooded person shouted at no one in particular, laughing. Was he talking about Luna's child, Double V, or me?

The pinkish glow of the Pod faded into gray. The shadows grew longer, like an old horror movie. My pronouncements spared me a few minutes, max.

"Please go back to your cells," Double V said. "Please, I'm begging you." It was not a good thing for a CO to use the word "please" or the word "beg."

Tapping came from the other side of the wall. The inmates on this side tapped something back. Was it Morse code?

If we survived the next five minutes, we would have one hell of a lawsuit against the jail. I just wouldn't be around to collect. Who did I name in my will? My family?

Not Jen, she wasn't family any more . . .

The tapping grew louder. Screw you Samuel Morse! My heirs could sue him for inventing Morse Code so the inmates could plan a riot.

The sun officially set over the other side of MDC. The hooded inmates kept whispering, definitely plotting something, like an insurgent military operation.

And yet, they waited.

"He's not so bad," one said from beneath his hood.

"Fuck him, he's a lawyer," his neighbor said. "He's the enemy."

When Dorothy landed in Oz the munchkins debated whether she was a good witch or a bad witch. I was both. Or perhaps I wasn't a witch at all.

"Oh, shit baby," Double V said. She wasn't talking to me.

I walked back over to the desk and stood by Double V. When they came after her, they'd have to get by me first.

How long would that take?

Would I really fight back?

God, I hoped I wouldn't cry . . .

"Bitch. Bitch. Bitch."

"Who wants to go first?" an inmate shouted. Someone had left a mop out by the toilet. A hooded inmate grabbed the mop, and starting mopping ominously. When did I ever fear a mop?

"Out, out damn spot," he said. He stared at me. "To mop or not to mop?"

Great. I would be raped by the one inmate who could quote Shakespeare.

HEY GOOD BOOKING

JUST WHEN AN UNEASY SILENCE settled over the pod, the lights came on and the outside door clicked open. An armed guard cautiously poked his inside, and then pointed his gun directly at the inmate holding the mop. "We're in lockdown. Into your cells, now!"

The inmate hesitated

"I'm serious!" The guard said. "And I'm going make the rest of y'all mop his blood off the floor."

That did it. The mopper put down the mop, and then backed away. The others slowly dispersed back toward their cells.

"I said now!" The armed guard reached for his gun. He cocked it. The sound echoed through the pod.

The hooded inmates mumbled one last time, then reluctantly returned to their cells, and pulled all extremities inside.

The cell doors closed automatically. Once the doors were firmly locked, the guard hurried to the desk. "You okay, V?"

"Yeah."

He finally took a glance in my direction. I was third on the depth chart of his caring. "You okay, Mr. Lawyer?"

"I guess," I said, letting out a deep breath. God, I hoped Luna and her child were all right.

Alejandro waved as his cell door shut. "You're one cool lawyer, *ese*."

"Thanks," I said. I'm glad he couldn't smell my underwear.

I walked over to Double V and escorted her out. She gave me a hug the moment we were out of the Pod. "You saved my life," she said.

"Just doing my job," I said. "Just like last time when you were my client and I was your lawyer."

"You were a shitty lawyer," she said. "You just got lucky."

That hurt.

Was I really a shitty lawyer?

• • • • •

The main entrance remained closed because of the lockdown. "We'll have to take you out through booking," a tiny guard, the size of a jockey said. Tiny took me down a strange corridor lit by amber emergency lights, like a Berlin fetish club. I wasn't home free yet. After a few more wrong turns in the dark, Tiny took me down another corridor to the booking area.

"Just be patient," Tiny said. "I don't know if we can let anyone out yet. You might have to spend the night here."

"You're not booking me, are you?"

"Should we?" Tiny turned to go. "Just wait here until we figure out what to do with you."

Inside a booking room, a photographer took a mug shot of a new inmate, as if contemplating a fashion shoot, looking for the best angle. The inmate still wore street clothes—a black leather jacket over a black shirt. With his deliberate stubble, he could be prepping for a photo session for a jeans company. His wore a black baseball cap for *Desert Demons*, the biggest movie shoot in New Mexico since *Terminator Salvation*. A gold statue lay next to his left leg. How did the booking guard miss that?

That statue was an Oscar! Who took an Oscar to jail?

The photographer stared at me.

"I'm not an inmate," I said. I flashed my attorney ID. "I'm a lawyer."

"I've taken a lot of mug-shots of lots of lawyers," the photographer said. "We just have to hold the exposure a little longer because they sometimes don't have a reflection, like a vampire. Just sit down and wait, they'll be back in a minute."

I sat next to the inmate. "Try to get my good side."

"I know you," the inmate said. He had blurred watery eyes and slurred speech to go with his strong odor of alcohol. At least his breath smelled good, like licorice. He must be drinking the 160 proof Absinthe that was now street-legal in New Mexico.

It took me another moment; it had been over ten years. "Sky Roberts," I said. "What the hell are you doing here?"

The Oscar stared at me. Sky "Sky High" Roberts won it for *writing,* of all things. He'd written a script about his dysfunctional life as a child actor—Robert Downey Jr. meets River and Joaquin Phoenix. This drunken asshole could barely spell his name, and he had an Adapted Screenplay Oscar of his Pulitzer Prize winning book?

I had my un-read self-published book, and a few un-read scripts, but these days I had trouble finishing "motions to reconsider conditions of release."

He spit. "I was minding my own business doing a movie until that cunt judge locked me up."

I didn't have to ask the identity of the judge.

He stared at me blankly. "You're that lawyer, right? From that old case when you represented that kid, yeah?"

I nodded. A long time ago I worked as a public defender in the small town of Aguilar, and he testified against my client while on location filming a movie.

"Well, you tell that cunt judge that she is so fucking dead." Before he could say anything more, he passed out on the floor.

"Did you hear that?" I asked the photographer. "He made a threat against a judge."

The photographer laughed. "Everyone who comes in here makes a death threat against somebody."

"Maybe he knows something about the kidnapping," I said.

Sky Roberts vomited and shit his pants simultaneously.

The photographer laughed. "He kinda has an alibi, doncha think?"

SMILY COYOTE

I FINALLY EMERGED FROM THE last doorway of MDC, maybe six in the evening. The darkness was total. The desert air tasted of freedom, but only for a moment. I knew why the airport was closed, as the wind blew dust straight from Arizona, and cactus shards pricked every exposed inch of my body. I felt like I had swallowed an entire Saguaro before I reached the safety of my car.

The authorities once found thirteen dead bodies buried in the desert around here. I didn't want to be unlucky number fourteen.

I had tried to call Luna again from the inside, but hit a busy signal. Could she be negotiating with the kidnappers? Suppose my stupid call waiting signal interrupted her negotiations? I hung up. The dust obscured the glittering Albuquerque skyline a few miles of desert away. The sandstorm felt biblical, like judgment day, or perhaps the eleventh plague.

I wasn't the only sinner out there. In the space next to me, a car vibrated from the motions of people dry humping. *How ghetto.*

Sitting, I felt a cracking sound. I squirmed to find a CD of the noted alternative artist/guitarist, Trevor McShane and cranked out the first track, a moody instrumental called "Albuquerque." After all this shit, I was still in Albuquerque, much like Martin Sheen was stuck in Saigon at the start of *Apocalypse Now*.

Feeling another sharp pang, I shifted positions and picked up the remnants of a tiny greenish rock from the car seat. It probably came from my recent trip to the Trinity site, where the first Atom bomb was tested back in 1945. I had proposed to Jen there, and the radioactivity had a half-life longer than the relationship. I really needed to sterilize my car, instead of shifting the debris from one seat to another. I put the rock in the glove compartment.

My entire case-load spread over my back seat nestled amidst the other debris of my life. Files, motions, orders mixed in with underwear, sweat socks and a stray screenplay. I had a Conflict Contract through the Public Defender's department, handling cases all over the state—cases the department didn't want or couldn't take because of ethical conflicts. The Public Defender Department kept Marlin Brando, the Godfather. Local contract attorneys got the Al Pacinos or even the James Caans. The out-of-town conflict contract guy inevitably got the Fredo Corleones of the criminal world. The state actually paid me less than Pacino's Scarface would get for selling a bag of crack cocaine.

I picked up the scattered pages of the *Legal Coyote* screenplay off the floor, and put it in a pile next to an aggravated battery case file. I liked aggravated batterers better than agents. Batterers were quicker at returning phone calls. Until now, crime paid, at least more than a one-dollar Hollywood option agreement.

Clunk.

I ran over something on the drive out of the parking lot. Looking in my rear view mirror, I couldn't see anything in the dust. I hurried out, just in case I had run over a body. In the glow of the red tail lights, I found a dead roadrunner. Real roadrunners were a lot smaller than their cartoon counterparts, and were definitely mortal. It was too windy to stay outside to bury it.

I hurried back to the car, and beep-beeped my horn in a fitting memorial. A dead roadrunner had to be a sign of something. Something bad. The coyote should never win.

I punched the air. Why had I hung up on Jen? When did I become such an asshole? After she broke my heart, of course. Still, I kept a special place in my heart for her, somewhere next to the left ventricle.

I dialed the 310 number. *"The number is currently out of service."* The airport was only five minutes from Luna's house, maybe I should pick Jen up after all.

My phone rang again.

Does this thing ever stop ringing? "Luna? Jen?" I shouted into the phone.

I could barely hear over the sandstorm. A tumbleweed the size of an SUV struck me head on.

I didn't want to stay so close to MDC, but I picked up the phone on the second ring. Tumbleweeds kept hitting me dead on, shook the car for a moment, then disintegrated in another burst of wind.

That, too, had to be a bad omen.

"Hello?" I said.

"Dan Shepard?" It was a woman's voice, but it wasn't Luna or Jen—*private number.* "With an 'a?'"

"That's me. Who is this?"

"I don't think you remember me. My name is Anastasia, like the Russian princess, but you might remember me as Nastia." Her accent sounded Russian, like Natasha from *Bullwinkle.*

"Nastia?"

"We met before, a few months ago, *da?*"

The image formed in my mind. I didn't know someone with a royal name like Anastasia, but I did know a Nastia. Pretty face, very short, part Eskimo or something. How did I know her again? She had blown me off for a date, like everyone else after Jen. I tended to forget women like that very quickly. "You're Eskimo?"

"My mother was," she said. "Inupiat to be precise. Remember I told you we could see America from my island, yes?"

I hummed an old Marine chant from *Full Metal Jacket*. *"I don't know but I've been told, Eskimo pussy is mighty cold."*

"How do I know you again?"

"Remember me from the Ends Zone?" The Ends Zone was a gentlemen's club off the freeway. "We talked for an hour that night. I told you 'It's always good to know a lawyer.'"

I went through a strip club phase after Jen broke my heart. On New Year's Eve, totally alone, I had nowhere else to go.

"On Stage One, escaping all the way from Siberia: Nasty Nastia"

A very short, very pale woman dressed in half a gymnast outfit did splits up on stage one to a rap-reggae remix of the Beatles' *Back in the USSR*. She did an upside down twirl, ten feet up the pole, as the rapper intoned *"The Ukraine girls really knock me out. They leave the west behind."* She had literally left gravity behind as she stuck a perfect dismount onto Stage One.

Just for that dismount alone, I dropped twenty bucks into her g-string—all that remained of the gymnast outfit.

She had indeed sat with me for an hour, maybe two, and I told her about writing a screenplay about the real story of Clayton Lonetree, the Navajo Marine in Moscow who was busted for espionage during the cold war. Unfortunately, everyone in Hollywood said neither Russia nor New Mexico were particularly compelling.

She had smiled at me, "You're compelling to me. And you're not that old." She even took my card.

"We were supposed to go out that one time," I said. "At Starbucks."

The image of the pale gymnast in her sweats pulling up to the downtown Starbucks and then driving away was imprinted my brain.

"I was tempted, yes. But I can never betray my *nastoyashaya lyobov*," she said. "My true love."

I remembered her text. *"U r cool, but I luv someone 2 much."*

"Let's not talk about true love right now. How can I help you Nastia?"

"Well my true love, my *nastoyashaya lyobov*, will save Luna's child."

I felt a chill through my spine. "How? Who?"

"You are still lawyer, *da?"* She said.

"I guess."

"You will meet again during the next week. You already know my *nastoyashaya lyobov*."

"I do?" I had the week from hell coming up — clients in Estancia, Crater, Las Cruces, Santa Fe, as well as a handful in Albuquerque. Did any have a fiancé named Nastia? Then again, all my clients' girlfriends this week had weird names. One guy's girl was Africa. Another was Asia. "What's your *lyobov's* name?"

Another tumbleweed flew by in the night.

"I can't talk. They might be listening to your calls. I'm at a pay phone."

Perhaps her exotic accent explained her cold war paranoia. I truly doubted that Boris Badenov wanted to tap my phone. "Just tell me how I can help you, Miss Nastia."

The sand roared even harder. I honked at the passing roadrunner convoy. They were heading away from MDC like rats deserting a sinking ship.

"You don't understand. I can help *you*. My *lyobov* can save Luna's child. You do want to save Luna's child, *da?"*

"Of course." I could play hero without even trying that hard. "Where is he? When can I talk to him?"

"My *lyobov* is unavailable." She had problems with her "l" sound; it came out sounding like a "W."

"Unavailable?" I asked. "Is he in a jail? In MDC? I just left there. . . ."

"Been in jail, out now," she said. "Maybe back again soon."

"Where?"

"I don't want to say," she said. She said "want," like "vant." "Not when I know you're on a cell phone. It's not safe. They can find out anything, *da?*"

"Who can find out anything?"

"The bad guys."

More tumbleweeds passed by my headlights, like wildebeest running from a National Geographic photographer.

"Hello?" I asked. "Are you still there?"

Did a tumbleweed just laugh at me? I heard traffic, sirens, coming from her end. "You have to go, miss," a male voice said from the other side.

"I don't have any more time," she said. "You'll see my *lyobov* this week. Soon. You'll know. You'll just know."

"I'll know?"

"You'll know when the time is right. My *nastoyashaya lyobov* will save the little girl."

"Good luck with that. And that's going to happen next week?"

"If everything works out, it will. Or soon. *Das vedanya.*"

Nothing more from the other end, as if the woman had been blown away in the wind.

"Hello? Nastia?"

Nothing.

This would all work out. I just needed to find one of my clients this week. He'd give me that clue that would break the case wide open. We'd give that clue to the FBI, and I'd be the hero.

Behind me the dead roadrunner suddenly came to life. Instead of crossing the road, it headed right toward me. It didn't yell out a "beep, beep," but I didn't want to wait. I slammed my foot on the ignition and drove like hell into the wind, crushing a few more tumbleweeds on the way. So the coyote didn't win after all.

My car finally escaped the zombie roadrunner once I sped onto I-40 at the Paseo del Volcan entrance. Heroes aren't scared of roadrunners, but my life resembled a Wile E. Coyote film festival: one failure after another. Even after I succeeded, the state inevitably convicted my client the next time. It was an endless loop.

Should I try to pick up Jen? Or was Alejandro right and it was all over? I was the Wile E. Coyote of love as well as law.

TWILIGHT BONE

THE DUST STORM BLOCKED ALL the bland subdivisions and truck stops on both sides of the freeway. I didn't pass any traffic in either direction. Odd for a Friday rush hour. More tumbleweeds than cars headed down I-40; the weeds actually drove better than most New Mexicans. At least they stayed in their lanes.

I tried to call Luna, and then tried to call Jen. The calls didn't go through. Maybe the sand swallowed everything electronic. I couldn't call nasty Nastia. Was she even real at all?

I looked down to double-check, unknown number.

I still hadn't made up my mind about picking up Jen when I passed under the massive Coors Boulevard interchange. Only in New Mexico would they name a major boulevard after a brewer. New Mexico usually led the nation in drunk driving . . . and deaths by lightning.

Although it was so foggy I couldn't tell, my Saturn must have crossed the bridge over the muddy waters of the Rio Grande, as the lights of the "Big I" interchange barely penetrated through the fog. The car drifted into the right lane and headed south on I-25. Luna's house was a mile further, the airport and Jen lay just a few miles past that.

The lights of downtown barely penetrated the sandstorm. The pyramid shaped summit of the tallest building in town glowed orange. On a night like this, the Albuquerque skyline belonged on a business park on the moon.

Approaching the main downtown exit, Martin Luther King Boulevard / Central Avenue, I finally reached Luna. "Jen called and said she's at the airport," I said. "Should I—"

"Pick her up!" Luna said. "She's in great danger. Get her here immediately. Keep this line clear!"

My pulse quickened. Jen scared me far more than the inmates did.

· · · · ·

Three miles south, the sign for Sunport Boulevard, the airport exit, appeared out of the mist. After a near-collision with a van, I headed east toward the airport's massive adobe fortress. With most of the lights off, and as the last stragglers headed out, the airport felt like Saigon during the fall. An electronic billboard announced: "closed for the night." This was the first time I could remember the airport getting closed for sand. A traffic cop signaled for me to turn around.

"I've got to pick someone up at the airport," I shouted into the dust. "She got left behind."

He shrugged.

I pulled the car alongside the Southwest Airlines arrivals gate near the East end of the barren terminal. There were several other people waiting for rides, but Jen stood there, alone, next to a stucco pillar, hiding from the wind like a teenaged runaway. Jen wore far too much make-up for her casual outfit of pink sweatpants and sweatshirt. Her sweat suit belonged on a young girl's teddy bear rather than a thirty-something woman. A black bra strap sneaked out over ripped fabric. Her pretty shoulder strained under the weight of a heavy big gym bag. Perhaps she'd been working out, then came here to turn tricks for stranded fliers on their layovers.

I hated the word *layover* when it pertained to Jen. When she started traveling to L.A., she talked about layovers in PHX, LAS and REN. I never understood how an Albuquerque flight could have a layover in Reno when flying to L.A. No. I had to stop thinking like that. I had no feelings for Jen any more. None for Luna either.

Jen entered my car. Her half-Korean, half-Hispanic features made her look a bit Hawaiian, but under the florescent lighting of the arrival area she could pass for an Asian version of Luna.

"I thought you had abandoned me," she said.

"I could say the same thing about you abandoning me."

I didn't know whether to kiss her. We had been engaged, but only for a month. Instead I shook her hand and squeezed her bare shoulder. God, just feeling that bare shoulder again brought back memories. Jen had the most beautiful left shoulder in the whole world.

"Heard anything?" she asked, struggling with her seat belt.

"No, Luna wants me to bring you to her loft. She thinks you're in danger."

"She's right."

"Someone named Nastia called me and told me she might know where Luna's kid is."

"Nastia?" Jen frowned. "That weird little Eskimo chick?"

"You know her?"

"You told me about her, remember? Right after we broke up, but were still talking. You went on for an hour. Were you trying to make me jealous?"

"I don't know. She made an impression on me back then."

"You sounded like you had a crush on her because she was a gymnast and her dad was a Jewish physicist in Siberia. You kept saying her life sounded so romantic—as if you were saying I was, like, not romantic at all."

I didn't want to bring up that old argument. "Could she possibly know someone who can help Luna?"

"How would I know?" Jen thought for a moment. The Saturn pulled out onto the loop road. "But she wouldn't call you unless she did. Let me think for a second on that one. I might know somebody who knows her."

The wheels turned in her forehead, but with her ADD, Jen's wheels turned in different directions.

"Watch the road!" she said. "You're just as bad as me, and they pulled my license."

"What's really going on here?" We looped around the parking structure after missing the exit to the interstate. *Those who forget the mistakes of the past are doomed to circle around the airport.* "Why didn't you call me when you got back?"

Jen waited until we exited off the loop road and descended west toward the interstate.

"Lots of bad things happened to me," she said. "I didn't know how happy you'd be to see me."

"I haven't heard from you in months. I did love you . . . once."

"I know."

"But that was a long time ago, in a galaxy far, far away. What happened to the job in L.A.?"

"Long story."

I'll always remember that night, the beginning of the end. We were in Santa Fe at an election party when Luna was running for judge. We met the President of the United States. Hell, he even flirted with Jen.

At the party Jen talked with Gabriel Rose, a Hollywood power player who kept spinning something about a big job in "development" at a major studio in Hollywood. He promised to pull some strings to get her into UCLA Law School for the spring semester. I couldn't get into UCLA by the way. "The University of Cute Little Asians," she called it.

I knew Rose; he had segued from entertainment lawyer to the production side. He kept telling her, "I can make you a star."

Jen believed him. She always had been a little bit gullible.

Within a few weeks after she moved, I got the dreaded "Time to Move On" phone call as my Christmas present. I knew couldn't really hold onto a shooting star like Jen. Alejandro's girl stuck with him through five felonies; Jen got a taste of Hollywood and I was a discarded script that wasn't compelling.

• • • • •

Jen said nothing until the Saturn was officially orbiting the interstate, headed north. "Everything fell through. I was out in L.A. for a while working for one producer, then another, all while failing out of law school. I came back with my tail between my legs. I didn't think you wanted to see me again."

I was about to say, *"I love you,"* but I didn't know anymore.

Jen vibrated with nervous energy while she texted furiously.

"I thought your phone was out."

"It comes and goes."

"Are you still drinking Red Bulls?" I asked. "Or what was that other one, Liquid Suicide?"

"Liquid Pesticide. And I think I'm getting the caffeine DTs."

"Who are you texting?" I asked. "Which of the million dudes in your life?"

"No dude. A woman who can help us get to Nastia," she said. "Why don't you ever trust me?"

Jen stopped texting to take a call. "Mom, I didn't leave after all, but I can't see you tonight. No, no news about Luna. Is Denise still with you? Good, let her sleep."

Suddenly a flurry of noise came through from the other end. Jen's mother was Korean, so I couldn't understand a word of it. Jen had sure pissed her mother off.

She hung up, and wiped a tear from her eye. "I'm kicked out of the house. So much for being an independent woman over thirty. My mom is cutting the cord."

"So why is she doing it tonight of all nights?"

"Well she's saying that with Luna's child kidnapped she's scared that they'll come after my daughter, too."

"I thought your daughter was still in the group home."

Jen had a daughter, Denise, from a previous relationship. Denise had some yet-to-be diagnosed disorder and, at age five, had not yet begun to talk.

"My mom takes her on a weekend furlough every once in awhile; she's a nurse, you remember, and she gets grandparent's rights."

"Can you take Denise out by yourself?"

"No, the litigation is still dragging on with the father's family. I can only see her with someone else present."

The father of Jen's child was a prominent lawyer who died under mysterious circumstances. His family never liked Jen. She had more drama than a Roman Polanski film festival.

"It breaks my heart," she said. "I still see her almost every day, but I don't think she's happy to see me."

"That's so sad."

Jen took a deep breath. "That's why this whole thing with Dew is getting to me so much."

"Dew?"

"Luna's daughter's name is Sacagawea. That became Sacka-dacka do, and then just Dew, like Mountain Dew, because it sounds better than Sack. Well I love little Dew. My own daughter hates me."

"I'm so sorry," I said. "I would have adopted her, if you ever got custody."

"It's too late now," she said. "Too late for a lot of things."

• • • • •

I missed the downtown exit amid the dirt and fog, and had to circle around at the next exit, Lomas Boulevard. The sandstorm blew only slightly less intensely down here in the valley, the air a touch more humid. We parked right on Central Avenue, the old Route Sixty-Six. In the sandstorm, Central Avenue had shifted out of the local space/time continuum. We were either back in the thirties, or in a post apocalyptic future where the only joint open was a taco kiosk serving *Soylent Green* chile tacos.

I moved to hold Jen's hand from force of habit. She had a scar on her wrist. I noticed a scar on her other wrist as well. Had she tried to slit them?

"What's up with your wrists?"

"I fell on some rocks while running," she said. "And I had to stop myself before I hit my face. It's not what you think. It's totally not what you think."

I didn't push. We dodged a few more weeds on the way to Luna's place, the Asylum Lofts. It was a looney bin all right. A developer had rehabbed this old asylum into chic lofts and condos. The asylum had lasted nearly a hundred years and survived fires and looting, but couldn't survive the yuppie invasion after the advent of the Santa Fe train. Since the last boom and bust, the building was now half-empty.

In the empty park behind us, the log cabin building of the Albuquerque Press Club sat on top of a woody hill. Barely a hundred yards from the interstate, the Press Club had played a hunting lodge in the forgotten movie, *Beer Fest.*

Down Central Avenue, right next to Pop n' Taco that appeared in the even more forgotten movie *Fanboys*. Tommy Lee Jones had eaten next door at Milton's diner for *In the Valley of Elah*, then searched for a killer a few miles east in *No Country for Old Men*.

Albuquerque was one big movie set that had never been struck.

•　•　•　•　•

Luna hadn't trusted me with her code. I pressed a buzzer, then stared at the renovated bricks, waiting for a response from the metal box. How did Luna afford this place? She finally had a stable income as a judge, but she had owned the place before then. Disgruntled lawyers spread rumors of dirty family money.

Luna had been one of the youngest DA's ever when she assumed the post as DA for Crater County; then the electorate voted her out nearly unanimously. She'd had rebounded nicely with a few big wins as a defense attorney, including her representation of Jen on murder and conspiracy charges.

Luna admitted she sent her name to the Judicial Committee on a whim. She claimed to be "thunderstruck" when the governor selected her over several more qualified and seemingly more connected candidates. She faced a contested primary next year. If she survived that, other candidates salivated at taking Luna down. Would the kidnapping help her get re-elected?

Probably not.

We waited in the wind, and dodged another weed or two. Jen shook, not just from the cold. "I don't know if I can go through with this."

"Why do you always get nervous when you see Luna?"

"I feel like the cheap Korean knock-off of Luna most days."

The door finally clicked open. The same clicking sound I'd heard in jail. We walked down a hallway, dodging ghosts, and I knocked on Luna's door.

A small Asian woman in a uniform opened the door, Albuquerque Police Officer Bebe Tran, an old friend. I didn't want to risk hugging Bebe; she carried a very big gun that probably weighed more than her. She nodded to me, and hurried back to the living room.

I called the place the Lunar Module. The Lunar Modules consisted of few rehabbed asylum suites, and the living room was an old multi-purpose room for the inmates. Industrial adobe chic interior design made the Lunar Module a little too hip for a rookie state judge. The place tried a bit too hard, as if ghosts possessed the interior designers. Many family photos hung on the walls. In the center of the wall, a blurry photo showed a doctor taking a little girl's temperature. Luna was the little girl. I had never met the doctor, Luna and Jen's father. After the "temperature picture," a few photos chronicled Luna running track at Crater High School, a remote town in western New Mexico. She framed her diplomas from the University of Colorado, right next to fames of news clippings of races won and lost. The far part of the wall showed family portraits of Luna with Dew, and Jen with her own daughter, Denise. Denise grimaced in her mother's grasp. Poor Jen.

Just below, another photo showed a little girl in an astronaut costume with her helmet off. Dew was a dead ringer for her mother, but had curly hair like a Hispanic Shirley Temple. She was four now, small for her age.

By the bathroom was a staged photo: Luna, Jen and a third half-sister, Selena. All wore the same space girl outfits, light sabers at the ready. Little Dew stood in front, as if she was their leader. What was that cartoon again—the *Laser Geishas*?

Luna had never revealed the identity of father of the child, not to anyone. She had gone through a wild phase a few years back. "As far as I'm concerned," she once told me over a few drinks. "Dew was a virgin birth, even though I was hardly a virgin."

Luna had various photos of her daughter in costumes—Dew dressed like Dora the Explorer, Dew as a cheerleader, and Dew as a princess at Disneyland.

I once won a trial for a child molester because the state had screwed up the date of the alleged incident.

"What are you going to do now that you're free," I'd asked the defendant.

"I'm going to Disneyland," he said.

I had a sudden feeling of revulsion for what I did for a living.

God, I hoped Dew was safe.

●　●　●　●　●

Inside, the living room, the small gathering resembled the huddle back in the G-Spot. I recognized a few. Washington, an African American US Attorney, was a former running quarterback from Notre Dame, stared at the phone as if scanning the opponent's linebackers. Officer Tran stood behind him as if waiting for a hand off. As a defense attorney, too much law enforcement made me nervous. Washington shook his head when he saw me, disapproving of Luna's taste in friends.

"Luna?" I asked. "We're here."

The huddle cleared to reveal a forty-something woman sitting on the couch. She did not get up, the weight of the world held her by the shoulders.

"Glad you came," she said. Luna acted more like Jen's

mother, as opposed to a sister. Luna had gravity in her a black business suit, like she never went off judge duty.

Luna's boyfriend sat on the couch with her and held her hand tightly. His other hand was on her shoulder, stroking it, almost too possessively considering the circumstances. The huddle re-formed.

He came over to us. It was Gabriel Rose the Hollywood ass-hole. I didn't know Luna was dating him now. "Good to see you again," he said. "We haven't seen each other since that picnic down at the Trinity site."

"That was a good time." I smiled at Jen.

If Luna was the upgraded version of Jen, Gabriel Rose was the upgraded version of me. He had a discrete nose job, hair plugs and laser eye surgery; he was Superman in an Armani suit to my polyester blend Clark Kent.

He did not make eye contact with Jen. "Ms. Song, good to see you again. I'm so sorry that Los Angeles did not work out for you."

"I'm sorry too," she said.

"Well, I'm here now for the duration," he said. "I'm one of the producers of *Desert Demons* with Sky Roberts."

"He's a walking time bomb," I said. "I saw him in jail. How did you get the state to invest so much?

He laughed. "Let's just say we've got a lot of money behind us, not just the State.

I grew curious. "Who?"

"You don't want to know. And don't worry; everything with Sky will work out fine. No big deal."

Luna kept talking to Washington and Tran. Everyone in room orbited around her. Washington and Tran grilled her about possible suspects, and she showed them a print-out of the thou-sand and some cases she'd presided over in just a few months.

"I think you could make a short list of people who aren't suspects," she said.

Luna finally excused herself from Washington and Tran, saying, "I don't know what the hell else I can tell you!"

"Calm down," Washington said. "We'll get the guy."

She stood and embraced Jen. "I'm so glad you're alive."

"Have you heard anything?" Jen asked.

"Not yet," Luna said. "How's Denise?"

Jen frowned. "No change."

"At least we know your daughter will live till her next birthday," Luna whispered.

"Let's not talk about *our* issues now," Jen said

"Dan, so glad you could come," Luna said. As if to spite Rose, Luna gave me a warm hug. "How was jail?"

I didn't want to talk about the lockdown, take away her thunder. "Sorry I was late. Traffic was a bitch. Are you all right?"

"Fine," she said. She hurried back to the couch and re-joined Rose as if he had his own gravity. He touched her shoulder possessively, like she was his daughter rather than his girlfriend.

No one knew what to say then so everyone stared at the cell phone on Luna's living-room table.

I coughed. Each of the men wore their own brand of cologne, the women their own perfume. The resulting smell was a chemistry experiment gone awry. My one-night fling with Luna took place well over a year ago, and it ended badly.

"All of you, I'm so glad you came," Luna said at last. "Even you, Jen."

I couldn't read Luna's glare at Jen, who said nothing. Washington headed toward the bathroom, whispering something into his cell phone.

"Still nothing," Washington said when he returned. "But I've got my best people on it."

"Thank you,' Luna said. "You're all my best people."

She didn't look at me or Jen. We pulled up chairs on the outside of the circle.

"How did it happen?" I asked.

"How many times do I have to go through this?" Luna asked. "It's draining me."

"Please tell us," Jen said. "I don't know anything either."

Luna hesitated, and then nodded. "I'd finished my docket. Officer Tran came with me for the warrant for Sky Roberts's arrest. I signed it. Dew stuck with me the whole time. It was three o'clock, and I was done for the day, so I wanted to sneak in a work-out at Midtown before dinner."

"I was supposed to take her to dinner," Rose said. "At the Kobe Burrito," he added. The Kobe Burrito was the most expensive place in town, home of the *hundred-dollar* burrito. Most of us only went to the Kobe Burrito once a year after a tax refund check came back. What the hell was this Hollywood asshole doing with our Luna?

Luna shivered. "It was this damn sandstorm; the lights went out in the parking structure. Some guys in ski masks pushed me down and grabbed Dew."

"Were the cameras on?" I asked.

"No, they got to the cameras, every single one. Obviously they were planning ahead."

"Did you see who it was?" I asked.

"Don't you think I asked her that?" Washington snapped.

More awkward silence. Luna turned her attention back to Rose. Washington looked at his wireless laptop computer as if the child was coming up on the screen. He pressed a few buttons as if each one held a clue. Tran made a phone call.

I might as well be invisible. "Somebody called me," I said. "It might be related to the kidnapping."

"Somebody called *you?*" Washington said derisively, still focused on his keyboard.

"It wasn't one of the kidnappers," I said. "This woman claimed that her 'true love' was one of my clients."

"Which client?"

"She just said I would be meeting him next week. Her name is Nastia."

"Nastia? That sounds like a whore name," Tran said. "I busted a girl named Nastia like twenty times last year."

"I don't know," I said, exasperated. "I have a lot of clients this week, all over the state. She said something about the dude being unavailable now, but that he could help me, somehow."

"I'm sure we can solve this case without you," Washington said. "We should have everything under control any minute."

He pressed a few more buttons on his laptop.

"All your clients are public-defender clients, right?" asked Tran.

"Right now they are. Once you get a contract, criminals don't want to pay you, if their cellmate gets you for free. When I was in the jail, one of the inmates must have overheard when Luna called me. They were all over the phones. Someone must have called someone who called someone else who then called back. It felt weird in there. The inmates sounded like they knew something was going down. Nobody acted surprised."

"How do you know this girl again?" Washington asked.

I didn't need to mention the stripper thing. "I told you I represent her boyfriend. I just don't remember which one."

"Well, I might as well talk to you," he said. "I have to follow protocol and follow every lead, no matter how remote, or how far from the source. Come by the FBI tomorrow around ten."

His eyes glared right through me. Everyone stared at each other, and then back at Luna. Rose continued winning the Luna sweepstakes. He stayed on the couch with her; she cried softly on his shoulder.

The phone on the table rang. Everybody jumped.

Washington put some kind of device onto the phone. He stared into his modified I-phone and pressed the screen with a stylus, and nodded at Luna.

She strained to pick up the phone, as if it was heavier than Sky's Oscar. "This is Judge Luna Cruz."

Silence on the other end.

"We have your child," the electronically altered voice intoned. "We have your child, Judge Luna Cruz." The kidnapper sounded matter of fact, as if he made ransom calls for a living and this was his third call for the evening list. He sounded like he was reading off a teleprompter.

"Who is this?" Luna said. "What have you done to Dew?"

"We know you have already gone to the police and to the FBI," the voice said, still on script. "Don't tell the media, if you want your child to live."

"What am I supposed to do?" Luna whimpered.

"We will call you tomorrow morning at seven. Follow our instructions to the letter or your child, Sacagawea Cruz, dies."

The phone went dead.

Washington touched the stylus a few more times. He listened into his earpiece, smiled hopefully for a brief moment, and then frowned, swearing under his breath.

"Nothing," he said at last. "These guys are professionals."

I stared at the picture of Dewand almost believed it was real..

"I'll stay with her," Rose said. "They're probably watching the house. I'm not law enforcement, so they're probably cool with me being here."

I didn't like the way he said, "cool with me." Kidnappers should never be cool with anyone.

"We'll keep the place under surveillance," Washington said. He turned to Tran. "It'll be APD, okay?"

"Sure," Tran replied. "You mean she's not big enough for the Feds?"

"Budget cuts," Washington said. "To our knowledge, this hasn't crossed state lines yet, so it might stay in your jurisdiction. My budget is cut to the bone unless it's terrorism."

More murmuring came from around the room. I couldn't think of anything else to say. I started toward the door; Jen hugged Luna one more time.

"I'm so sorry," Jen said. "I'm so sorry." She had this endearing quality of repeating herself when stressed.

"I don't think it's your fault," Luna said.

"I don't know," Jen said. "I don't know."

Jen took Luna's hand. "Just have faith Luna, no matter what. Geishas forever."

"Geishas forever," Luna said. She didn't look like she had much faith.

• • • • •

Jen and I hurried down the ghostly hallway toward the exit. "She might not be there anymore, but I just got a text from someone who might know where Nastia is."

"Who?"

"My friend Mia. I don't think you know her. At least I hope you don't know her."

"Let's go," I said. "Why didn't you tell the FBI?"

Jen frowned. "I don't trust the FBI."

"I'm not sure I'm the type to play hero."

"We don't have a choice," she said. "If you say a word to anyone, especially Luna, I'll like totally be dead."

SONG SUNG BLUE

"FASTEN YOUR SEATBELT," I said to Jen in my car.

"That's a line from a movie," she said. "*It's gonna be a bumpy night*, something like that?"

"No, I really need you to fasten your seatbelt."

Even while we were engaged, Jen and I had cycles in our relationships, like a sine curve or cosine curve, one of those curves from sophomore math. She had an annoying habit of disappearing, than re-appearing.

Jen attended law school off and on; she took a course here and there, would get an A in one and then drop out of others. I'd helped her with a few papers, I was ashamed to admit, but she usually did better with her own writing, on the rare occasions when she put her mind to it.

"What kind of trouble are you really in?"

She just shook her head. "You don't want to know."

We approached the "Big I" interchange between I-40 and I-25. We could go north to Santa Fe, east to Amarillo or west to Los Angeles. The Ends Zone lay to the north.

"Go straight," she said.

I kept heading north. "So how do you know Nastia?"

Long pause.

"I work with her," she said.

I looked at Jen's little pink outfit and black bra. It all made sense now. "Work, as in present tense?"

"Yes, as in present tense. There's a reason I didn't tell you I was back. I'm just a waitress at the Ends Zone, okay?"

"Okay," I said. "You don't have to be so defensive."

"I told you I got myself in trouble," she said. "I think it has something to do with my job. All my fault. All my fault."

We parked in the Ends Zone lot where someone got shot every summer. Luna would sure kill Jen if she knew her sister was working at a strip club, even as "just a waitress."

●　●　●　●　●

I followed Jen inside. A bouncer wanded me down, just like at jail. Ironically, the metal detector wand at the strip club was more sensitive than the one at the jail.

The bouncer asked if I wanted the calendar that was on the front counter. On the cover, a small box held Nastia's face, half-Russian, half Eskimo, although technically *Inupiat*. She had radioactive green eyes and wore a lot of make-up over her pale skin, like a ghost in red lingerie. In the light of the club, her whiteness made the picture resemble a photographic negative.

"Is she here?" I pointed.

"Not no more," he said. "I don't think that bitch is ever coming back."

Jen dragged me inside. "Don't ask any questions yet."

Past the lobby, the Ends Zone was as classy a strip club as Albuquerque could handle, although it was a far cry from anything in Vegas or even Phoenix. It could barely qualify as a *gentlemen's* club rather than a regular man's club. The tablecloths on the tables and scented candles took away the smell of sweaty women and even sweatier men. If not for "Daisy" up on Stage One, and the women grinding away on laps, this felt like a sports bar in a boring suburb.

"They're filming that movie here," Jen said. "*Desert Demons*, based on that game. This is supposed to be an ex-pat club in Dubai."

Three men in black outfits huddled in a corner, a dancer on each lap.

"They're probably closing a pay or play deal on the next movie," Jen said. "I think they're throwing in a few lap dances with the first dollar financing."

"How do you know?"

"I know," she said. "Some asshole tried to include me in such a deal last week. I told him to fuck off; I was just a *waitress*, not a bargaining chip. I gotta go change. I have to be on the clock if I'm talking to someone. You know the rules, right?"

I didn't answer as she headed toward a back room. I knew the rules all right, from my Ends Zone phase after Jen left me— every night for two weeks straight. I quit coming after I met Nastia on New Year's Eve and vowed never to return, well, at least for another year. My goal was to make the *fiscal* New Year of July first at least.

So much for New Year's resolutions.

I recognized a few of the dancers around the room. Before my conflict contract, gentlemen's clubs were a prime client source. I represented Daisy on a DWI charge and Destiny, who was on Stage Two, on a string of drunk driving cases and a domestic violence or two.

That's why I got the public defender contract. Dancers were the worst clients. I'd do domestic-violence charges for free for dancers as my pro bono requirement for the year. Daisy had once called it a *pro boner contract,* so I wanted to avoid even the appearance of impropriety. She got busted once for prostitution, when she worked for the *Cute Sixty-six* prostitution ring, where the girls not only provided tutoring for athletes, they also provided sexual services. I told her she needed to pay me more than the three-hundred an hour she charged as an alleged "cutie."

"I graduated from Brown University," I said. "You go to the community college, and your time is worth three hundred dollars an hour? I'm worth more than three hundred an hour."

She didn't agree. "You're not that cute," she said, "and besides, you don't have to do even half the disgusting things I had to do."

"You don't know the half of it," I said. "You've never seen one of my sentencings." Thank God for the regular income of the public-defender contract. Dancer clients were too high maintenance. Invariably once the case was over they always went back to their evil drug-dealing boyfriends. After all, I was just their lawyer, not their lover.

• • • • •

I sat by Daisy's stage. She took off her shirt to reveal the handiwork of an overzealous surgeon. "Guess what I finally invested in?" she asked as she put her hardened boobs millimeters from my face.

"*Plastics*," I said, pretending to advise a young Dustin Hoffman in *The Graduate*. Her chest alone probably had enough plastic to keep a factory fully running. She stumbled off the stage at the end of her song.

A woman in a black "waitress" t-shirt emerged from the locker room and headed toward me. "You gotta order something," she said. "Or they'll evict you. The meter's always running here. We got that new 160 proof Lucid Absinthe at twenty-five dollars a shot now."

I checked at my watch. "Just a coke."

"The soda or the drug?"

"The soda."

"I can dance for you if you want," she said. "It's gotta be a VIP."

The waitress wore glasses and belonged in a library this time of night, especially since she sported a plaid school-girl skirt. Thankfully, she hadn't gone for the augmentation. The fact that she was almost the only woman in the room with her clothes on somehow made her sexier. "I'm waiting for someone," I said.

"*Waiting for Godot*?" she asked.

I smiled with recognition. "You're in school, right?"

"I'm just slumming to pay for my Master's in English Lit," she said. "A feminist perspective on the existentialists. *Nietzsche is peachy—*"

"*But Sartre is smarter.*"

I tipped her an extra dollar for a literary allusion, and nursed my can of Atlanta's finest.

Five women holding gym bags marched into the locker room, looking like a basketball team. The girls deliberately de-sexed themselves. In the outside world they were college students, nurses, and even legal secretaries like Jen. They psyched themselves up with nervous pre-game chatter.

One Latina was a French maid; another was a schoolgirl from the Hogwarts campus. A state law apparently required belly rings and Chinese characters tattooed on their back. One woman sported a tattoo of her naked body on her back, so you could never forget her appearance in the front.

The Friday afternoon crowd of businessmen slowly morphed into the Friday night crowd of lonely computer salesmen and rowdy gang-bangers celebrating the big drug deal.

Tonight, nervous energy emanated from a table in the corner. Even though they already had girls on their laps, several other girls hovered on the periphery. The guys wore t-shirts and matching baseball hats that read *Desert Demons*. Unfortunately, the logo showed Sky Roberts's face gazing out of the bars of a jail, the rest of the Earth exploding behind him.

The girls were out for quick cash, or even better; a speaking part with at least four lines so they could qualify for the Screen Actor's Guild.

"You SAG?" one guy asked an aging dancer.

"Don't worry, I'm getting a boob job next week," she replied.

The existential waitress came over to me again. "You with the movie people?"

"I once wrote a script," I said. "I can make you a star."

"I'll pass," she said, sounding like a bored producer. "Could I get you another coke, Godot?"

"I'm fine," I said. "I have to drive. I figure I'm at a point-oh-two for caffeine; they're busting dudes for point-oh-four these days."

She smiled. "You must be *the* lawyer, right?"

"I'm *a* lawyer," I said.

She lingered a second at the table, but then a gigantic Native American man came over and gave her a bear hug, lifting her off the ground. She managed to keep her beer bottles upright. He wore a white cowboy hat that perched precariously over his long black hair like an iceberg.

"Hey, Cowboy," she said after he let her down. Cowboy? I wasn't sure if she was being ironic with him; he didn't seem like the type for irony. He smiled like a little boy.

"Hey, Mia," he said.

That must be Jen's friend. They disappeared into the VIP room before I could follow. A big bouncer blocked the velvet rope. "No pay, no play."

• • • • •

When Jen finally emerged, she wore a long pink wig and the black lingerie that had lurked under the pink outfit. She balanced on the world's highest heels, making her nearly my height. With her make-up, she was that futuristic cartoon character from Luna's photo: Laser Geisha Pink. Her large purse could hide a light saber or two.

I stared at her damn left shoulder again and remembered why I fell in love with her. Moments like this. As Jen tip-toed on her heels, she exuded power and danger.

Then she stumbled over someone's foot and I grabbed her wrist before she fell.

"You saved me," she said.

"It's my job." I looked into her big brown eyes.

"We gotta go to the VIP room," she said, finally breaking my gaze. "We'll be safer there."

"I don't know if I feel comfortable with this, Jen."

"Call me Pink out loud," she whispered. "I don't want everyone to know who I am. We're just going to talk, don't worry. But you're going to have to pay. I'll get a manager over here."

We sat a table in front of the VIP room and waited for a bouncer to let us enter. Would they wand us down again, or just check my credit?

I recognized the manager immediately. I got Gustavo a dismissal on a domestic violence, or was it a deferred sentence on a DWI? We pretended not to know each other. He swiped my credit card for the bare minimum, a hundred dollars, plus a ten-dollar service fee. Good news about my credit card, there was no maximum limit.

That was a bad thing, too, at thirty percent interest.

"You can tip if you want," he said, pointing to a blank space on the slip.

I growled at him. He certainly hadn't tipped me for getting

him his deferred sentence. He gave me a handful of *zone dollarz,* wooden chips that acted as currency around here. I probably went through a whole box of those chips the night Nastia had been here.

• • • • •

When Gustavo left, Jen took my hand and pulled me inside the "VIP Zone." We were the only ones there except for Mia and the Native American giant.

He smiled at Jen. "Next time, Pink," he said. "One day I'll convince you to cross the line to the dark side."

"You know I don't dance," Jen said.

"Every woman is a dancer," he said. "She just don't know it yet. In times of economic uncertainty people do a lot of things they said they'd never do."

Jen laughed. "Not as long as I'm still breathing. I've got morals, you know."

Mia still had her shirt on as she sat on his very large lap like Princess Leia flirting with Jabba the Hutt. Cowboy turned his attention entirely to Mia.

Jen whispered, "He's an Indian named Cowboy Begay. Pretty funny, huh? He's a tribal cop out in Crater for the Crater Band of Navajos. Comes here all the time since his wife died. Feds shot her by mistake."

Cowboy Begay might as well have been a cop named Sue. He didn't have any alcohol with him. He looked like a straight shooter. This was his only vice.

The next song started. Mia stripped down to her bra, and took off her glasses and began dancing for Cowboy the Indian. Cowboy closed his eyes as if summoning back his lost love. Mia didn't actually do a lap dance, didn't even totally undress, just brought her body close to his, touching him slightly, blowing in his ear.

It felt rude to watch something so intimate, so I turned to Jen. "So what's really going on here, ummm, Pink?"

She put one leg over my lap, as if holding me down, but not moving.

"Keep that thing in your pants," she said. "Nothing more will happen." The bouncer glanced in on us, nodded at her, and then stood guard outside.

"Okay, this story is kinda weird," she said. "My whole life is kinda weird."

"Just tell me."

"Well, I had a lot of money and, well, power at one time," she said.

"You knew the President. Did you and he sleep together?"

"No, not even." She smiled a Mona Lisa smile. "But I did know the Hollywood people."

I noticed she didn't deny sleeping with any of them. She continued after a deep breath. "They all have places out here, connections up in Santa Fe. Well, through them, I had the connections to convince the powers that be to give Luna her judge job."

"You?" How could this silly girl in high heels and a pink wig have any power whatsoever? What magic powers did Laser Geisha Pink really have?

"I also know a lot of people who know a lot of things."

She gestured at the dancers sitting by the movie people. Jen didn't seem the blackmail type, but I didn't push it.

"I won't ask," I said. "So if you have these superpowers, why the hell are you back in the Ends Zone in Albuquerque, America?"

"Let's just say that the good times didn't last. I'm not what you call a good businessman, I mean business woman. I got into deep debt to a lot of people you don't want to owe money to."

"I got job, and tried to put my money away, but I got debts that no honest man can pay," I sang, quoting Springsteen.

"Put your make-up on, and try to look pretty, and meet me tonight in Atlantic City," she said. "That was your favorite song. Well, I had debts that no honest woman could pay and I'm finding out that you can only call in a favor *once*. I did it all for Luna, well, most of it. I burned a lot of bridges, so when my turn came there was like nothing left to burn. I'm mixing metaphors again."

"I don't care," I said. "Is Luna dirty?"

"No, of course not," Jen said. "Never. Never. I bet they're sending her a message that they can get to her. I had no idea how ugly it could be. God, I fucked everything up."

She cried for the rest of the song.

The bouncer stuck in his head in again. "That's one song, Pink."

"She's not dancing," I said.

"Doesn't matter," he said. "If she ain't waitressing, she ain't paying her debt and that's stealing. You know this place is like a cab, here the meter—"

"—is always running. I know." I was about to protest but instead I handed a *zone dollar* to Jen. Jen handed it to the bouncer.

"Put that on my tab," she said. "I owe them a lot of money and they deduct from my paycheck."

The bouncer left in a huff.

"Why do you owe them money?"

"I crashed my Prius into Gustavo's Corvette. Long story."

"Were you drinking?"

"No, I had a lot on my mind. Driving while *Thinking*. Well, texting actually. It's even worse. I got charged with reckless, criminal damage to property and leaving the scene. Gustavo and I worked out this *arrangement* when he tracked me down, so it never went to court. He even posted my bond, long as I work off my debt for getting his Corvette fixed."

"Why are we in here, really?" I asked her.

"We're waiting for Mia."

Mia contorted her neck around. "It'll be a minute. I'm kinda busy right now."

Jen asked me to re-tell the story about Nastia. She listened intently.

"You have weird taste in women."

"Tell me about it."

• • • • •

After the third song, Cowboy paid Mia in crisp bills.

"Same time next week?" he asked.

"Same bat time," she said as she put her outfit back on. "Same bat channel."

A tear glinted in Cowboy's eye. "I don't think you realize how much what you do means to me."

"I realize," Mia said. "Lord knows I realize."

Cowboy gave Jen a hug, too. He wiped a tear away from his eye, and suddenly reverted to his bad ass cop persona. He pushed Gustavo out of the way.

"Sorry, guys," Mia said. "Cowboy can be very persistent."

"So why are we here?"

"Don't get your hopes up," Mia said. "It's not what you think."

"So what's going on?" I asked. "What's really going on?"

Mia sighed, almost post-coital. She hadn't been faking it. She liked Cowboy more than she let on. Or perhaps the money had given her the glow. She reluctantly put her glasses back on. "I got to get back to serving drinks." She laughed as she played with the *dollarz* coins. "Talk about mixed emotions."

"I get it," I said. I gave her a few *zone dollarz.*

Jen nodded at Mia. "Remember how you called me and told me that Nastia was in today? You know that Russian Eskimo girl?"

Mia raised an eyebrow. Jen gave her another insistent look. "Remember what we talked about on the texts?"

Mia finally nodded. "Yeah, she was in here earlier today. God, I'm losing track of days with my mid-terms coming up. She gets a call from someone and totally freaks out."

"When did this happen?"

"About five today. She took off like a bat out of hell. I don't think she even changed back into her street clothes."

"Do you have any idea where she might be?"

Mia thought for a moment, as blood slowly flowed back up to her brain. "Nastia hangs at one of the *Desert Demons'* sets on weekends," she said.

"Hangs?"

Mia smiled. "Lonely guys with money away from their wives in Hollywood. Do the math."

"So she didn't really like me for me?" I said.

"Duh," said Jen.

"Where are they filming?"

"They've filmed all over the state. They did the desert scenes over at White Sands, and the military stuff at the Missile Range near Cruces. But now, they're down to one major set-up in Santa Fe at the prison and one over in Crater County at the refinery. I think she's at the Crater set. Everything's kinda on hold right now, with Sky's fate up in the air. If he goes to jail for a long time, it's all shot to hell."

"We'll try to find Nastia tomorrow," I said to Jen. I turned to Mia. "Did you ever see who she was with?"

Mia frowned. "I don't know. She was with a lot of people. Chicks too."

"Anything else? Tattoos?"

"Most of the people she hung with were in and out of jail. Does that help?"

I formed a picture in my mind, then another, then another, then another. "That sounds like every one of my clients."

"Sorry, I can't be more helpful."

"So do you know anything about the kidnapping?" I asked. "Did Nastia say anything?"

Mia thought for a moment. She stared at Jen, then at the door. Gustavo looked in, then stuck his head back out.

"Yeah, about a week ago Nastia said someone told her something really big was going to go down. Maybe she meant the kidnapping."

I frowned. Maybe everyone in the whole state really did know that something bad was going down. Everyone except me.

"Mia, back to the bar, now!" A voice came over the loudspeaker.

"Anything else?" Mia said after the bouncer peeked in again. "If I don't get back on shift, Gustavo will fine me and add it to my tab. Or worse, stop paying the bond on the reckless driving."

So much I wanted to ask but I couldn't think of a question at the time. "I don't know."

Mia nodded at us both, and then left. "Hope Godot finally comes for you," she said, then disappeared out the door.

Jen frowned. "Is there something between you two that I don't know about?"

"Private joke," I said. "When did you get so jealous of me?"

Jen shook her head. "Who me?"

Another couple came into the VIP room and Gustavo re-entered. "So are you going to work a full shift, Pink?"

One of the side effects about being a defense lawyer is that you actually give a shit about people you shouldn't give a shit about. Jen was too smart, with too much potential to be earning her living lap by lap. Servicing a table was only a few inches away from serving a lap.

"How much is your pay-out for the night?" I asked. I wasn't quite sure what a pay out was, or if that was the correct term, but I tried to sound like a Mac Daddy, if that was the right term.

"In times of economic uncertainty, don't fuck with another man's livelihood," he said derisively. "The bitch owes me."

I reached for my credit card. "Dude, I'm paying for Jen *not* to dance or even waitress tonight. Will three hundred be enough? I'll even throw in a tip."

Gustavo took the card, and then turned to Jen. "You understand this is just one payment. You still owe me forty-seven hundred! I paid your bond, bitch."

"Forty-six seventy," I said.

"The tip don't count."

Gustavo ran the card right there, then left.

"Dan, I need one more favor," she said. "You know my mom kicked me out and I have nowhere to stay . . ."

• • • • •

I bought Nastia's calendar on the way out, much to Jen's chagrin. I turned to the centerfold of her in the remnants of her gymnastics uniform while suspended upside down on the pole. Nastia's legs could probably grasp onto the pole through an earthquake.

Why couldn't Jen be like that?

YELLOW KRYPTONITE

I lived in the Bosque Apartments on Central Avenue, where a gaudy stretch of Old Route 66 crossed the Rio Grande. The faux-adobe complex could pass for the Taos Pueblo on Percoset, with its jutting angles and hidden staircases. The building looked modern and ancient, ruined and renovated, all at the same time.

The neighborhood was the demilitarized zone in the battle of *Feng* versus *Shui*. East of the complex there was a verdant golf course; to the west, the Bosque, an area of cottonwood trees that lined the Rio. The tourist district of Old Town, founded 1706, lay only a few blocks away.

Unfortunately, the last three hundred years had not smiled on this part of town. The old motels from the *Grapes of Wrath* days once housed the Okies stuck on the journey from east to west along the mother road. One organization had the mistaken idea to take homeless kids, put them in a motel and check on them once a week. Needless to say, the teen runaways frequently broke into neighborhood homes and cars. The grapes of wrath had become raisins, and on the next block over they had even fermented into vinegar.

My apartment sat on the second floor, and we stumbled up the narrow stairs bumping into each other, but in that nice sort of way, like drunken strangers in the night. Close to ten, at night, I needed to hold my head up in my hands from the stress and exhaustion.

"The minimalist look, huh?" Jen said, referring to my utterly blank living room. I did have a stack of framed movie posters lying on the floor. "And you wondered why I never moved in with you?"

"Follow me," I said. "Everything I own is in my room. Could you give me a second to clean? I wasn't expecting company. You're my first guest up here since . . . well, since you."

Jen entered the room but couldn't find the light switch. She nearly tripped over a running shoe that was perched precariously on top of a briefcase, which was on top of the other running shoe. All of that leaned against an upside-down framed painting; a pink abstract Jen had done during her art class at the community college.

After she left, I couldn't decide whether to hang it or hide it, so I just left it there.

I reluctantly turned the light on. Thank God, the cockroaches didn't emerge from behind the painting.

"Just turn the lights off," she said.

She sat on my couch, and pushed away some underwear. "I'll take your couch. I'm going to pass out. Do I need to wear a hazmat suit?"

"I'll take the couch, Jen."

She got up off the couch, came over and grabbed me by the hand and pulled me down onto the bed.

"Just hold me, Dan," she said softly.

Outside a full moon floating over the slow cruising traffic of Route 66 provided a bit of illumination. We *just held*.

But before we could relax, a high speed chase on Route 66 passed by. We stiffened, worried that the SWAT team would hurry up the stairs and bust us for—

Bust us for what? We were two adults, a little battered by life, lying on a bed holding hands. Jen took a few deep breaths and her chest heaved up and down. Any movement on my part would ruin the moment.

"I feel so safe with you," she said. "Why did I ever leave you?"

"You tell me."

"I hope Dew is all right."

"There's nothing we can do now. For Dew."

"No there isn't, is there?"

She cried for a moment, and then wiped away a tear.

"Who are you, Jen?" I asked. "Who are you really?"

"I'm Laser Geisha Pink," she said. "You know the picture of me, Luna and our other sister, Selena. We're the Laser Geishas. Well, that's who I want to be."

"You really don't like being yourself, do you?"

For a brief moment the moon went beyond a cloud, and traffic stopped at a far-off light. Jen was engulfed in darkness.

"I'm a total fuck-up in everyday life. My only real friend in the world is Luna. And now you again, I guess, but I know it's going to take awhile for us to get back to where we were. You've got to admit, as Pink, I have superpowers. As a sexy waitress, I can make evil men reach for their wallets and cut them down to size with one turn of my hips."

The cloud parted, the headlights flowed again. "You've had the opposite effect on me, Laser Geisha Pink," I said.

She smiled. "So if you could be a superhero, who would you be?"

"Isn't it obvious?"

She named about twenty obscure heroes. "I don't know those," I said. "I don't even know the difference between the X-men and the Watchmen."

"Well, who do you see yourself as?"

"Superman, of course."

"Superman? He's like so totally old and lame."

"Well, I can relate to him. I'm a mild-mannered dude in everyday life. People even say I look like Clark Kent."

"Well, your glasses are off now, and you aren't so super."

I wanted to make a joke about circumcised steel, but stopped myself. "And I have this complex about saving damsels in distress, yet I can never reveal my secret identity to the women I love."

"I do get it now," she said. "You can be Superman if you want to. But what's your weakness? Every superhero has a weakness."

"Yellow kryptonite of course."

"Yellow kryptonite? What's that?"

"Asian girls with issues." I squeezed her arm. "Like you."

"That's like totally racist," she said. "But really true in your case."

We talked the rest of the night. We didn't have sex. That would have changed too many things. I found myself spooning her in spite of myself.

"Don't fall in love with me again," she said.

"Too late."

Was I joking? I didn't think so.

SATURDAY
Song: "Meet Me at the Mesa" by Trevor McShane

DOCKET IN MY POCKET

MY APARTMENT WINDOW FACED DUE east, so the sun mugged me right at six. I checked the other side of the bed. In the indentation, I smelled perfume and cigarettes from the club.

And then I saw her. She was in a towel, her hair still wet from the shower. Unfortunately, she held up a hammer. She tapped it in the air, as if testing her killing technique on a skull. My skull.

Would she kill me in my bed?

I wasn't truly awake yet. She could easily get me before I forced my body up. Was this really happening?

She then dropped the towel. I saw her from behind, but I couldn't drool before half a dozen episodes of *CSI Miami* flashed through my brain. She'd use the towel to hide the blunt trauma on my brain, and then clean up the blood. Something like that.

I was too groggy to formulate a strategy. Maybe I deserved to die. If so, getting killed by a naked woman with a hammer was certainly a cool way to go.

But instead she picked up a nail with her other hand and used the towel to deaden the sound as she knocked it into the drywall. She then repeated it even more softly for a second nail. If I was asleep, I probably wouldn't have heard it.

She then hung her painting on the wall, right side up.

"What are you doing?" I asked.

"It was bugging me," she said. "I can be anal sometimes."

"I can see that."

She put the towel back around her.

"Where are your keys?" she asked, bending over a pile. "Oh, I just found them."

I wasn't awake enough to protest. She dropped her towel, grabbed a pair of my sweat pants and a Brown University sweatshirt, and hurried toward the door with my keys in her hand.

"Jen, what are you doing?"

I didn't hear her response and my car sped away before I found any clean clothes. I had a different wardrobe for each of my courthouses and judges. All the cities, all the jackets, and all the ties now lay on the floor. Unfortunately, Albuquerque's tie lay next to Alamogordo's jacket.

• • • • •

Jen pulled into my parking lot after fifteen long minutes. She carried in all my files, plus coffee and a loaf of banana bread from a nearby Starbucks.

"We've got to get going on this," she said. "You said one of your clients next week knows something. Well, we need to organize your files. And we can't organize shit without Starbucks."

She fueled up on a big swig of a *double-sized vanilla flavored energy drink.* Flush with caffeine, guarana, and just a touch of Taurine, she then cleared all of my laundry and began organizing my files, somehow attaching each random piece of paper to an unmarked or even wrongly marked file.

"Just shower," she said. "You like totally smell terrible. Is your superpower a nasty smell that knocks people out? Do you meet clients here?"

"Most of my clients are in jail," I said.

"I can see why. They don't want to come here."

I hurried into the bathroom, with the intention of taking the world's quickest shower, but vanity took a hold of me. Stress sure took its toll on my pores and sweat glands. I used every single potion in the medicine cabinet, squeezing the remains of facial scrub and three shampoos and body washes to make myself smell good. I cut myself shaving in the shower, and my jaw bled.

I didn't want Jen to see me bleed. When the bleeding stopped, I finally emerged. Everything had changed.

Jen had made giant strides during my shower, and had banished the clothing to the closet and the files to the cabinet. "This is the way you practice law?"

"I keep everything in my head," I said. "I have my panic attacks two weeks in advance so I can be cool in court."

"Ever been held in contempt?"

I laughed. "The only person who's ever held me in contempt was your girl, Judge Looney Toons. I had the DA sign off on a continuance but she wouldn't grant it and nearly locked me up. I have a few cases before her next week, by the way."

"Hopefully this will be resolved by then," said Jen. She had already turned on my computer and hit up "nmcourts.com," to double-check my court settings. She inputted a calendar file, and then scribbled everything down into my small black calendar.

"Monday you've got Luna's court at eight-thirty. Minnie something or other," Jen said. "Is Luna actually going to hear it?"

"They won't let her out of her docket," I said. "Didn't you see the news the other day? A bunch of cases were dismissed the last time Luna took a day off and they didn't have backup to do the trial. The media went nuts."

I remembered the signs of protesters: JUSTICE CAN'T TAKE VA-CATIONS! They had a picture of Lady Justice wearing a Hawaiian

shirt— sitting on the beach while behind her the city of Albuquerque burned. The local bloggers had had a field day, so even
a kidnapping might not be enough of an excuse to dig Luna out
of her hole.

Jen shook her head. "And then you have to be out in Estancia
by eleven for a Tyrone Johnson on a drug case, for his conditions-
of-release hearing. That's sixty miles away. You're gonna have to
violate the laws of time and space to get from one court to another."

"Usually when I violate the laws of time and space, I manage
to get a deferred sentence."

She smiled. "Can you do that for me, sometime?"

God I loved that smile. "For you, I get space dismissed, and
then credit for time served."

"If you could put time in a bottle, you would probably break
it," she laughed while opening up both files. "Could it be either
of those? The one who called you? Didn't you say that Nastia
told you her dude was in custody?"

"She said he was 'in, but out,' something like that. I get the
feeling that for this dude jail is like a revolving door."

"Minnie is out of custody, and she's a girl, so she's probably
out, right?"

"As far as I know."

"Tyrone Johnson's case is at eleven. You really sure you'll
make it on time?"

"I'll try."

"Could Tyrone Johnson have a girlfriend like Nastia?"

"I doubt it. He's a black guy who cooked meth. I just don't
see it. As far as I know he's never been before Luna. How about
Tuesday?"

"Tuesday you got Jonny Braun, embezzlement." She
frowned. "What did he embezzle?"

"The guy was a janitor at an adult bookstore and secretly put DVDs in the trash every day as he walked out. Of course he was on camera when he did that. That's as un-cool as it gets."

"A conflict contract attorney isn't much better."

"Well, I get paid to clean up someone's messes," I said. "I'm like a public defender, but without the dental plan. Wednesday I go down to Cruces, right?"

"First, you go to Alamogordo for a change of plea on a drug case in the morning, then Cruces in the afternoon. In Cruces, you've got an aggravated batterer: Tyler Dandridge." She flipped a few keys on "nmcourts.com."

"No big deal."

"Hey, online it says there's a motion to amend. I didn't see anything in your file."

"Sometimes they forget to mail them to me." I said. There was something about Las Cruces and the Third Judicial District. Mail between Las Cruces and Albuquerque came up I-25, which passed through a region that *conquistadores* called *Jornada de Muerto,* the Journey of Death. I often had visions of mail trucks dying en route. "Sometime the mail gets lost. I'll deal with it when I get down there."

She laughed. "You're like those guys who drive up in the Arctic, those ice road truckers."

"Except I have to do a two day drug trafficking trial at the end of the ice road."

"Shouldn't you do some kind of response motion or something?"

"I'll do it the night before and bring it with me. I'm sure I'm still cool."

Jen shrugged. "Speaking of drugs, Thursday you're in Santa Fe. Your client's name is Cody Coca. That's his real name?"

"Ironic, huh? A coke dealer named Coca. I don't make up the

names. Actually it's a fairly common Northern New Mexico name."

"Trafficking, and tampering. Nastia might like a trafficker, but not a tamperer. That sounds too wimpy."

"He was the guy doing the flushing. Felony flushing."

"You've also got your own ticket. The one in Moriarty for speeding through the canyon. I remember you telling me about it when you were bragging about Nastia."

"It's just a phone hearing. I'll do it on the fly."

"A lawyer who represents himself has a fool for a client or a fool for a lawyer."

"I'm nobody's fool."

"Yeah right, fool. Then Friday you've got like three cases, all of them in Albuquerque. Different courts—one in Metro, two in District."

"I'm betting he's one of them."

We went through the list for Friday—all heavy hitters. Alejandro, the client from the jail, on armed robbery; Benally, on battery; and Cortez on attempted murder, which had pled down to something else.

"Just attempted murder," Jen said. "Attempted murder is like totally lame."

"The victim's still in the hospital."

"How do you defend these people?"

"Didn't you used to be one of those people? Luna defended you on something."

"Long story," she said. "I was innocent. Well, I wasn't guilty."

She typed up a quick summary of the names of all my cases for the week. She tried to print it out, but my printer was jammed. She swore lightly, and then copied all the names down perfectly onto a piece of notebook paper, and then copied them onto the Ends Zone calendar. Thankfully, Nastia's face wasn't on March.

Next Jen indexed all the defendants online, typed a few more keys, and then frowned. "That's weird. None of these guys has ever appeared before Luna."

"So what does that mean?" I asked.

"Well, I have no idea which of your clients would know anything."

I frowned. I wasn't going to get to be the hero after all. I looked at my watch, nine-thirty. "I have to see Agent Washington at the FBI."

"Can I come?"

I didn't know what to say. I caught another glimpse of that perfect left shoulder, but I didn't want to seem too eager. "I guess."

"I don't want to be alone," she said. "With you, I feel like nothing can harm me. Hell, even my scars are healing."

MASSACRE AT STINKING SPRINGS

As we drove north to the FBI building, I turned to Jen. "We're kinda like the Rosencrantz and Guildenstern of this case. We're on the outside."

"*Hamlet*, right?" She said. "They were the old friends of Hamlet who were sent to him to see what he was really up to."

"You're smarter than you look."

"Not that smart. What happened to Rosencrantz and Guildenstern?"

"They died."

"Couldn't we be like Romeo and Juliet?"

"They died, too."

The FBI building overlooked I-25, just down the frontage road from the Ends Zone. The Zone did serve lunch, so perhaps an agent occasionally entertained an informant over there, or maybe they held bachelor parties for agents.

I tried to drive into the lot, but was quickly rebuffed. "Park in the east lot!" the big guard at the gate shouted as he pointed to an empty lot. His guard box could withstand several suicide bombers and probably a direct hit from a Kamikaze.

We parked in the most distant space, and then headed into a roaring March wind. We showed the guard our IDs as he stared at Jen's exposed skin.

"Aren't you cold?"

"I'm trying to show that I don't have concealed weapons."

"You got goose bumps," I said. "Is that from fear or cold?"

"Both," she said.

"Only Shepard," the guard said through the ominous intercom. "The floozy stays behind."

"She's not a floozy," I said to the air.

Dejected, Jen walked back to the car. She wanted to say something, but the guard buzzed me in through the gate past a very high fence. I crossed a dying lawn to enter a modern building with vague Spanish accents. Inside, a sign by the bulletproof glass read, NO ELECTRONIC DEVICES IN FBI SPACE.

FBI space? We weren't in a building. We were in a "space."

The small, rounded lobby could pass for the bridge of a prototype of the *Enterprise*. The walls glistened in metallic tones; the doors were either a shiny wood or a dull brass. I noticed not one, but three black video cameras. Directly above me a sprinkler probably sprayed poison gas as needed.

I showed an ID to a receptionist who was behind the bulletproof glass. She looked like she should be working at a mortgage company as she read *People* magazine. Unfortunately, no magazines graced the lobby. What magazines would you expect to see in the FBI lobby anyway?

A bronze plaque on the wall described the namesake of the building: a special agent involved in a shootout at a place called Stinking Springs, New Mexico, somewhere on the reservation. The man was the first special agent to die in New Mexico.

I sat in the spaceship lobby, feeling naked without my phone. Bored, I listed every fictional FBI agent in my head, starting with Elliot Ness and ending with Mulder and Scully from *The X-Files*. Outside, Jen paced in the cold, stopping every few moments to wave to me.

"Don't wave to the FBI," I said out loud. "Jen, put some clothes on!"

She yelled something. Unfortunately, here in space no one can hear you scream.

"Can I go outside for a minute?" I asked.

"No," the receptionist said. "Once you're inside, you can't leave until you've been cleared by an agent to go back. Once you're in, you're stuck."

• • • • •

Special Agent Jorge Washington finally entered the lobby like a blitzing middle linebacker. Even on Saturday, he dressed in a blue blazer, red-and-white tie, and white shirt, like he just came from a political rally . . . or a book burning. He even had a shiny a red-white-and-blue flag pin on his lapel. He could pass for a senator speaking at a church.

He noticed Jen walking around outside and waving. "That girl is trouble," he said. "Come with me if you want to live."

He escorted me into a very small room off the lobby. This room was little more than a cloak room. He looked at me as if he viewed me as an X-file, one of those crappy stand-alone episodes.

"So you got a call from someone named Nastia," he said. "But you don't know anything about her or what she knows. Why do you think that's so important? Why should I care?"

"She thinks she knows something. One of my clients might know where the kid is."

"Which one of your clients?"

"She didn't say."

Washington shook his head. "Luna means a lot to me," he said. "We went out for a while."

I felt a tinge of jealousy as I noticed a big gun holstered to his side. "I didn't know that."

"I hate to use the cliché, but this one is personal."

"Clichés work because they're true," I said. A teacher had told me that in a film class. "It's personal to me, too."

He showed one quantum of solace. Only one. "I don't understand why she's fucking that asshole Gabriel Rose."

"Maybe we have a common enemy then."

"Maybe." He let his guard slip, a single tear formed by his eye, and then he wiped it away with his heavy hand.

I told him everything I had, which wasn't much.

He frowned. "I would be remiss if I don't follow every lead. I want you to keep in touch with me. Tell me everything. Even if you don't think it's important. Okay?"

"So do I get a Junior G-Man badge?" I said a little too flippantly, a line from an old kids' show. What was a G-Man exactly?

"That's your problem, you're never serious." Washington got right in my face. "If Luna's child dies because I didn't do everything in my power to save her, I'll have to take it out on someone."

I half-expected him to hit me right there.

"I'll walk you to the gate," he said instead.

• • • • •

Washington lit a cigarette when we exited. It must have been a special top-secret cigarette prototype as it defied the wind. "It's a no-smoking building," he said. "Don't tell Luna."

"About the meeting or the smoking?"

"Both."

When we got to the gate, he pointed at Jen, who was now pacing even faster. "We have a file on her. You and Tokyo Rose back together?"

"She's Korean not Japanese. I don't know if we're back together."

Jen wilted from a cold gust. My urge to rescue her increased. If Washington came after her, I'd take a bullet for her right there. He stayed outside smoking, finished one cigarette and then another.

I hurried to Jen, and gave her a hug. "Why didn't you sit in the car?" I asked.

"You took the keys, asshole. That's what I was trying to tell you."

"I'm sorry."

I fumbled with the keys before remembering to be a gentleman. Then I held the door to let her in.

"I tried to call my mom, but she's not picking up. Can I go check on her?"

"Your mom still have that crappy home in the 'war zone,' just off Zuni Street by Highland High School?"

"Yeah. She'll never leave; she loves it there. I've got a bad feeling she might be in trouble. Even when she hates me, like now, she always picks up."

I had a bad feeling too. We didn't say another word.

Back at FBI Space, Washington finished his cigarette and lit a third, then blew the biggest smoke ring I'd ever seen. I subconsciously patted down my body to see if he had put a trace on me. Then Washington took a call, and smiled.

BURNING DOWN THE HOUSE

WHEN WE DROVE SOUTH ON the interstate, I had to make another choice. "East on the Forty to San Mateo, or south down the Twenty-five to Central?"

"You should get on the freeway," Jen said. "Then get off on the San Mateo Boulevard exit."

"But traffic on San Mateo is a bitch in the morning. You gotta go by the Wal-Mart Super Center. No, I could stay on Central, then cut over and get on Coal and follow it until it gets to Zuni."

"It's still early, there won't be Wal-Mart traffic yet," she said. "Most of the way you can just jam on San Mateo."

"But there's that long light once you get off the freeway at Indian School Road."

We faced a life-or-death situation and here we argued about traffic. "Whatever," I said, taking us east on the freeway, then exiting on San Mateo Boulevard. Smoke came up in long plumes from the south.

"I sure hope that isn't my house," she said.

"I'm sure everything is fine. This neighborhood is on fire every other night."

"That's why I like you," she said, when I grabbed her hand. "You make me feel safe."

"No one's ever told me that before. Well, you make me feel like I'm always in danger."

She shook her head. "I know. I know. I know."

"I was kidding," I said. "But then again, part of me would like a guardian angel."

She didn't respond. Her moment of safety had quickly ended.

We finally turned onto her street, and found a pile of rubble where a modest stucco home once stood. Unlike the FBI "space," this house couldn't withstand a Kamikaze attack. Firemen sprayed the final cannons of water as if performing last rites. They stopped spraying as we exited the car. The house had expired.

Jen's mother, Nurse Song, was standing on the edge of the road in a daze, crying.

Jen ran out of the car. "Mom, are you all right?"

Nurse Song mumbled in Korean, before switching to English. "I'm alive."

"Where's Denise?" Jen asked. "Where's my daughter?"

"She's at the group home," her mother said. "That big guy from the group home picked her up."

Except for a few Korean artifacts that I spotted in the rubble, the house, and everything in it, was completely gone.

Jen and her mother talked quietly to each other in Korean. Well, her mom talked Korean and Jen answered in English. Their anguish was palpable; her mom really loved this place. I gave them some distance.

Jen had grown up here. Now her room was just ashes. She walked to the edge of the yellow caution tape, but didn't cross, just stared at the remnants of a baby carriage in the debris.

"They're trying to kill me!" she shouted to no one in particular. "They're trying to kill me!"

She gripped the yellow tape as if it were the bars of a jail cell. I tried to read her expression and failed. She let go of the tape, and gave her mother a hug, then whispered more words.

Officer Tran showed up and asked a few questions. Jen pushed her away and hurried back to me.

She closed her eyes as if thinking of something. "Dan, I need an hour alone with my mom, to make sure she's okay. Meet me over at the group home. I need to check on Denise."

Nurse Song spoke in Korean to Jen, who picked up her phone and began texting furiously with her little fingers.

"I'll take care of everything, Mom," she said. "Everything."

MOMMY DEAREST

I DRANK MY STARBUCKS HALF-CAF for the next hour and then met Jen at the group home, which was near the university. This home was more of a treatment center for special needs children, but it had a nice ancient adobe vibe to it. The *conquistadores* could send their special needs kids here while off on conquest.

Jen sat in a visiting area staring at a five-year-old girl who did not quite return her gaze. I stayed out in the lobby, but could see though a glass window.

"Mommy loves you," Jen seemed to be saying to the little girl. "Mommy loves you."

The girl smiled for one moment, but otherwise did not respond. I turned to the burly Native American next to me. "Do you work here?"

"Yeah, I'm the 'do everything guy,'" he smiled at me. "I know you. You represented my wife once. You got her *ag bat* down to simple battery."

I sensed an advantage. Maybe I could get him to reveal something that should be classified. "What's up with that little girl?"

"No one knows. She's not autistic or retarded. The tests show someone is home inside there. She just doesn't want to talk yet. It's like God hasn't made a decision to commit to her yet."

God hasn't made a decision yet. I sure hope God hadn't already decided about Dew as well. At least Jen had committed to her daughter. Jen bent down and kissed the girl on the forehead.

"She's a troubled spirit," the man said. "She's sane, but her soul is mad."

"That's kinda harsh to say about a five-year-old."

"I was talking about the mother."

Jen reached out to touch her daughter, but the girl pulled away. Jen began to cry, but her child still did not react. The *Do Everything* man went inside and indicated that Jen had to leave.

Jen still had tears in her eyes as she entered my car.

"Are you all right?

"I don't want to talk about it," she said. "I'm the worst mother in the world. God, I hope my daughter isn't harmed, too."

"Is there anything I can do?"

"Drive down Central," she said. "We need to talk to Luna."

• • • • •

I blinked, and we were in Luna's place at the Asylum Lofts. We tried to buzz in, but a female voice answered. "Who's this?"

"It's Dan."

Officer Tran came down and opened the door. She led us up without another word.

Inside the Asylum I tried to give Luna a hug, but she put up her hands. "We've tried to call you," I said.

"I'm not picking up unless it's the kidnappers."

I had no idea how to respond to that. I felt very awkward.

"Dan, can you give us a minute?" Jen asked.

• • • • •

"This is total bullshit," Gabriel Rose said into the air, pacing furiously down Central Avenue just outside the Asylum. It took me a moment to notice his blue-tooth earpiece. "We'll have to close down in Crater if the shit-storm hits. We can keep shooting the riot up in Santa Fe with the second unit. But that's it. This whole thing is fucking ruined."

He threw his phone down with rage.

"Is something wrong?"

"A little privacy, okay?" he shouted at me after picking up the phone. Disgruntled, he walked even further away, around the corner of the building into the park behind the Asylum. I just shook my head. I think my criminals were saner than the lawyers I knew.

• • • • •

He returned a few minutes later. "Sorry," he said. "The whole world is coming down."

"Don't worry about it." I didn't know how else to respond. He wasn't exactly a friend. If he married Luna and I got back with Jen, we'd be in the same circle; hell, we'd be in-laws. We'd be family.

I sat with Rose out in the front yard and watched traffic fly over the Martin Luther King Bridge. A train sounded its horn as it arrived from Santa Fe. The train whistled again, and then kept heading south.

I broke the ice when the train was finally out of ear shot. "I ran into your old buddy, Sky Roberts, in jail."

Rose shook his head. "Apparently the cops ran into him too. Twice in one week. He was my first case in New Mexico. I walked him on aggravating assault."

"Just call it *ag assault*," I said. "Like real lawyers do."

He laughed. "Yeah, you're a *real* lawyer."

"I keep it real," I said. We both laughed, pretending to like each other. He had represented Sky Roberts when that asshole was a co-defendant of my first public defender client in a case down in Aguilar—the case where I became the *Rattlesnake Lawyer*. "I didn't think I'd ever run into you again."

"New Mexico grows on you. You get a lot more for your money here. Especially now that I'm in a relationship."

I didn't like the way he said that, implying that he had bought Luna. Rose made me think "what if?"

What if I had stuck it out in Hollywood? What if I hadn't spent money on stupid things and invested wisely? What if I actually believed in myself, even half as much as he did?

His teeth were much cleaner. His personal trainer had made his muscles bigger, so his expensive clothes fit him better. His high priced medication had minimized his ADD and depression. I didn't even want to think about what else was bigger.

Time to change the subject, before I checked myself into a real asylum. "How's the movie going?"

"Haven't you been listening to the news? It's hard to believe that a two-hundred-million-dollar production rides on the fate of Sky High Roberts. If that little fucker goes to jail for a year, the banks will call in all the loans and the State will pull back the financing. If the judge considers it a second DUI and he does a week, no big deal. But if the judge calls it a third, or God forbid a fourth, it's a mandatory six months. But the judge is being a total fucking bitch."

"Who's his judge?" I asked, playing it cool.

He pointed up, toward Luna. "I love her so much, but you can see why she's called Judge Looney Toons. But I still love her. You know why?"

"I have no idea."

"She actually believes in something. I'm not used to people like that."

"What does she see in you?" I asked.

He laughed. "I believe in myself and she hopes it's contagious."

I wanted to punch him right there, but lucky for him, my phone rang. I was embarrassed to pick up my clunky cell phone in front of Rose. I knew he'd smirk when he saw it, and he did.

Private number. "Hello?"

"It's me. Nastia."

I returned the attitude to Rose. "Do you mind?"

He shook his head. He wouldn't budge. "I got here first," he said.

Reluctantly, I crossed Central Avenue and stood in front of a crumbling yoga joint sweat pouring out the walls.

"Dan, I don't have much time, are you there? Can you hear me?"

When I was as safe a distance as possible I spoke into the phone. "Nastia, what's up? Where are you?"

"I'm in Crater tonight. Like that McShane song, "Meet Me at the Mesa." More like at the Mesa refinery. I heard from my *lyobov*."

"What did he say?"

"Nothing yet, but my *lyobov* knows what's going down. We gotta meet, *da?*"

"Where?"

"In the town of Crater. By the new truck stop next to the casino. I'll find you there."

"Please tell me what's going on!"

"I can't over the phone," she said. "I heard what happened to your friend, Jen. The bad guys mean business. Like the old KGB, *da?*"

"Who are these guys?"

"I don't know."

"So why does your *lyobov* want to help if it's so dangerous?"

"My *lyobov* will do anything for me. *Anything*. It just takes a while to get – how you say—the ball rolling."

The line went dead.

When I walked back across the street Rose resumed talking into the air. Something about completion bonds. He kept talking as I tried to buzz back into the Asylum.

Tran answered. "We're still working things out. Stay there."

She hung up on me, and a wave of depression and impotence washed over me.

Rose kept talking, whispering the occasional "I'll deal with it," into the phone. He smiled after he hung up. "I've got to go up and take care of Luna. You go down and take care of your own girl."

"That's the thing. I don't know if she is my girl."

• • • • •

I waited outside on Central Avenue for another hour. The neighborhood had gentrified with the condos and all, but bad dudes still lived in the crumbling Route 66-era motels. Drug deals and prostitution still went down here.

Get your tricks on Route 66.

A cop eyed me as if he wanted to bust me for loitering with intent.

Jen finally came down. "She doesn't want me to stay."

"Tran?"

"No, Luna."

We looked at each other for a long minute. The chemistry between us was definitely back. She took my hand. Damn it felt good to hold hands again. Thankfully her wrist scar had heeled a little more since this morning.

Maybe I could save this girl from herself. Or at least bandage her up after she cut herself again.

"So you want to come with?"

"I'm all in," Jen said. "I'm always up for a wild goose chase. Let's roll."

"You really think Nastia can help us?"

"We don't have anything else, do we?"

TRICKS ON 66

"JUST GIVE ME ANOTHER MINUTE," Jen said. She made calls and texts, sometimes simultaneously, all while pacing up and down the garish stretch of Central like a streetwalker on uppers. Getting her tricks indeed. The street was empty except for several panhandlers. They smiled at Jen with a weird kind of professional courtesy.

God she had a great rear end. What was that country song, women sometimes looked the best when they were walking away from you? I didn't remember whether the singer was happy or sad.

Jen closed her phone and walked toward me. She smiled. That special place in my heart next to the left ventricle had now expanded all the way to the aorta.

Jen said she had to go take care of her mother. She called me after an hour. "I'm running late," she said. "A lot to take care of."

"With your mom?"

"With my life."

I had spent half of our relationship waiting for Jen to take care of her life.

"I need to find out how bad I've screwed it up," she said.

"Well, call me when you've fixed everything."

• • • • •

I took a nap. I was watching the NCAA tournament on TV, cheering against Duke, a college that had rejected me for law school, when a cab pulled up. A knock came at the door.

"Are you sure you want to come with me?" I asked Jen. She wore a tank top with the Geishas on it. Too much skin for such a windy day.

"I'm starting to like hanging out with you," she said. "It's like I never left."

"But you did leave," I said.

"My mistake."

"There's two minutes to go," I said. "Let's wait 'till the end."

The game went into overtime, of course. We found ourselves clenching hands on my couch. I looked into her big brown eyes, and then at that damn bare shoulder. Should I kiss her? No, not yet. Plenty of time for that later.

• • • • •

We finally set out west on I-40 about five in the afternoon. As the color drained from the landscape on top of Nine Mile Hill, the earth resembled an unfashionable section of the moon. I held her hand. We had a comfortable silence in the last of the light as we descended into the next valley west of Albuquerque. A roadside billboard advertised a woman's boxing match featuring Heidi "the Navajo Hammer" Hawk at Crater Casino. Heidi had made cameo appearances in my life since my Rattlesnake Lawyer days. She was one of my first clients, then an old girlfriend's roommate at the hospital. She even knew Luna back in Crater County. From the chiseled abs on the billboard, at least someone I knew could take a punch.

Right around Tohajiilee, at the edge of the desert, the darkness kicked in, both inside and outside.

"Do you think Nastia's in danger?" Jen asked.

"Well, the people we're dealing with have kidnapped a kid and burned your house down. I'd say they were pissed."

Neither of us broke the uncomfortable silence as we ascended another lunar hill. "Let's talk about something else," I said. "Anything."

"Why didn't you move on after me?" Jen asked.

"I never met the right person," I said. A stock answer, like a mountain climber says he climbs mountains because they're there. "I mean, a stripper like Nastia sure wasn't Ms. Right."

"No, really. What about Luna? You two could have made it. There was a window before she met Rose and you were with her before."

"She's the perfect woman. Unfortunately, she's looking for the perfect man. She went out with a weight lifter for awhile that was Mr. Universe for Albuquerque."

"That's crap," Jen said. "Most of her men have hardly been perfect. This guy she's with now, Mr. Hollywood, is like a total asshole."

"But he's a very rich and successful total asshole," I said. "Well, it's weird. I feel that no woman could really love me until I am rich and successful. Even if I am an asshole."

"But you *are* successful."

"I'm a just public defender without the benefits. I wrote a self-published book that no one read. I'm all alone."

"You blame me," she said. "Didn't work out for me, did it?"

"Did you and Rose do it while you were out there in Hollywood?"

"Nah," she said. "I think he's gay. He never made a move on me."

"Why would anyone not make a move on you?"

"You flatter me too much," she said. "I'm not that hot."

"Then why is Rose with Luna?"

"Why does anyone want to fuck a judge?"

"Why?"

"So the judge doesn't fuck them. You know that."

We kept driving west on the empty interstate. By this time on a Saturday night most people have already made it to where they're going.

"So what about you?" I asked. "What really happened in L.A.?"

"I'm just a girl who can't say *yes*."

I laughed, even if she wasn't joking. "I had a girlfriend who said 'I like people who like themselves. Opposites attract.'"

"It's not that. I've just always felt like damaged goods. My mother always said I let her down. And my father, don't even get me started about my father."

"So you're looking for Daddy in your dating life?"

"No. I'm looking for you." She squeezed my shoulder. "But if I sleep with you, will I end up in a mental hospital like that one chick you dated, Ophelia?"

"I can't promise anything."

"Then we'll have to wait."

A few miles later we passed by the famed Golden Road Casino, to the south. Jen immediately stiffened. I remembered our last trip here, a year ago, on a lazy summer Sunday on the fourth of July weekend. I checked my watch.

• • • • •

Eight months earlier . . .

The Golden Road Casino tried to evoke the hey-day of Route 66, but what was a hey-day anyway? One could almost imagine the auto denizens of Radiator Springs in Disney's *Cars* playing here. In the fanciful art on the wall, a bunch of junky autos engaged in playing a friendly game of poker. The Volkswagen Bug held a full house.

Since it was Fourth of July, the casino was decked out with patriotic glitz: red, white and blue everywhere. Since this was an Indian casino, I wondered if they were overdoing it a bit, technically we were in a sovereign country after all, here on the rez.

Jen and I scattered to different parts of the casino. She went to the red section, I went to the blue. My public defender check was late, as usual, so I settled for putting a five dollar bill in the penny slots, and gambled one penny a line. Jen made a pit stop at the Players Club window. Apparently she had a line of credit at the casino. How could a girl like Jen have a line of credit?

I found an old machine called *Risqué Business*. If three of the characters line up in a row at one time, you received a bonus. For the first time in my life, the buzzers rang. . .I won three hundred and fifty credits. I jumped for joy.

"We gotta get out of here," Jen said, emerging from nowhere.

"But I won."

"You won three hundred and fifty pennies. Don't spend it all in one place. Hand me your keys and meet me at the car."

"What's going on?"

"You don't want to know," she said. "But it's serious. They think I stole a watch from the jewelry shop."

"Did you?"

"I gave it back. You've got to believe me. They still want to hold me and check all the video on computers to see if I stole anything else and hid it."

I hesitated for a moment; I held her wrist, as if I was a lie detector. She was calm, too calm; perhaps she was telling the truth. I quickly slipped her the keys and pretended to stare at the screen.

Jen disappeared. I bet the max credits and soon lost everything.

After waiting another moment, I nonchalantly walked out the front door. Big men in tribal casino security outfits pushed passed me on their way in.

Inside my car, Jen scrunched down in the back seat. She jokingly made a motion toward my crotch. "How'd you like some hot fugitive sex?"

"Not tonight. I have a headache since I don't know what's going on."

"Don't ask," she said. "I had a friend who helped me get out the back way. We've got an hour to kill before they give up."

"Shouldn't we just drive away?"

She pointed to a roadblock at the entrance to the freeway. A tribal policeman manned the roadblock and gave a quick glance at every car leaving. The Golden Road was a cul-de-sac. We were trapped here for the duration.

"So now what?"

"There's something I want to show you."

We hiked around to the back of the casino, far beyond the spotlights. Within moments, we reached a big sand dune that glistened in the moonlight. I touched her shoulder.

"See if you can catch me," she said, as she ran up the sand.

The girl must have been training hard in her spare time; she made it to the top before me, and then stopped for a moment of panting. Her heavy breathing almost sounded like an orgasm.

"You're faking, right?" I asked.

She finally caught her breath. There was a smell of perfume mixed with the cigarettes of the casino, with just a tinge of desert root. God, it smelled good.

"So why are the tribal cops out to get you?"

"They're not really," she said with a smile. "But they've got to pretend they're looking for me. The whole thing will blow over in a couple of hours."

"So who's really after you?"

She laughed. "Nobody. Everybody. I don't even know sometimes. I just don't want to wait for the video."

"What would the video have shown?"

"That I'm innocent... or at least not guilty."

She loved saying that, even though I had no idea what it meant. Not guilty of what? I looked in her eyes again, as they reflected the lights of Albuquerque in the distance. The full moon crossed in the range. We sat and watched the commotion down below at the casino.

"Riding the storm out," I said. *"Waiting for the thaw out,* REO Speedwagon."

"A song way before my time," she said.

I hugged her. Korea was the land of morning calm and Jen was the calm at the edge of this evening shit storm. Her serenity was contagious as the wind died; even the sound of the freeway couldn't penetrate our little bubble. Sitting near her, for just one moment, we felt we had an entire frontier separating our little nation of two from the rest of the world.

We sat there on the sand, pretending we were on a beach overlooking a stormy ocean. Eventually the commotion died down below. The roadblock lifted and the cop sped off to another emergency. The casino grew calm in the moonlight. I listened to Jen breathe, and watched that perfect chest go up and down.

"Do you want to go now?"

"Not yet." She kissed me.

I kissed her back.

There on top of the sand dune, glowing from the distant lights, we made love for the first time. Something over-powered me. "I love you," I said.

What was I thinking? I was in the middle of the desert with a fugitive I barely knew.

"I love you, too," she said. "I was going to get you a watch when they started freaking out and said I was trying to hide it."

"You were going to steal a watch for me?"

"Well, you're always late. It was silver and turquoise."

"That's sweet," I said. "But don't break the law on my account."

We spent the night together on that dune. Thankfully it was a warm night, or perhaps our little nation of two had its own geothermal power. She liked playing with my ears for some reason. She laughed at my silly jokes, and even got my obscure reference to Lemmiwinks, a gerbil in *South Park*.

We awoke to the sound of motors and she held me tight, terrified.

"Is this it?" she asked, closing her eyes. "Have they come for me?"

Something flew over us.

A pair of all terrain vehicles leapt the hollow in the dunes we lay in. Like us, they shouldn't be out here on tribal land, and they pretended not to see us.

We had returned to the scene of the crime a few weeks later, and she actually bought me the silver and turquoise watch in cold hard cash.

• • • • •

Back in the present, I checked that turquoise watch again. We were more good time driving west on the interstate into the spring sunlight, I tried to pick out the sand dune to the north, the exact spot we made love for the first time. Hopefully the sand buried any evidence of our rendezvous. Unfortunately, my eyes failed in the darkness. After we had passed through the Golden Road Casino's jurisdiction, and back onto New Mexico land, Jen smiled.

"So how many casinos are you banned from?" I asked.

"I'm not sure," she said. "Do you count the ones in Vegas and Reno? Well, they love me in Crater's casino. That's like the only place where I win."

"How often do you go there?"

"Not that often," she said. "I was there a few weeks ago when I was an extra in the movie."

"Who did you play?"

"A dead girl."

DMZ.com

A FEW MORE MILES OF desert freeway west, and we finally arrived at our exit. It felt like a war zone, except here *four* competing adversaries struggled for dominance. The truck stop lay at the southern tip, like the home plate of a baseball diamond. To the north, the vast expanse of the old Mesa refinery formed a vast metallic outfield. To the east, at first base, lay the Crater Casino. To the west, at third base, movie people had erected makeshift trailers and double wides for a movie camp for *Desert Demons*. Signs in Arabic lined the entrance. They must be filming a big action sequence at the refinery. Was this supposed to be Iraq?

Each base had its own no trespassing signs, like the DMZ between heaven, hell and purgatory.

"What's going on here?" I asked.

Jen smiled. "It's complicated. This is the checkerboard part of the rez. They told me the scoop last time I was here, a while ago on the way back to Albuquerque."

"Who owns what out here?"

"The refinery is on Indian land. The movie camp is on private land, but the film people also have to pay the tribe to film on the refinery. They have to pay the private landowner to stay there, too. The casino is on Indian land of course, but the truck stop is owned by a rich white dude. I heard he's pissed at the tribe."

"A tourist could eat fatty food at the truck stop buffet and fill up with expensive gas, gamble, breathe toxic fumes, and then hopefully get filmed being blown up in a refinery while pretending to be in Iraq. Great weekend."

"I did that about a month ago," she said.

"And why were you here again?"

"I was an extra for one of the scenes. A harem girl who got killed."

"A harem girl?" I asked. "I'm dreaming of you in a Jeannie outfit."

"I'm not a whore for real, okay?"

"Did you meet any movie stars?"

"Sky, of course. And the producers—a rich Mexican guy and an Arab. They both wanted me at the same time, but I said *not even*."

Before she could fill me in she smiled and called, "Yo Cowboy!"

Cowboy Begay, the tribal cop, stood filling up his squad car at the station. A state policeman filled his car on the other side. The two stared at each other with icy tension, probably from day after day of jurisdictional disputes.

Cowboy's mood visibly lifted when he spotted Jen. "Hey, Pink!"

Jen hurried to him and I followed. "We're looking for Nastia," Jen said. "You know, the girl from the Zone. She's the Russian Eskimo chick from the Ends Zone. "

Cowboy stared at the refinery for a moment. "*Inupiat*," he said. "There's a major difference. I saw her getting gas here a few minutes ago. I think she might be turning tricks at the movie set. Glad I don't have to monitor those assholes."

"What? The little ho hurting your tax-free casino, Cowboy?" the state trooper taunted, butting into our allegedly private conversation.

"The casino money goes to the tribe."

"Well, I'm not in the tribe," the trooper said. "It ain't paying for my gas."

The two men locked eyes in a staring contest. This had been going on since Frontier days, in their past lives.

"So who you got your money on in the fight tonight?" the trooper asked. "Want to make a side bet?"

"I'm betting on my home girl, Heidi the Navajo Hammer Hawk," he said with a smile. "Always bet on red!"

Both men holstered very big guns amidst a lot of flammable chemicals. Were they going to have some kind of draw? But before the two cops' personal feud could escalate, gunshots rang out for real, to the north near the refinery.

"It's over there!" Cowboy said, pointing toward the club. "Yours or mine?"

The trooper pulled out his radio. "Whose jurisdiction?" he shouted.

We could see the dark shapes of men running from the movie side toward the refinery. Others headed into the refinery from the casino.

"The refinery's on my side!" Cowboy shouted.

"Then you take it." The trooper smiled. "I don't want a shoot-out this close to shift change."

"Stay back then," Cowboy said, as he headed toward the refinery.

"Do you need back-up?" one of Cowboy's deputies asked, a surprisingly squeaky-voiced man for someone so big. It was hard to tell if he was Native or not.

Jen pointed to a short, dark-haired girl in the distance who was standing by a trailer on the camp side, smoking a cigarette.

"Smoking on a polluted day seems redundant," I said. "Here, next to an oil refinery, it's suicidal."

"That looks like Nastia," she said. "I'll go get her."

I sure couldn't identify Nastia from this far away. This Nastia was much shorter than I remembered, but then she had probably worn major heels at the club. I started to follow Jen, but the state trooper grabbed me. "Let her go."

What did he mean by that? I leaned forward, but the trooper didn't release his grip. "Sir, you need to stay back. Everything on the other side of this truck stop is restricted land . . . restricted by somebody."

What should I do? The trooper kept staring at me. He was heavy and I could outrun him, but I couldn't outrun his bullets.

The shoot-out continued on the far side of the refinery, maybe a quarter-mile away. Figures ran in all directions in the eerie green lights of the complex. Two more shots rang out, then countless ricochets. For a second, the ground rumbled. I could run away right now, but I knew I'd better wait for Jen.

On-lookers emerged from the casino on the west side. More came from the movie set to watch on the eastern flank. What was this, entertainment on a Saturday night here in the boonies? Jen and Nastia disappeared into the crowd in the distance.

Nastia the Eskimo gymnast— I couldn't see her face any more in my thoughts. It had been months ago and I'd only seen her for an hour, max, in a dark club. What the hell was her connection to this? Who was her, what did she call it, her *lyobov*? Perhaps the bad guys wanted her dead just for talking to me

The state trooper stood by us, keeping the crowd steady with a hand on his revolver. He had his radio on maximum setting; the ear piece probably broke a long time ago. His radio spewed random reports from inside. "Two people. . . . Armed. . . . Possible kidnapping. . . ."

More ricochets off the metal of the refinery. A hissing noise came from one of the tanks. If it went, there would be an inferno.

The people on the casino side darted back into the building.

More movie folks came out of their trailers to watch. A few even started filming with phones; perhaps they needed B-roll for the movie.

State trooper vehicles pulled into the parking lot, their sirens blaring. Until Cowboy formally asked for assistance, the state cops could only wait in the parking lot. A handful of tribal cops emerged from an annex to the casino and ran deeper into the refinery area.

"We'll handle it from here," a tribal cop shouted to the state troopers. "Stay the hell back from our jurisdiction."

I wanted to do something, but what? Nastia had tried to contact me. This was my fault somehow. My nausea grew worse. The refinery might as well be belching smoke inside my gut. Was Nastia dead? Did this have something to do with me and Jen?

A long pause, then the trooper's radio crackled. "We got one down! One down!"

I heard a squeaky voice say "She walked right into the shot. I told her to stop! I told her to stop!"

The trooper spoke into radio. "Do we have clearance to go onto the refinery?"

"Not yet," the dispatcher replied. "Not until you get clearance from tribal police. It's still their crime."

The refinery hummed, the machinery beat relentlessly like a bad industrial rock band from the nineties, a Nine Inch Nails cover band on meth, perhaps. Or was it that Trevor McShane song "Meet Me at the Mesa?"

"One down!" the radio stated. It sounded like Cowboy. "One down!"

The machinery halted. Maybe someone had pressed the "off" button. Then a smoke stack let off one good belch of fire, like a dragon that had waited to a fart until company had left.

Silence.

Wind echoed through the metallic canyons.

Finally, a voice on the trooper's radio said, "All clear."

"Can we enter Indian land?"

The dispatcher replied, "Not yet. You do not have clearance to enter the reservation."

"I've got a dead female," I recognized Cowboy's voice.

"She walked right into me. I told her to stop!" the squeaky voice said.

I shuddered. Nastia was probably dead. There went my only chance of helping Luna.

The state trooper forced everyone to stay back while a tribal ambulance pulled up to the refinery. A team of EMTs wearing the Crater tribal insignia rushed into the complex.

I fumbled through my wallet until I found my bar card. "I'm an attorney," I said.

"I don't care," he said. "Show it to the cop over there."

A very big tribal cop stood just in front of us. "This is sovereign Indian land. Our rez; our rules. Unless you hurry up and study and take the tribal bar, you ain't no lawyer over here. I can't let you pass until we get the okay from Cowboy."

Hopefully Jen followed Nastia into a trailer. They were both safe, right? I jumped as a car honked and cut through me like another gun shot.

"Have you see, Jen?" I asked the tribal cop. "Have you seen Nastia?"

"Who?"

Jen had probably gotten impatient and gone back to my car. That was probably her honking to get me to hurry. Did I leave her my keys? I forgot. I had to find out what happened to her and Nastia.

• • • • •

Finally, after an hour, the tribal EMTs emerged, pulling a stretcher.

"Who is it?" I asked Cowboy when he finally got within earshot.

Cowboy frowned and shook his head. He pulled back the top of the sheet to reveal the woman underneath. It was Jen. She didn't move. Blood stains were everywhere, a bullet hole in her head. There was another bullet through her bare shoulder. For some reason that was what got me. My mind couldn't process this.

Jen's dead?

Luna lost a sister.

Nurse Song lost a daughter.

Denise lost a mother.

I lost my best friend . . . maybe more.

Jen's dead?

She sure as hell wasn't moving. I sank to my knees and threw up—everything in my stomach, everything in my heart, and half the memories in my brain.

As I stumbled up, I heard ringing in my ears. Had the gunshots deafened me? No my phone decided to ring at yet another bad time. I stood still. Not again.

"God damn it! Get your phone," Cowboy shouted as he zipped the bag, covered Jen's face again, and urged the EMTs to move on.

I wiped away the tears from my eyes and the crap from the sides of my mouth. I saw a private number. It could be Nastia.

"Dan Shepard?" a squeaky male voice asked.

"Yes."

"Will you hold for Saul Podell of the Morris Williams Agency? He really loves your *Legal Coyote* book."

"He does?" I asked. "I don't understand."

"He wants to set up a meeting about turning it into a TV series. Is now a good time for you to talk?"

Part 2

RED DUSK

ON THE OTHER END OF the line, Saul the agent raved about my book in a thick New York accent. "It's so good that it's inspired me to write again," he said.

I mumbled something in agreement. How many times had I heard that line? All I could think of was Jen. I told him now wasn't a good time, but I would love to come out there, not this week, maybe the week after.

He laughed. "You call us when you're ready to come."

"I thought it was supposed to be 'Don't call us, we'll call you,'" I said.

"No, the ball's in your court, call us when you're ready."

I hung up. Hopefully all of my balls would land before then. Luna would get her child back. Jen would come back to life. I stood there completely numb, staring at the refinery as it let loose a barrage of smoke, looking for Jen's spirit.

A cop finally approached me. "What's your relation to Jen Song?" he asked.

I didn't know what to say. I hadn't slept with her, well, not in awhile. She certainly wasn't my true love, or *lyobov*, or whatever it was. She was with me for now, but we had never settled on the definition of what that meant.

"Just a friend," I said. "For a while we were engaged to be engaged."

"Past tense?"

"We broke up a while ago, but were in the process of getting back together."

"That don't count. I got nothing to say to you," the tribal cop said. "But don't go nowhere. I'm sure Cowboy wants to give you the whole nine yards."

"The whole nine yards?"

"His rez, his rules."

"You guys keep saying that."

• • • • •

I sat at the truck stop on a bench. Washington drove up with two other FBI agents. They must get a discount rate on blue suits, white shirts and red ties. He silently grilled me, staring with those G-man eyes as if water-boarding me.

"What the hell happened?" he asked.

"I tried to get her to stay here," I said.

"You can't tell Jen anything."

I couldn't tell if he blamed me or not. I tried to follow as the agents moved closer to some newly erected crime scene tape, but the tribal cops pushed me back. I cowered in the corner. Without Jen, I had no more mojo.

Cowboy stood up to the FBI. He wouldn't let him onto his scene without the proper paperwork.

"It's a major crime!" Washington said. "It's under the Major Crimes Act."

"It's an accidental shooting," Cowboy replied. "It was a suicide by cop."

Suicide by cop? I thought again about Jen's scars. It all made sense, unfortunately. Life was too much for her and I deluded myself in thinking I could save her. The squeaky deputy was nowhere to be seen. If he was Native and the shooting took place on the rez, then a whole set of jurisdictional rules applied that I had forgotten since my one semester of Indian law. I nearly threw up again, but there was nothing left in my stomach, or my heart.

"Suicide or not, if tribal cops were involved in a shooting, that comes under Major Crimes."

The two sides kept arguing. I tried to get closer so I could hear.

"You, lawyer! You stand over there." A tribal cop pointed to a spot in a corner of the parking lot.

"Can I go to the bathroom?" I asked the cop.

"Maybe you should do it in a cup. See if you're dirty," he said. "I see bloodshot, watery eyes."

"I've been crying. I just lost my . . . best friend."

"Just use the unit over there," the cop said, pointing to a portable toilet.

• • • • •

After an hour Cowboy came over to me, still in bad ass cop mode. The squeaky deputy still hadn't appeared on this side of the line. Washington made a few more phone calls in his car, and finally drove away.

"You win, Cowboy," he had said.

Reporters and other hangers-on crowded around the yellow tape.

"You will not pass," Cowboy said, like Gandalf in *Lord of the Rings*. "Lawyer, you come with me."

"Am I under arrest?" I asked.

"Should you be?"

Why do people keep asking me that? I expected him to smile to indicate he was joking, but he didn't smile at all. Everyone treated the lawyer like one of the criminals.

"Have you called the next of kin?" I asked.

"We'll let the FBI do that," he said. "They have to do something."

• • • • •

The tribal police station was a little adobe annex grafted to the side of the casino. From the outside, this brown box, barely the size of a convenience store, didn't look like it belonged to a casino, as if official law enforcement was an afterthought out here. This was the Wild West after all.

We entered through an outside entrance. Inside, the office had primitive equipment, worse than most small police stations I'd been to in New Mexico. Even the furniture looked like something John Wayne would sit on.

"This is your station?"

"The Feds shit on us these days. You know that," Cowboy said.

As chief of police, Cowboy rated a crappy desk in the back of a temp building. A picture of his late wife, a pretty, though heavy-set, Navajo woman showed her nearly buckling under her turquoise. In another picture, two children wore Redskins sports jerseys and posed with Heidi Hawk, the female boxer. I considered raising the issue of whether Redskins was a derogatory term for a football team, but now was not the time.

"Why were you and Jen here?" he asked.

Could I trust Cowboy? His weather-beaten face indicated a man out of time; he should have been a warrior in frontier days. Now he guarded a casino and a refinery in a jurisdiction the size of mall parking lot.

"I'm waiting," he said.

I told him the story, racing a mile a minute.

"For a lawyer, you're a terrible witness," he said. "You didn't mention the strip club."

"I don't think you need to put that in your report, or the fact that I saw you there."

"A lot of stuff isn't going in my report. I knew Nastia. She danced for me a couple of times. Like I said, she worked the movie camp once in a while, too, if you catch my drift. Outside my jurisdiction, so I couldn't bust her. So much stuff goes down with the movie people."

"Where is she?"

"She just vanished into the night. There's an All Points Bulletin out for her."

"You think she's a bad guy?" I asked. "I thought she was helping me."

"We don't know yet. Don't have any idea who she really is. This is real complicated."

"Washington said this is a *major crime*," I said, referring to the landmark Major Crimes Act, which gave the Bureau jurisdiction on Indian land in special cases. "Doesn't the FBI take over?"

"Once they get a court order signed by a Federal judge, they sure do," said Cowboy. "I don't see a Federal judge around, do you? Right now we don't have a *major crime*. Like I told him, we have an accidental death, possibly a suicide caused by an Indian cop on Indian land."

"Did you shoot her? Did the deputy with the squeaky voice?"

Cowboy betrayed nothing. "Like I said, until a Federal district judge rules otherwise, it's an accident. I'm in charge."

"You didn't answer my question."

"I know."

"Can I talk to the deputy?"

"No. And trust me on this; he's a lot more scared of me than he is of you."

I tried to look at Cowboy. He was a friend of Jen's from the club. He was on her side, right?

"So what do I do?"

He smiled. "Stay here at the casino tonight in the hotel. We'll put you up. Just like you was a high roller. We'll even get you into the fight tonight."

"I don't know if I'm in the mood for a fight. I'm the lowest roller I know. Why do you want me to stay?"

"I don't know yet," he said. "I'm waiting for further instructions."

"From who?"

"The Feds call it the need to know basis—and you don't need to know."

ALWAYS BET ON RED

THE CRATER INN WAS THE ugly step-sister of the casino complex, a two-story faux adobe building built on the cheap, like an architectural Indian minstrel show. The walls desperately needed stucco. Cowboy shrugged when he noticed my discomfort inside the building. "Hey, it's for the tourists. Our people don't stay here."

Cowboy took me to the front desk and talked with the concierge. "Get him into the fight, but give him the cheap seats."

The concierge put me in a first floor room with a view of the freeway exit. I think the room's regular price was less than the cost of the all-you-can-eat buffet. Trucks headed for California roared past me on Route 66. Part of me wanted to join them, to get away from Jen's ghost.

Despite the late hour, I called Luna. "I know already," she said. "Washington called me. I've lost everyone who's close to me. I don't know how much more I can take." She muffled the line. "Gabe, Jen's dead."

"Did you call her mother?" I asked.

"I did already," Luna said. "Her mother wasn't really surprised. She said Jen spent her whole life with a target on her."

"Is there anything I can do? Anything?"

"I've got my own crisis. I hate to say it but perhaps Jen is in a better place."

She hung up.

I felt serious guilt. Washington blamed me. Did Luna blame me as well? Why couldn't I have made Jen stay in the car? Why? Why didn't I follow her? Oh, because a heavily armed state trooper grabbed me.

I took the world's longest shower, hoping my guilt would wash out with the complimentary herbal shampoo and conditioner. I gagged and nearly threw up another time, but caught myself.

Jen couldn't really be gone, could she? And what the hell happened to Nastia?

I tried to console myself with the Hollywood news, but how many times had I heard that bullshit before? With God as my witness, I'd give up a deal for a series based on my book if it would bring Jen back.

Wouldn't I?

I hesitated for a second, but the answer was clear. I wanted Jen back more than even a first look development deal on the studio lot.

By nine o'clock I couldn't stare at the TV without going insane. There was a story about the shooting, but the newscaster also mentioned the championship women's fight. All publicity was good publicity for the casino, right? And speaking of casinos, the hotels supposedly pump in air so you can't sleep and want to gamble. Come to think of it, the air here felt a little too fresh. The walls started closing in on me and I jumped off the bed.

Cowboy had comped me for the fight —a good an excuse as any to leave the unfriendly confines. Besides, I wanted to observe Cowboy. I didn't trust him. He mentioned that "everybody" would be there. Could everybody include Nastia? I doubted it, but perhaps I would find someone guilty by association.

"The ring's the thing by which to catch the conscience of the king," I paraphrased Shakespeare.

• • • • •

In the casino lobby, a long line snaked from the showroom entrance. Metal detectors stood at the end of a waiting area filled with glass boxes containing headdresses and pottery. Unlike the patriotic excess of the Golden Road Casino, the Crater band went out of their way to let you know you had left America behind.

Many of the Native Americans in the crowd shook their heads at the quality of the displays.

"Navajo pottery sucks," said a young man. He wore a Laguna-Acoma High School t-shirt.

"Don't be dissing my mama's pottery," a Navajo replied.

Security stopped them before it got out of hand. Fight nights brought out the testosterone; insulting a man's mama's pottery could be fatal. My God, I would have loved to have taken Jen here to see all the tackiness!

A ticket waited for me in the will-call line. Just last week a famous R & B act performed here; I certainly saw no *miracles* in this cramped venue the size of a school gym. Nothing *supreme* either, just plenty of *temptations.*

I had been to only one boxing match before and I expected to see a lot of mobster types with their molls. I wasn't disappointed. One even wore a pink wig.

Was that Jen's wig?

No. This woman looked Navajo rather than Korean.

Several truckers lined the cheap seats. I sat in the back row of the stands, with a group of gang kids, wearing "505" jerseys, the area code of New Mexico.

"How did you get out of jail?" said one to the right of me as he shouted to the guy on the other side of me.

"I said my mama was sick," the man on my left replied. "How about you?"

"My *tia* died again."

"Your *tia* dies every fight, *ese.*" Left snickered at me. "You're that lawyer, right? You were cool in G-7."

"Thanks," I said.

"Well don't say nothing about us being here," Right said.

"Mum's the word," I said.

"Who are you here with?" Left asked.

"I don't know," I said. "I'm looking for someone."

"Don't see anyone looking for you."

The crowd certainly didn't dress as well here as they did in Vegas. Here they favored turquoise bling over gold.

"Damn there are a lot of ugly chicks here," Left said.

"Most of them look like dykes," Right said.

"Hey, shut up!" A pretty blond woman in the next row turned around. "Dora's my girlfriend. So don't be saying shit."

Late arrivals raised the percentage of females in the stands and many of the women were there with dates—female dates. A banner announced the main event: Heidi "the Navajo Hammer" Hawk, versus Dora *"La Culebra"* Lilly, a gigantic blonde Amazon.

I looked again at Heidi on the poster. Through amazing training, this one-time paint sniffer had become one hundred sixty pounds of steel. She sported a serious Mohawk, even though she was Navajo.

"Now to sing the national anthem," the tuxedoed announcer called. "Former *American Idol* contestant—New Mexico's own Anna Maria Duran y Villalobos."

I gasped. Anna Maria was another former client. It was old home week here in Crater County. Anna Maria entered the ring wearing a long black dress. She sang the anthem first in English, then did a verse in Spanish, then one in *Dine,* the Navajo language.

Finally, the announcer introduced the main event. "Ladies and Gentleman, let's get ready to . . . tummmmble!"

He knew he couldn't legally say the copyrighted, "Let's get ready to rumble."

Dora Lilly made her entrance with a mariachi version of *Bang Your Head*, even though she was a tall, burly white girl with bleached blond hair. She could pass for a female version of Mickey Rourke's character in *The Wrestler*. I wondered if the silicone in her fake boobs were enhanced with iron.

"Bang your head," Left sang along with the song.

"Wake the dead!" Right sang the next line.

The song abruptly ended and the lights went off.

Distant drumming announced the Navajo Hammer, like an army coming over the range. The drumming grew louder and louder. I remembered the Florida State Seminole chant, but it did not compare to the real thing, a real war chant sung by real warriors. At first only the Navajos chanted, but by the third verse the rest of the crowd figured out the words. Soon everyone, all races, sexes and sexual orientation went wild as the drums grew louder and louder.

The beat contained strong *medicine*, in the Native American sense of the word. I wanted to believe in the medicine of the drums. Somewhere in the depths of hell these drums could wake the dead.

Once everyone joined in, Native and non, male and female, innocent and guilty, the drums got even louder. The crowd went into a fever pitch as an entourage emerged from the depths of the casino. Something shiny floated above the crowd: a very big man carried a golden championship belt. God, why couldn't I carry a belt for a living?

I closed my eyes and stomped my feet to the beat. *Bang your head*! I wasn't in the casino any more. I was at a ghost dance in the underworld.

A cheer erupted. . . .

Everything was possible if I just kept my eyes closed. The medicine could work. Bring her back! Bring her back! Bring her back!

Bang your head!

Wake the dead!

The cheers grew even louder.

Could it be? I opened my eyes.

No, the drums' medicine had not woken the dead. Heidi came down in her turquoise robe emblazoned with her sponsor's logo, *Navajo Repo,* a tribal company that repoed cars on the rez.

"Don't fear the *Repo!*" someone shouted.

Heidi slapped hands and then took a victory lap around the ring. And the fight hadn't even started yet.

I stared at Heidi. She kept making cameo appearances in my life and in the lives of other people I knew. She sure would make an interesting lead character in a book someday. I already had a title: *Navajo Repo.*

I spotted a woman ringside who resembled Nastia, short and pale. How did Nastia look, really? I had never seen her in a good light. In any event, I was pretty sure this was the woman from the truck stop a few hours earlier. I needed to get a good look at her. "Excuse me, could I borrow your binoculars?" I asked Left.

"Get your own eyes! It's the Navajo Fucking Hammer! She's our homegirl, *ese.*"

The bell rang, and the fight began in earnest. The crowd roared with every Heidi Hawk uppercut. I had to get to Nastia, if that was indeed who it was. I pushed my way down the stands, but a huge security officer stopped me when I reached the bottom. The mystery woman must have seen me as she headed toward the casino exit.

Barely five feet tall, she ducked under the bobbing heads of the fight fans. I followed, but accidentally stepped on a few cowboy boots in the aisle. Someone pushed me to the floor. In the meantime, the mystery woman vanished into the depths of the casino. I picked myself up and rushed for the exit.

A security guard touched my shoulder. "Once you leave, you can't come back."

"I'm not coming back," I said

In the casino, I tried to follow through the maze of slot machines. A roar of triumph came from the showroom. Heidi must really be hammering. The slot machines actually shook, and then switched into tilt mode.

Several patrons swore and I heard more than one say, "I lost all my money."

The casino floor grew even more crowded as a big party emerged from the buffet, and I ran into a gauntlet of obese patrons. I almost put my hands on a woman to push her away, then noticed she was on a walker.

I mumbled an apology.

"Get your head out of your ass," the old woman shouted.

I still couldn't see the short woman under the towering machines. Up ahead, the doors to the main exit swing open and a gush of desert wind came into the casino. When I finally hit the main exit, Cowboy came out of nowhere and put his gigantic hand on my shoulder.

"Get back to your room," he said. "You've caused enough trouble for the night."

"Who was that?" I asked.

"Not who you think," he said. "Let her go."

• • • • •

Back in the room, I lay on the bed and stared at the Native American artwork and cried. Then I flipped on the TV to muffle the sound of my tears and found a marathon of episodes of the Laser Geishas on an obscure cable network. The show was an acquired taste. Did they deliberately dub the show that badly into English?

I didn't know whether the funny names of the villains based on obscure literary references was supposed to be smart, dumb, or so dumb that it had to be smart. Just like Jen.

I could see why she loved the show. Deep down it was about values and friendship. The Geishas were Geishas by night. For one hour a day, right at sunset, they had super powers. They could avenge anything, but then they returned to status quo. One important theme was cooperation. Pink, Blue, and Green all had to come together to have the power of each other.

What about Denise? The staff member at the group home said the staff didn't know what was wrong with her. Would Denise even know her mother was gone?

And poor Dew. Poor, poor little Dew. I remembered her dressed up like a Geisha of her own— Laser Geisha *Lavender*.

In one episode, there was a little girl who got kidnapped. I turned it off before finding out the ending. These shows always had happy endings, right?

•   •   •   •   •

I went out to the parking lot as the sun rose the next morning. The reddish mesas and buttes of the high desert came to life with each powerful ray. A train thundered off in the distance and echoed off the distant canyon walls. *Meet me at the Mesa* indeed.

A greenish stone jabbed me when I sat in my car so I put it in the glove compartment instead of littering. I then stared out my car window at the magnificent red rocks, glowing in the rising sun.

I prayed. With God as my witness, I would do everything possible to save Luna's child. I would avenge Jen's death, even if I took the rest of my life doing it.

Unfortunately, I still had to survive a week of practicing law.

SUNDAY BLOODY SUNDAY

WHAT ELSE TO DO IN Crater on a Sunday? I hummed the U2 song, Sunday Bloody Sunday to myself. That was about a massacre in Ireland, but it somehow felt appropriate. I certainly didn't want to gamble this early in the morning and an all-you-can-eat brunch of burnt bacon, greasy eggs and green chile just made me nauseous.

I returned to the little adobe police station annex. Cowboy sat at his desk, his uniform was wrinkled and sweaty, and there were five Styrofoam cups on his counter. He must have worked through the night.

"Are you going to tell me what's going on?" I asked.

"No."

"Do you need anything from me? Am I free to go?"

"I better follow at least some protocol around here." He fingerprinted me, took a DNA swab, and even took a handwriting sample.

"Do you need me to identify Jen's body?"

"We'll get her family to do that," he said. "You're not family. We're going to keep the body for a while for an autopsy."

• • • • •

I needed to get the hell out of Crater. Without Jen, New Mexico had become one giant crater for me. Maybe Beverly Hills wouldn't be so bad. I found a station doing a U2 marathon. I liked "With or Without You," but couldn't handle "Sunday Bloody Sunday" when it came on for real.

At ten in the morning I headed east on I-40 to Albuquerque. Driving like Superman, desperately hoping to stop the rotation of the earth and turn it back one single day.

My phone stayed silent during a thirty-mile dead spot in the high desert. When I got back in phaser range, it rang.

"Dan, it's Anastasia. I mean Nastia."

Anastasia was her real name; Nastia was the familiar version. Anastasia seemed more appropriate at the moment.

"*I killed the czar and his ministers,*" Mick Jagger once sang in *Sympathy for the Devil.*

"*Anastasia screamed in vain.*"

"Where are you?"

"I can't say. Don't try to find me. I'm on the run. Sorry about Jen. I know she was your . . ."

She paused as if thinking how to say it. "She was your friend, *da?* She was my friend, too. She worked with me a few weeks."

"Thanks," I said. "Was that you last night at the fight?"

"You saw someone you thought was me?" She said nothing for a moment and I could hear her breathing. "You weren't supposed to see anyone."

"So was that you, or wasn't it?"

Silence.

"Maybe. Maybe not."

"Are you safe?" I asked, once it became obvious she wouldn't continue.

"I don't know," she said. "I can't talk much longer."

I didn't want to push it. The woman sounded distraught.

"My *lyobov* will see you this week. My *lyobov* will know where you are at all times."

"You keep saying that. What's really going on here?"

"I don't know yet. I'm just as lost as you, but I'll think of something. It's always darkest before the dawn, *da?*"

The call died.

Every mile I passed another wooden cross with flowers on it, each representing someone killed in a car crash. This portion of I-40 was one of the most dangerous stretches of highway in America. At every cross I saw Jen.

● ● ● ● ●

I dropped by the Lunar Module. Luna sat on her couch with Nurse Song.

Luna gave me a loose handshake when I entered. Nurse Song didn't even bother. Her gaze indicated that she blamed me for Jen's death. Hell, I blamed me for Jen's death.

"Jen was always going off on wild goose chases," her mother said.

I don't know if that made me the wild goose or not. Had I enabled Jen? No, she enabled me—enabled me to actually care for a change. I couldn't think how to respond to that. "I tried to make her stay with me."

"You shouldn't have gone to Crater in the first place," Nurse Song said. "It's all your fault."

"You know what the worst part is?" Luna asked. "I still have to work tomorrow."

"I actually have a case before you in the morning," I said. "If you can't get out of your cases this week, I don't think I can either."

Neither woman said anything.

"Your case is the least of my worries," Luna said.

"I can't believe you're working."

"I have to. I'm on thin ice with the press, thin ice with the public. My career is on the line. But it's not about me; I have one hundred cases tomorrow. One hundred people are expecting me to rule on their lives with fairness and impartiality. I owe it to them. I owe it to justice."

We all stared at the photo of the little Laser Geisha on the wall.

"Have you heard anything about Dew?" I asked.

"I got another call," she said. "Last night. The kidnappers told me I should go to court tomorrow, keep working and not say anything to anybody."

"Did the kidnappers tell you to rule a certain way?"

There was an uncomfortable silence and Luna's face puffed up so much she turned her back to me.

"Don't ask me that," she said to the opposite wall. "Don't *ever* ask me that!" Then she snorted, as if I had asked if she'd cheated on the bar exam.

"I'm sorry."

"Maybe it's time for you to go," she said. "See you in court, *counsel.*"

She enunciated the word "counsel" as if it was a swear word. No lawyer liked being called counsel, much like no senator liked being called "my good friend." A lawyer knew bad things were coming forthwith when he got called *counsel.*

"Yes, *your honor*," I replied.

MONDAY
SONG: "The Eagle Flies" by Trevor McShane

IT'S NOT DOCKET SCIENCE

I DIDN'T SLEEP SUNDAY NIGHT either. My phone rang several times at odd hours, always private or unknown numbers. I kept my phone right by the bed. Several times I missed the ringing, but even worse, when I did answer, I found silence at the other end.

"Nastia?" I asked the first time.

"Jen?" on the second.

Neither replied.

• • • • •

At six, I decided to leave my bed and stumble into the shower. Bret Favre had the best game of his life after his father died. Kobe Bryant scored fifty while facing felony charges in Colorado. I would force myself into that kind of zone, and *compartmentalize* myself, whatever that meant.

It was easy to find things now that my clothes were organized. Jen had even put in a light bulb, so I could pick out matching pants and jackets to avoid more "diversity suits." I went with black, of course — black suit and black tie against a white shirt to look like a hit man from *Reservoir Dogs*.

I did have a pink tie. Mr. Pink was a character in that movie, but I went with the black. Mrs. Pink was gone, after all. I almost put on my rattlesnake cowboy boots, but I didn't feel like the rattlesnake lawyer any more. The thirty dollar black shoes from Wal-Mart seemed right, as I was just a Wal-Mart lawyer who had everyday low prices. The shoes were probably made out of the silicone used in Dora the boxer's fake boobs.

As I drove toward the courthouse, it snowed, like God spreading Jen's ashes. Downtown Albuquerque stood at around, five thousand feet; the snowline usually began in the heights. A few days a year the lower parts of town received this light dusting, while the dumping took place a few miles uphill.

New Mexicans couldn't drive in even an inch of snow, so traffic crawled down Central Avenue. The old Route 66 had become Route Six Miles an Hour.

I arrived at the Second Judicial District Metropolitan courthouse at eight A.M. and parked at the bank across the street. Metropolitan court handled misdemeanors, as well as arraignments for felonies. I wanted covered parking inside the massive concrete parking structure, but that space might not exist. I kept driving around anyway. *Parking for Godot*; Jen's death made me feel even more existentialist than usual.

My phone rang, and I saw a state government number. "We're rejecting your billing," a secretary from the public defender department said. "We couldn't read your writing. You'll have to re-submit."

"It's always something," I said. "I heard you guys do it deliberately so you don't have to pay on time and the state can collect the interest ." Indeed, at the end of fiscal year, the department rejected nearly every invoice on bizarre technicalities.

The secretary laughed. "I'm just following orders. Besides, Dan, you'd do this for free, right?"

I hung up. "Yeah, right."

• • • • •

The Metro courthouse building didn't belong in New Mexico. This nine-story tapered building of marble and glass should be the capitol building of a breakaway communist republic flush with oil money. Many of the players involved in construction of the courthouse received major time in a conspiracy case. However, corruption worked well occasionally; at least some of the money actually went into the building.

Water flowed from a bronze statue of the scales of justice that stood in front of the marble building. Quotations regarding justice lined the stone floors. I had no idea what to say about justice, right now.

A building this nice should have a dress code. Unfortunately, the throngs of people who entered for their DWI or domestic-violence criminal cases dressed like they were already headed straight for jail, or straight to hell. DWI drivers sometimes chose t-shirts with pictures of Chevy trucks under their Jack Daniels caps. The accused wife-beaters actually wore sleeveless "wife-beater" t-shirts.

People waited outside the door in the cold morning air. Today it seemed as if the entire metropolitan area was lined up to get into court. Everyone in Albuquerque was guilty of something today.

Luckily, the lawyers and other officers of the court had their own line through the detectors. Even though I entered this courthouse at least twice a week, the private security guard still made me show an ID and my official New Mexico State Bar Card to prove my identity.

"You sure you're a lawyer?" she asked. "I don't see you on the computer list."

"That's Shepard with an 'a.'"

"Thank you, sir." The guard had a picture of her kids on her uniform. I always used to joke and ask "Same kids?" But no one laughed any more. No one had a sense of humor in New Mexico these days.

I took the elevator up to the seventh floor, even though it felt like a moving coffin.

With each floor, I pondered whether Luna would really show up today. Everyone said she skated on thinner ice every day. Considering the backlog of thousands of cases, a metro judge needed a signed death certificate faxed to the head judge to get excused from a hearing.

I hurried all the way down the marble hall with its grand view of the ten thousand foot Sandia Crest out the large glass windows.

"It's all downhill from here," I said. Even though the cases in this building were all misdemeanors, the lawyers dressed in gray metallic pinstripes, like they were spun from silver. Private DWI lawyers could make a fortune getting cases dismissed by working the time limits. They moved slowly, as if they were prancing down a catwalk like a model who didn't get out of bed for less than a few thousand dollars.

Minnie Dumond, my client du jour, waited for me outside the courtroom door. I certainly didn't feel like a hit man, high class or otherwise. Her mother and father sat on separate benches. Apparently they had a restraining order against each other.

Minnie was barely eighteen and weighed two hundred pounds—especially with the five heavy gold hoop earrings in her left ear. I once called her "Minnie the Demon" by mistake, instead of Minnie Dumond. She was biracial, possibly tri-racial, a definite mix of African and Indian, but Gandhi Indian, not local. She sold jewelry at a booth on the Air Force base. She proudly showed me a pic of her work once. Her jewelry mixed all her cultures and wasn't bad. Yet it couldn't be *that* good, or else she'd hire a real hit man, or at least a real lawyer.

"Mr. Shepard?" Minnie the Demon shook my hand. "Is everything going to be all right?"

Her hands felt cold and clammy. She didn't care about Jen's death or any of the other tragedies in my life. She just cared whether I could save her

I dressed like a hit man, so it was time to act like one and kill her problems. Court could be as simple as jail sometimes. Minnie the Demon had a problem. The State of New Mexico paid me to solve it. Case closed.

I opened her file right there in court for the first time in a while. The case at hand, or to be precise, the case at arm, was a domestic-violence case between two lovers. Minnie had allegedly bitten her boyfriend in the forearm. Needless to say, drugs and alcohol had been involved.

"Do I have time to take a pee?" she asked. "I heard Judge Looney Toons once locked someone up for going out to use the bathroom. Then I heard she locked up someone else for peeing in court."

I checked my turquoise watch. "I'll cover for you with the judge. Don't worry. But make it quick. And remember to flush!"

· · · · ·

"I can't believe that they wouldn't let Luna take a personal day," I said to the courtroom's public defender, a well-dressed young man with a ponytail. Ironically, he had been accepted into Georgetown, where I'd been waitlisted. He took this high-paying, low-stress job because he wanted to, not because he had to. I couldn't remember his real name, so I just called him Georgetown. He actually dressed better than I did; more like a Gordon Gekko Wall Street lawyer than a PD.

Georgetown shrugged. "The kidnapping took place on a Friday afternoon. Jen's killing took place on a Sunday. Metro court protocol requires her to make a non-emergency request one business day in advance. A while back one judge had a heart attack, but didn't call it in. He was removed from the bench by the chief judge."

Georgetown gestured at the masses of humanity waiting out in the hall. "And today's a Zoo Docket. Plus, she's covering another judge's Zoo Docket as well."

Across the street in District, they called these dockets "Zoo Dockets," but this was more like a circus on speed.

Before we entered the courtroom, the two biggest sheriff's deputies on the force stopped us cold. "No one can get inside without a reason."

"Reason?" I nodded to him. "We're third on the docket. I already showed my ID downstairs."

"I wasn't downstairs, so I don't care. Mr. Shepard, could you kindly show me your ID again?" the larger deputy said.

I shrugged. "I'm still me. I think."

"I'm serious," he added.

I took out my lawyer ID and showed it to him, then pointed to our third position on the docket.

"See, we're on the guest list."

"Don't block the aisle," he said.

●　●　●　●　●

Inside, the courtroom was packed with the usual clients and their usual lawyers. Several cameramen had set up in the back, a few with national logos. Were they here for me?

"You in the black suit," a cameraman asked me. "Is she gonna do Sky Roberts first?"

"I don't know," I said. "She kinda has her own schedule."

I checked my turquoise watch, looked at the empty bench where Luna was supposed to sit, and swore softly under my breath. I tried to calculate speeds and distances in my head. Court for Tyrone was scheduled for Estancia by eleven, sixty miles away through a snow-packed canyon. I had no time for a circus, even one on speed.

My life could be worse, however. Georgetown had thirty-five clients. Five were named Martinez and three Garcia, yet he already had everything briefed for the day. He could still get it up for his clients. Perhaps that's why he got into Georgetown, and I had to settle for American University.

If law schools were women, Luna was Georgetown, and Jen was just American University, my underwhelming alma mater. That made Nastia some unaccredited law school out in L.A. Then again, a lot of really smart people went to unaccredited law schools out in L.A. and they made a lot more than I did for stupid conflict contracts.

• • • • •

Court did not start at eight-thirty as it was scheduled; Luna had a tendency to run late, especially when she took one of her long morning runs on sunny days. She sometimes wore sweats under her robe, and always wore running shoes.

On the seventh floor, the two courtrooms on the east side of the building started five minutes early, and the two on the west side had clocks that literally ran six minutes slow. Sometimes you needed a degree in temporal mechanics to know whether a nine-o'clock case on the seventh floor would occur before an eight-o'-

clock case on the third. If district court time management came into play, or worse, district court in other jurisdictions, the calculations could require the super-collider's atomic clock. My math scores were much lower than my verbals on the SAT, so I calculated wrong most of the time.

I had various names for the process: the physics of justice, docket science, or just court calculus.

"Where's the damn judge?" The cameraman asked. "We gotta get something in time for the mid-day news."

"She's tied up at the moment," the court monitor replied, cowering behind her desk up front. I called her the monitor lizard, because she had a greenish complexion and constantly stuck her tongue out of the side of her mouth as she read the latest court gossip on the computer screen. "It says here that the Chief Judge sent a squad car to pick her up."

I tried to keep Jen off my mind. Minnie grabbed my shoulder with a sweaty hand. "Am I going to be all right?"

"What?"

"Am I going to be all right?" she asked. "You're like a million miles away. This is about *me*, this isn't about you."

I nodded. "You're right."

Minnie's father, a thin man wearing a Motel 6 polo shirt came over. "Is Minnie going to be all right?"

"I hope so."

Minnie's mother, a heavy-set black woman who looked like a "before" picture of Oprah came next from her own bench. "Is my baby gonna be all right?"

I was about to lose my temper, then stopped myself. I couldn't blame them for caring. To them, Minnie wasn't a defendant; she was their baby. Well, she was my two hundred pound baby, now. "I sure hope so."

I tried to be positive, but it was hard. If Mary had come over and asked me "What's going to happen to Jesus?" before his trial in Jerusalem, I would have said something like "I've got some bad news about the trial, but some good news about the appeal."

I mentally forced myself to play lawyer for the morning. I found the Assistant District Attorney, a graduate of something called Western Pacific Law School out in South Central L.A. Western Pacific sounded more like a railroad than a law school. Maybe he should be loco-motioning rather than litigating.

Then again, the DA's office rejected me, because they didn't think I was committed enough. Hell, I had been rejected everywhere for commitment issues; that's why I took the damn conflict contract. It was an endless succession of one night stands in the courtroom.

Western Pacific was barely five feet tall, and wore a red and white striped jacket that he must have stolen from his son's bar mitzvah. This asshole was a better candidate than I?

"Where's your alleged victim?" I asked.

"On the way," Western Pacific said.

"Well, we're third on the docket. If you don't have a witness by the time we're called, I'll move to dismiss."

Western Pacific didn't change his expression. Metro prosecutors were very pragmatic: winning or losing didn't depend on their ability; they got their paychecks regardless. Office policy prohibited them from dismissing cases, even if all their witnesses were dead.

We were in a race. If the alleged victim showed up and testified about the bite, Minnie lost. If he was late, Minnie walked. Justice here depended on traffic patterns and parking spaces, and on the line at security or the wait for an elevator. It wasn't docket science, it was a docket crash.

I turned my phone off. Luna seized any attorney's phone that dared to ring in her courtroom. She threw someone in jail on a second ring. After her demeanor towards me last night, I sure couldn't risk it.

· · · · ·

Commotion sounded from behind the door. The clerk sounded surprised. "All rise?" she asked, a question, not a command. She was not sure who would emerge from the wings.

The door opened a crack, and then it closed. "Am I really ready for this?" a voice asked from inside, unaware that the acoustics carried the words into the courtroom. Finally Luna entered the courtroom, wearing her robe with something even blacker underneath it, but the material was frayed, as if she'd ripped it in rage. She looked as if she hd aged twenty years over the weekend.

Everyone stayed up until Luna sat down. She stared at the gallery.

"Tell them to sit down," the monitor lizard whispered.

"Be seated?" Luna asked, unsure. The crowd was unsettled by her demeanor, but complied. She picked up her first file. "Our first case we'll do by video. *State versus Sky Roberts*."

The TV cameras immediately turned toward the video screen in the corner. In high security situations, the court sometimes held arraignments by video, and the inmate stayed safely locked up at MDC, seventeen miles away. The video on the big flat screen behind Luna was blurry. It showed a gray room at MDC, but it could be in the Russian *gulag* for all we knew. A burly guard took Sky to a podium; he wore a red *High Risk Inmate* jumpsuit.

"Go big red," I muttered to myself.

Since a lawyer has to be in the courtroom usually a public defender handled video arraignments, but in this case a big time attorney now stood at the empty podium.

Sky wasn't in jail, for the DWI case *per se*. He had already posted his bond long ago. He was now in for violating conditions of release.

"Your honor," Sky's attorney said. "I must ask you to release Mr. Roberts forthwith. This latest incident was a minor relapse."

I laughed as I thought about this minor relapse. Sky had vomited right in front of me.

The lawyer continued. "My client has already spent the weekend in jail. That should be sufficient. He has many arrests, but no actual convictions."

"And you stand by that, counsel?"

"I do," the lawyer said. "And I must state the fact that a two hundred million dollar production is resting on my client's immediate release. Think of the hundreds of production jobs that will be lost if he is not released forthwith."

The lawyer liked the "f" word all right.

"Well, I don't believe you, *counsel*," she said.

"Officer Tran?" Luna pressed a button. Tran emerged from behind the walls and stood at the podium as if she was the real prosecutor, not the cop. "Your honor, as you requested, I researched Mr. Roberts's legal history, including his convictions in Vietnam while he was filming *Body Bag II* with director Lee Donowitz."

Sky actually smiled. Apparently his drunken binge in Ho Chi Minh City brought back a few happy memories.

"Your honor, he had a conviction for drunk driving and was found with an underage prostitute in Ho Chi Minh City. He received a deferred sentence, but that is still a conviction for our purposes."

"*Me so horny*," Sky chanted, laughing directly at Tran. "Ho Ho Ho Chi Minh."

Sky's attorney began again, "The production schedule of—"

"Counsel, be quiet, and make sure you client is quiet as well," Luna said.

Tran continued, icily. "In addition, Mr. Roberts has a conviction of driving under the influence in one of the United Arab Emirates, and there is still an active Interpol warrant for his arrest."

"He was driving drunk in a country where alcohol is banned?" Luna asked.

The attorney mumbled something on Sky's behalf, something about mis-speaking in his earlier statement.

Luna interrupted him, just by lifting her gavel. "I said quite clearly that I would sign an order putting him into custody if he lied to me. I would consider it direct contempt. And you realize that once I know of an active warrant, even an international one, I cannot let him go. It's against all judicial ethics."

Defense attorneys in the back mumbled something about "Judge Looney Toons."

Luna frowned. "Did you seriously think I would not have Officer Tran go to the Internet movie data base and do a search of every jurisdiction where he has filmed? Did you think I didn't know about Vietnam and that he filmed one of the biggest war movies of all time over there? We're just lucky that we have someone here familiar with international law like Officer Tran."

"I didn't think international convictions counted," the lawyer said.

Luna said. "Counsel, he killed a family of four in an auto accident in England. I do check out *tmz.com*."

"I was just getting to that one, your honor," said Tran. "Technically he is still on probation over there. Again, it's been deferred, so counsel was technically right."

"Thank you, that will be all," Luna said, talking to the screen. "State? Any response?"

Western Pacific then woke up, read standard items about conditions of release. Someone else had definitely typed this page for him as well. Western Pacific droned on about the arrests, and then had one moment of brilliance. He stood up and put the paper down. "Your honor, if you'll look behind Mr. Roberts on the screen you'll see several dozen inmates. They are not movie stars. Most of them have less of a criminal record than Mr. Roberts. In all likelihood, you will not release those defendants."

More sounds of assent from the inmates standing behind Sky on the screen. Damn right!

Inside the courtroom, several people began swearing under their breath, and it grew to a collective grumble. No one in this room had even starred in a high-school play, much less won an Oscar. The defense attorneys, who normally hated Luna, mumbled that their clients deserved the same treatment as Sky.

Somehow Luna kept it together. "Order, order! I will not exclude the convictions, arrests, deferred sentences or whatever they are."

"I will not tolerate Mr. Roberts's blatant disregard for his conditions of release. He also had to undergo random testing. Needless to say, he failed."

Sky kept laughing. "That's my skull," he said. He pounded his forehead with his cuffed hand like Jeff Spicoli in *Fast Times at Ridgemont High*. The dude must still be high. Lord knows they got some good stuff in jail.

Luna didn't laugh, and there was silence in the gallery. A defendant had just mocked her in open court. She frowned and put her head in her hands. Perhaps she waas crying. "I stated for the record that if you lied to me, Mr. Roberts, I would hold you in direct contempt for six months. I am duty bound to report you to all the international authorities to see if they wish to extradite you."

"Whatever," said Sky. "They don't want me. You know it. Get me to a real judge."

Luna banged her gavel. "I order that Mr. Roberts remain in custody without bond pending trial. You can take that up with a real judge. Mr. Roberts, you will stay in custody until the other jurisdictions decide whether they wish to extradite."

Luna took a deep breath and closed her eyes. This was only a "conditions of release" hearing on a misdemeanor DWI, so why so damn serious? She glanced at the monitor lizard and pointed to the garbage can.

The monitor lizard bought a garbage can to Luna's side of the bench. Luna looked down at the can for a moment as if a demon was about to exit her throat. She counted to three, and through sheer force of will, held everything down.

The entire courtroom held its collective breath. Luna nodded. The courtroom exhaled. She had regained control of her body, at least for the moment.

"Mr. Roberts, I will give you six months contempt for lying to me. When you looked me in the eye and told me you had no other convictions, you held this entire system in contempt. You laughed at the orders of the court, you laughed at me, but most important you laughed at the law. So I will return the favor and hold you in direct contempt. That is *my* discretion and that *cannot* be appealed to a higher court."

Western Pacific smiled as if he was personally responsible for this great legal victory.

"You cunt!" Sky shouted. For an Academy Award winning writer, he sure had a limited vocabulary.

"That's another month," Luna said.

"You fucking bitch," Sky Roberts shouted. "You total fucking bitch. I thought you were supposed to take care of this."

"Take care of what?" Luna asked.

The screen showing Sky went dead. We would never know what Sky wanted Luna to do. Did Luna cut the video off? Did someone on the other side?

A chill went up my spine. Sky might not be a kidnapper, but something smelled really bad. Why the hell would he think he could get away with it? Gabriel Rose had mentioned the movie's financing. Who would want to back a movie that depended on the services of the most unreliable actor in the world? Sky High had brought the movie down low. When I had asked who the financiers were, Rose told me I didn't want to know. Well, I sure as hell wanted to know now!

Sky's attorney smiled. "It's only Metro. I'll have this stupid judge reversed in an instant." He actually said that out loud.

Luna frowned. "Wrong thing to say counselor. You took an oath and you lied to me. Even as a stupid judge I have the power to sentence you to one day in jail on direct contempt."

The audience gasped. A lawyer hadn't actually gone to jail on contempt since last year when a district court judge had me arrested for saying "fuck" in court.

"Fuck," I said out loud as the lawyer was handcuffed by the deputies.

Thankfully, no one heard me or I would be in jail as well. I watched as the lawyer was taken back into the depths of the jail by a guard. There but for the grace of God went I.

Luna shivered as if she had given herself the death sentence, then she took a deep breath and got back to business. "Next case?" Luna said. "We've got *State versus Tommy Lee*. Wasn't he the lead singer of an eighties hair band? That's set for trial. Mr. Lee, are you here?"

I checked my turquoise watch. Not much time left. This was a held over traffic case, set for trial. If the guy wanted a trial, the wheels of justice would grind to a halt.

Neither Tommy Lee the rocker nor Tommy Lee the criminal appeared in the courtroom.

"Speaking of eighties hair bands," Georgetown mumbled in my ear. "Guess which one she's going to mention now?"

"I have no idea," I said.

"*Warrant*," Luna said with a frown at Georgetown and a bang of her gavel.

It was our turn. The victim still had not shown up and hadn't called in.

Luna was still green. I couldn't read her expression. Did she still blame me for Jen's death? Did Luna like me or hate me now? All I know is that she had already sentenced three straight people to jail, Sky, his lawyer, and now Tommy Lee. Would she go four for four?

"Next case. *State versus Minnie Dumond*." Luna mumbled the last name of my client, clearly rattled from Sky's case. "State, are you ready?"

"Not yet," Western Pacific said. "Could we have some more time?"

"Defense is ready," I said. Were we? I looked back just as Minnie entered from the outside. She must have gone number two.

This time Western Pacific read his scribbled notes on a folder about attempting to contact the victim, but admitted he might have sent it to a wrong address. He argued something about weather conditions and the difficulty of parking. He felt cocky; he just had a movie star locked up. He didn't expect anything different to happen with a necklace maker.

I should feel guilty about my next words, considering I would soon drive like a madman to a court sixty miles away. "I move to dismiss your honor. People don't show respect for your court if they don't make it here on time."

Luna almost cracked a smile. Perhaps she felt like she wanted to throw me a bone.

"I'll dismiss the case," she said. "You're free to go Ms. Dumond. You too, Counsel."

"Thank you, your honor," I said.

She smiled. "You be careful out there, Counsel."

"I will, your honor," I said.

Luna's bronze skin remained green. Her brown eyes were streaked with blood. I glowered at Western Pacific. He beat Sky's lawyer, but he didn't beat me. He didn't care. He'd kept Sky Roberts in, and that would probably get him laid back at the office.

I went up to the bench. Close up Luna looked even worse. Western Pacific followed me, just in case I uttered a word about a pending case behind his back.

"Your honor that took guts on your decision with Sky Roberts," I said. I couldn't bring up anything about the kidnapping in front of Western Pacific. Was Luna willing to sacrifice her daughter for justice? "Are you sure you know what you're doing?"

Luna ignored Western and instead looked directly at me. "Jen told me to have faith. Those were the last words she said to me. For some reason I have faith in justice and faith that someone, anyone, will . . ." She hesitated. "Somebody, somewhere will save the day so I don't have to sacrifice my ideals, so I don't have to violate my oath. I didn't take this job seriously enough, but now I realize that I can lose it, I know how important justice is. I don't know why, but I have faith. Faith in the system. The rich jerk gets treated the same as the poor jerk."

That quote certainly didn't belong in marble down on the courthouse floor, but I liked it nonetheless.

In that moment, I felt Luna's faith. The moment passed

quickly when a few more defendants crowded into the court-room, searching in vain for seats.

"The court will take a recess now," Luna said. She turned to the monitor lizard. "Could you tell the Chief Judge that I am deathly ill, and bring another judge down? I'm done. I can't do this any more."

Done for the day? Done for the week? Or done forever?

Luna slammed the door behind her before the monitor lizard could ask anyone to rise.

"Leave the courthouse now," I said to Minnie the Demon, "before she changes her mind."

Minnie went to each bench and hugged a parent.

We walked toward the elevator just as the alleged victim showed up at the metal detectors. Minnie was a regular angel when she spotted the man removing chewing gum wrappers by the metal detector. It was clear that Minnie wore the pants in the family; her boyfriend looked like a bad poet.

"I love you baby," she shouted.

"Me, too."

They hugged. They both danced with joy. Was that the lam-bada? Apparently they had long since reconciled.

What's the difference between an accused underemployed artist and me? She had someone who loved her.

After a long hug, Minnie then hugged me goodbye.

"You saved my ass," she said. "I owe you one."

I laughed. I repeated a line from *The Godfather*. "Some day, and that day may never come, I might ask a favor from you."

"Anything."

"Do you know Nastia?"

"The Eskimo stripper?"

"Yeah?

"Nobody knows Nastia."

She turned away as if scared. Oh well, at least I could cross one name off my list. I was about to say I wasted the last two hours of my life, but with one final look at Minnie resuming her hug, I couldn't help but smile.

And yet as I walked away, Minnie started feuding with her boyfriend. She slugged him one, right there in front of the guards. They were on her in moments.

So much for me saving the day.

HAMLET OF ZUZAX

I DIDN'T HAVE TIME TO stay. It snowed harder outside the court-house. I shuddered, imagining the white carnage a thousand feet higher up in Tijeras canyon.

I wanted to call the clerk's office in Estancia, let them know I was running late, but a cop pulled up behind me. I couldn't risk seven days of community service for violating the Albuquerque phone law by talking on the phone while driving. Hell, Jen got in that accident and had to pay off Gustavo. I sure didn't want to work in a place like the Ends Zone.

I filled up at a station at Broadway and Lomas. Nearby, standing next to each other, were a Starbucks, a McDonalds' and a convenience store. They might as well be three Americas. A yuppie exited the Starbucks with a drink with whip cream; a mother came out of the McDonalds, her kids clutching Happy Meals; a bum stood outside the convenience store, chugging a half-crushed energy drink, he must have taken from the trash. I sometimes met with clients at McDonalds. I never met them at Starbucks.

Traffic crawled up Fifth Street to the entrance onto I-40 as if a whole courtroom had just emptied out all at once. What was that Trevor McShane song? "The Eagle Flies?" This eagle was stuck on the runway.

The snow worsened with every mile east on I-40, the old Route 66. By Tijeras Canyon, a thousand feet higher on the eastern edge of Albuquerque, the dusting of snow affected traffic. Route 66 became route 55, then 50 then 45. People didn't want to speed in the snow. Probably a good thing, I was a frequent flier in traffic court in all of the jurisdictions along the highway. My phone hearing on a speeding ticket for heading through the canyon was set for Thursday. I'd deal with it then.

I sure got my tix on Route 66.

A trooper waited under the bridge at his usual spot, I slowed to ten miles under the limit. He waved at me. I waved back.

I flashed back to my first trip through the canyon, when I was headed to the small town of Aguilar for my first job as a public defender. I loved the twenty-mile stretch through Tijeras canyon––the over-thrust of Sandias to the north and the slightly smaller Manzano Mountains to the south—it felt like Colorado. With snow on the ground, this could be a ski trip to Vail.

My reverie ended at the hamlet of Zuzax. No, I didn't know how it got its name. Traffic crawled by the inevitable accident in the construction zone. A haz-mat truck slid on the icy roads.

A shivering deputy directed us onto the old Route 66, the frontage road, past several rustic gas stations. The East Mountain area of Albuquerque had become a real estate Shangri-la. Californians, Arizonans, and even a few Coloradans loved mountain-style living within commuting distance of Albuquerque at a fraction of their old prices.

I just loved saying the "Hamlet of Zuzax," even though I wasn't sure of the actual definition of a hamlet. Zuzax had a gas station and a few homes in the distance. Some hamlet.

"To be or not to be," I said. I wanted to turn back, but I was stuck in the two-lane traffic. Cops diverted us onto the frontage road.

After doing the math on speed versus distance I called the court, but didn't get though. Leaving a message was no excuse.

Everyone else on the docket had already done the same thing. Maybe they would cut me a break for weather.

Nah. . . .

I always imagined taking Route 66 east, switching to Interstate 66 in Virginia and going to my ancestral home of Washington D.C. More recently, I wanted to take Route 66 west. It became Santa Monica Boulevard. If I took a left on El Camino in Beverly Hills, it would take me right to the Morris Williams Agency.

● ● ● ● ●

I passed a Wal-Mart and a "travel center" in Edgewood, although the town could also be "Edge-plains" as well, it depended on your point of view. The travel center's billboard advertised rattlesnake souvenirs. Rattlesnake souvenirs. I hoped someday people would be able to purchase rattlesnake-lawyer souvenirs here in the hamlet. Maybe a lawyer in boots could hold a skull lamenting poor Yorick, and that he knew him well.

I blinked and seemed to magically teleport to the Moriarty exit. I sure didn't have any memory of the drive through the whiteness. Moriarty was one of those Route 66 towns that were too tough to die. I passed a Chinese buffet. I had a rule: no Chinese food in towns smaller than fifty thousand people, unless there was an engineering college.

Perhaps I should just stop at the local courthouse and pay the damn speeding ticket. The only way to get out of a ticket was if a cop didn't show and cops out here always showed. Well, supposedly a Los Alamos physicist got out of ticket because he proved that sunspots had affected the radar gun, but he had NASA send in weather satellite data to prove it. I was no physicist, and I had too much on my mind to worry about Thursday's silly little phone hearing.

I cursed as I checked my turquoise watch and quickly headed south on Highway 41. The landscape was more plains than desert. Under the snow, this could be the steppes of Russia—except for the mobile homes and warehouse churches.

The Russian vibe reminded me of Nastia. How did Eskimos, excuse me, the *Inupiat* people, stand the cold? Cold wasn't the absence of heat; it was a real force. Just like evil wasn't the absence of good.

Was Nastia was a good guy or a bad guy? Hell, I didn't know if I was a good guy or a bad guy.

A few more miles south through the steppes on Route 41, I took the turnoff for the Torrance County courthouse on the edge of the village Estancia. The surprisingly modern courthouse contrasted with the small bungalows and ranches in the distance. For some odd reason, one rancher had a real World War II PT boat landlocked across the street. The courthouse itself felt like an alien fortress plopped down into the dust bowl of the thirties.

There was already an inch or two of slushy snow mixed with the mud. Thank God for cheap shoes after all. Inside, a sign read No Weapons, but the metal detector was turned off and no guards were at the door. Ahh . . . small town life.

As I walked past the clerk's office, the women inside shouted a hearty hello. "Hey Dan! We saved a Power Bar for you."

The Power Bar gave me a slight dose of power. The single corridor in the courthouse bulged with the crowd. Judges here heard criminal, civil and even divorce cases. The magistrate court sat at the end of the hall next to the two district courtrooms. This meant the name changers and speeders had to wait in line with the murderers. It felt very democratic . . . with a small "d."

I liked being in Norman Rockwell America—good hardworking folk who were often involved in farming, people who had lived here for generations, both Anglo and Hispanic. This was a red state all right. Did that make this Norman *Rodriguez* America?

No full-time judges served out here so nothing happened Monday through Wednesday. One judge came all the way in from Socorro on Thursdays, another came from Truth or Consequences on Friday. Luna probably had walked away from more cases today in Metro then these judges saw in an entire year.

A large man in a western-cut suit came out. "Mr. Shepard, the judge got tired of waiting for you! We had to start the sentencing on the murder case already. You'll have to sit tight."

Normally this was one of my favorite small towns. I'd had a few jury trials out here and had done surprisingly well. I once had a column here in a local paper, and the people had laughed at my jokes, or at least had never complained about me. Everyone treated me well when I got gas at the single station, or had a burrito at the local sandwich shop.

Today's judge did not wear his judicial robe, because the courtroom was too hot. Judges' moods could vary with the temperature. He had gone to Harvard and somehow ended up here in the heartland. You can take a judge away from Harvard, but you couldn't take Harvard away from the judge. "You're late," he snarled.

I wanted to tell him about the traffic in the canyon. Or perhaps "Traffic was a bitch," but that sure wouldn't work out here. I knew I wouldn't have enough time to go to the bathroom. Instead I mumbled something about delays in Metro court. "I'm ready to begin."

"It doesn't matter; you'll have to wait until we finish the sentencing on the Jones case."

The judge checked the outdated computer screen and then issued me a contempt charge, with a hefty fine.

"That's more than I'm getting on this case, your honor."

"Then you should have left on time, don't you think?"

"Sorry," I said. I started to edge to the bathroom, but the judge gave me a dirty look. I would have to hold it.

"Let's get back to the case at hand" the judge declared.

The District Attorney was in the midst of recounting gruesome testimony about a murder. He went on for forty minutes about how the defendant, eighteen year old Eric Jones, had chopped off his brother's head while high on meth, and then thrown it out the driver's side window, all while driving a hundred miles an hour on I-40.

Mary Ann Romero, famed national expert on insanity, then got up to testify that the defendant wasn't crazy, just anti-social. She went on and on. . . .

"Ms. Romero, could you just sum it up?" the judge asked. "What's going on deep down inside him?"

"Deep down inside him, he's no good," she said.

I half expected the gallery to sing, *"He's no good, he's no good, he's no earthly good."*

The defense attorney, an aging conflict lawyer named Kleinfeld, rose. "Your honor, the District Attorney said the defendant threw his brother's head out the driver's side window. Actually, it was the *passenger* side window."

The judge glared at him. "Is that all you have?"

"Nothing further, your honor."

Kleinfeld sat down. His close was one line about a window? I always found something good about everyone and Judge Harvard made it easy for me when he gave Eric Jones a life sentence, then twenty more years, just in case. If possible, there would be a guard with a stake waiting by the grave if Jones ever rose from the dead.

The sixty-year-old Kleinfeld in his rumpled tweed coat and brown tie with mustard stains on it, mumbled. He did not shake his client's hand as the guards took the man away. Was that what I would become?

Had I become a lawyer like that, already?

• • • • •

"Are you ready to proceed?" Judge Harvard asked me when the courtroom cleared.

"I guess so, Your Honor," I said, scrambling up to the bench. I prayed I would make it through the hearing without wetting myself. Kleinfeld left his files up there, abandoning them as he had his client.

I turned to the man sitting next to me, my client, Tyrone Johnson, an elderly African American man with a shaved head. He could pass for a blues guitarist the Beatles ripped off. Tyrone was very dapper in his old-but-elegant glen plaid suit. It took me a second to recognize it. It was *my* suit. I gave it to him during our last jury trial, and he had held onto it for court.

I bought the suit on sale a few years ago after seeing a member of the royal family in a suit just like it. Unfortunately, not a single tie in my closet matched the clashing patterns of the fabric.

Judge Looney Toons had even made fun of it in court once. "Counsel, you should call that outfit a 'diversity suit.'"

The diversity suit didn't breathe very well in Albuquerque's dry heat. However, in Estancia, Tyrone could pass for His Majesty's Minister of the Exchequer.

This hearing was about conditions of release. Tyrone wore an ankle bracelet, for electronic monitoring. He had an additional bracelet that measured his blood alcohol, and still another bracelet from somewhere else. Perhaps he wore the third monitor just for show. The bracelets made a noticeable bump in the glen plaid by his leg. He played with them in some sort of ritual.

"Can you get these damn things off me?" he asked. "I can't wear cowboy boots."

"I'll try, but the State is against my motion."

The prosecutor wore ostrich, or possibly emu, boots, and they weren't just for show. He swore his real name was Tex. Round here, a name like Tex along with Emu boots worked wonders with jurors. His sleek western suit would fit in perfectly at the stock show auction for a Kobe beef herd coming into Amarillo. He handed me a three-page witness list. A witness list for a release hearing? This wasn't just shooting fish in a barrel for Tex; this was shooting fish in a barrel with semi-automatic weapons. Justice wasn't blind out here, Justice was personal.

Tex called the chief of police to the stand. The chief told of Tyrone's long history with the police.

I sprang to life. "But other than this current charge, he has no other felonies."

"No."

Tex then went down his list in alphabetical order. Unlike Western Pacific, he had prepared his list himself. Also unlike Western Pacific, he actually cared about the results. They ate what they killed out here. Tex had all four officers of the local police force, his next-door neighbors, including the man in the overalls, even Tyrone's high-school teacher, a bent-over woman in her nineties, who wanted nothing more than to speak her piece before she died.

"I taught him freshman year in high school," she said. "I've been his neighbor for twenty years now, and he's still a terrible person."

I mentioned Tyrone's recent actions were the stuff of rumor, like running meth houses for twenty years all over the county. He had never been convicted of a violent felony and whatnot. Sure, he had a bad reputation, but with each witness I repeatedly

mentioned the presumption of innocence until proved guilty beyond a reasonable doubt, just like a legal zombie.

Why did the prosecutor try so hard? My client would probably plead out in a few months anyway. This was just a simple
release hearing. Law was a sport out here, and they wanted to
run up the score.

Judge Harvard stopped the prosecutor after nine witnesses.
We didn't have to hear from the doctor who treated Tyrone for
God knows what diseases.

Tex smiled at me. He owned this courtroom. I was just a legal
tourist.

"Counsel?" The Judge said to me. Didn't he know I had a
name: a first name and a last name? "Any closing remarks?"

Tyrone whispered in my ear. "If you keep me out, I've got
something for you."

"What?"

"Keep me out and I'll tell you. It's about your girl, Nastia."

Nastia? Could Tyrone be the one? Doubtful, but I sure had to
try. Time to make it personal on my end.

"Your honor," I said. "I kept hearing about all the bad things
my client has done over the last forty years. However, with the
exception of not watering his lawn, he has complied with the law
during the time he has been out on *this* case. That's all he can do.
Not one positive test, with two bracelets on, and he's kept in contact with pre-trial services. What more do you want him to do?"

The Judge stared. "And?"

"And?" Tyrone whispered to me. "You gotta keep me out, I
promise I'll be good. I promise. I'll tell you about this Nastia
chick."

He knew about Nastia. "And, if umm . . . necessary I will personally vouch for him. You can hold me in contempt if he doesn't
comply."

Judge Harvard banged a gavel. "I will continue the release Tyrone Johnson, and I will indeed hold you personally responsible if he fails. I would keep your checkbook handy if I were you, Mr. Shepard. In fact, I'll cancel your contempt. Why don't you write a check for Mr. Johnson's ten thousand dollar bond immediately, and we'll only cash it if he fails to show."

The crowd gasped. I didn't know if that was legal or not, ethical or not, but I had to put my money where my mouth was.

• • • • •

Tyrone and I sat alone in the bathroom as I finally relieved myself. I felt like I was pissing gasoline. I didn't like showing any vulnerability in front of a client. In these confined quarters, Tyrone smelled bad and the suit smelled like ammonia that was often used in manufacturing meth. If he had concealed a weapon of any kind, he could kill me before the guard came back, if the smell didn't kill me first.

He reached into his pocket and handed me two pieces of paper. I finished up, wiped my hands and took them from him.

The first page was a fax cover sheet from my stationary marked "Attorney Client Privileged" with a fax number from an Albuquerque office supply store. The time stamp was about ten minutes after my hearing in Albuquerque. I had probably hit the canyon by then.

The second page had a case heading for *State versus Tyrone Johnson* and again was marked Attorney-Client Privileged. A note addressed to Tyrone read, "Please make sure when you are in private to tell Mr. Shepard that Nastia tried to call him in metro court but could not get through."

Fearful of Luna's contempt, I had turned my ringer off in metro court then forgot to turn it back on. I turned it on and found numerous messages and texts, but couldn't check them out in this location. My phone's provider worked great in Hawaii, but here, just fifty miles the other side of the mountain, the earth swallowed everything electronic.

I admired Nastia's ingenuity. The State could not legally read attorney-client letters. She could get to me this way without leaving a paper trail. By the time someone got a court order, hopefully she would be long gone.

"Just because you're paranoid, doesn't mean the sky isn't falling down," read the handwritten fax.

The sky? Did she mean Sky Roberts?

The next line was equally cryptic. "The moon made it worse."

The moon? Did she mean Luna?

Before I could ponder, Tyrone got up and shook my hand. "Thank you," he said.

"Tyrone, my friend, someday—and the day may never come– –but someday. . . ."

He smiled. "Don't worry, I got you covered."

I wanted to wash my hand again, but decided against it.

He then took the papers from me, ripped them up and flushed them down the toilet. "You can never be too careful," he said.

THE LAND OF CHILILI

I TOOK THE BACK ROAD out of Estancia to avoid the construction of I-40 and any potential hazardous spills. Rural Route 55 went east through the plains on a straight shot back to the Manzanos.

I made a hard left onto Route 337 north, through the infamous Chilili land grant. Yes, that was really the way it was spelled— *Chilili*. Wasn't that where Puff the Magic Dragon was from? A sign announced something about the treaty of Guadalupe Hidalgo in 1841. I wondered if I was still in New Mexico, or even America. Outsiders never took this road. If you were an outsider driving out here, you were already lost.

Unfortunately, I came to an abrupt stop at the next hamlet a few miles north, just north of the land grant. A sheriff's deputy stood in the middle of the road. Had I missed the turn-off back to civilization? This hamlet had one church, one gas station/store and three abandoned cars.

The Deputy stared at me. "You ain't from around here, are you son?"

"Is it that obvious?"

"Well, we got a funeral going on," the Deputy said. "You gotta wait till the church empties out."

Every single person exiting the funeral stared at me. No, I wasn't from around here. This highway's nickname was the Salt Missions Trail, whatever that meant. I thought about Lot's wife at Sodom, and stared downward rather than looking back.

Time stopped until someone tapped on my window making me almost bust my seat belt. A disheveled man kept tapping, metal chains on his hand. Who was he, Marley's ghost? Was this my Christmas carol with all the ghosts of my past coming back trying to get me to change my ways? Well, technically it would be Spring Solstice carol.

It took me a moment to recognize this ghost. I had represented him: a convicted drunk driver named Stewie, and he wore a jail uniform and still had chains. Had he escaped?

Stewie's bulk hid the petite correctional officer standing behind him. "He needs to talk to you," the CO said.

I opened my window and a blast of cold air and bad breath flooded the vehicle.

"Thank you for getting me out for my brother's funeral," he said.

I had indeed filed a request for a furlough last week. Once I fax-filed motions, they left my brain without a confirmation slip. "No problem."

"I owe you one," he said.

"We love you, Dan," Stewie's mother shouted.

Perhaps I *was* from around here, after all.

• • • • •

With the funeral procession in my rear-view mirror, I put my foot on the gas, eager to escape the boundaries of the Chilili land grant and get back to America, if it was still around. I still hadn't heard any details about Jen's death. I finally found a local news channel. It reported there still were no details on the "possible accidental shooting" on the *Desert Demons* set.

"Jen Song, a stripper had died. Possibly in a suicide by cop."

She was a waitress not a stripper, damn it! She wanted to live!

Cowboy was just covering up an itchy trigger finger from one of his deputies.

My mind raced faster than the four cylinders of my car's engine. I looked down at my speedometer again. Twenty-five miles over the limit, I was now legally committing the crime of reckless driving, a full misdemeanor with a mandatory seven days in jail. An oncoming car honked at me. If I hit them while driving this fast, it would be vehicular homicide, a third degree felony.

Grief was not a defense to vehicular homicide. I might take myself out, but I sure didn't want to hurt anyone else.

I had to get off the road, for the safety of myself—and others. I slowed down, searched for a rest stop, but this land was all private property, and about as private as you can get. Stopping on the side of the road could be construed as trespass in a land where everyone had assault rifles. Some even had aggravated assault rifles.

Up ahead, a telephone tower; I should have phone reception by now. I wanted to check while driving, but the road zig-zagged. Snow covered the shoulders.

I finally stopped at the first public lot, a hiking trailhead on the edge of the Manzano Mountains. The Manzanos were lower than the Sandias. The Sandias weren't technically part of the Rockies; more like the little brother who had never amounted to much. That made the Manzanos the inbred part of the mountain family—more hills than mountains, not particularly lush, nor particularly desert.

Both my mind and my right calf demanded a break before returning to civilization. What did Gandhi say about Western civilization? *That it would be a good idea.* I wasn't convinced.

In the trailhead parking lot I exited the vehicle and sat down on a boulder. Sitting in these wooded foothills relaxed me as much as possible . . . under the circumstances.

Radiation might pass through me, sitting this close to the tower, but at least my phone worked again. Nurse Song had left a message.

"You called?" I asked when I reached her.

"Yes," she said. "Jen's memorial service will take place on Saturday in the Japanese gardens in the Botanic Park."

"I'm invited, right?"

"You can come if you want," she said. "Jen won't mind."

Then she hung up.

● ● ● ● ●

I stared at the mountains. *The sky is falling.* My sky had fallen all right. At first I wanted to find the killer and get vengeance, but I was no ninja warrior, or even a laser geisha. The snow started up again; perhaps the sky was falling after all.

Didn't my tax dollars pay for something called the FBI that handled these cases?

I called Agent Washington. "It's Dan Shepard. I got a tip from a client that there might be a link between the kidnapping and Sky Roberts getting held today."

On the phone, Washington's voice sounded deep enough to have its own gravity. The radio wave struggled to escape his side of the phone as if it was a black hole. "And how did you hear this?"

"From a reliable source. I'm a criminal-defense attorney. I have a lot of reliable sources on the other side of the law, and I can't reveal their identity."

Washington's voice went even deeper. "We're already investigating that link. Thank you for your cooperation."

If he said anything more, the sound waves did not escape his orbit. For a moment, Washington's voice caused the snow to shake, as the mountains echoed with each syllable of the word "cooperation."

So much for accomplishing something by Saturday, before Jen's funeral. Nurse Song sounded reluctant when she invited me, so I didn't want to come empty handed. The whiteness of the Manzano Mountains made me sigh.

I picked up the faxed page again. Nastia must be fairly sophisticated and intelligent to know how to monitor nmcourts.com. If her dad really was a dissident Soviet physicist, she probably had a semblance of a brain to protect herself.

Unlike Jen, Nastia was pro-active. I liked that. She talked about her *lyobov,* like she meant it. She didn't have ADD when it came to men, despite her unfortunate choice in careers. Just because she sat on dude's laps, didn't mean that she lost her heart.

My phone buzzed and I saw a text from Hollywood about setting up my meetings. "My boss is heading to Cannes for a month," Allen Koenigsburg, the assistant, texted. "It's now or never."

So much for them waiting for me to get back to them. I was the flavor of the week. I better make the call to the direct line.

I hit a few keys and reached Allen, "Are you out in L.A. now?" he asked.

"I'm somewhere in the Seventh Judicial District of Hell." I told him about the two hearings. It felt strange talking to someone in the sun, as I stood there in the snow.

"It makes me want to practice law again," Allen said.

"You practiced law?"

"I worked for a big L.A. firm for a year, my first year out of UCLA."

He mentioned the firm's name; they had rejected me, of course.

"You're still practicing?" he asked. "Your life sounds so much more exciting than reading scripts."

"You don't know the half of it."

We confirmed my appointment for next Monday, mid-morning. I had never heard of the person I'd meet. Still, I'd heard of his shows and of his Emmy awards.

"You're in the big leagues now," Allen said.

"I'll believe it when I see it." A squirrel ran on top of my car.

I hung up. I felt guilty about thinking about Hollywood at a time like this, but Jen wanted me to go on with my life. At least, I hoped she did. Maybe someday, if the stars aligned, I'd write something about her. I got back on the Salt Missions Trail. Maybe it should be the Salt Mission Impossible trail.

TUESDAY
SONG: "No Love, No Hope" by Trevor McShane

MASTER CRATER

THE SNOW MELTED BY TUESDAY.

"Spring is back with a vengeance!" the weather reporter reminded me when I woke up at my apartment that morning. I had barely slept last night. I checked my hair after I showered. I was going gray. I think I had aged a year in the few hours spent with Jen. Now, as Trevor McShane had sung, there was *no love, no hope.*

Stress and fatigue made me sluggish. I grabbed the nearest boring blue suit, and then stopped. Which tie? This was my outfit for Crater after all, which was even more remote than Estancia. Do I wear a solid blue tie or one with "patterns and shit?" Rural people hated busy ties. I found a novelty tie with a cartoon representation of all the attractions of Route 66 that might work. I stayed with the cheap artificial shoes, however. Did that make me the silicone lawyer?

At least the roads were already clear this late in the morning; even the high country snow disappeared under the onslaught of the hot spring winds roaring up from Mexico. The winds pushed me out to Crater on I-40 at warp speed.

Upon arrival, the movie camp bustled with activity, but not in a good way. The grips and gaffers were all helping break camp, cursing Sky Roberts with every breath. "At least we can get one more day of shooting at the prison, with or without Sky," a gaffer said to his co-worker.

"Yes, but after this crap with Sky High Roberts, no one will ever want to shoot in New Mexico again!"

"Old Town Crater" sat about a mile from the exit, in even more barren country. Crater was Luna's ancestral home. On one wistful occasion, she told me she'd like to retire to Crater and escape the limelight. Her mom's home had been boarded up for years, but she could sell the loft and live in Crater like a queen. I picked out a potential Luna Mansion immediately, one of the few non-trailers in town.

Luna told me her dad started the medical clinic here. Then the state condemned the clinic and replaced it with a municipal building that housed basically every government function—local, state and federal—for the thousand or so people who still lived in the greater Crater metroplex, an area the size of Rhode Island.

Old Town Crater was basically a dead hamlet with boarded-up store fronts, except for one liquor store. Rather than "to be," the town had gone with "not to be."

To make it worse, the refinery smell, that weird gasoline smell, drifted down here. I never liked the smell of napalm in the morning.

The "courthouse" had two rooms. One was the courtroom, and the other a lobby partially filled with cubicles. Each cubicle contained a governmental service ranging from welfare to domestic violence. Both the lawyers and the citizens had to wait in the lobby, next to the animal control officer's cubicle with its pictures of abandoned puppies.

"Spay and neuter your pets," read a caption, right next to the jury check-in. Someone had crossed "pets" out and scribbled in "jurors."

A CO brought in Jonny Braun in his Crater Detention Center outfit, and he could be a lost puppy about to get neutered himself. He couldn't post the one hundred-dollar security bond. Someone on the outside merely had to post ten whole dollars.

I didn't laugh. If I went to jail, would someone post ten whole dollars for me?

"Nice tie," he said. People smiled at the tie. I sure couldn't wear something like this in Albuquerque on the seventh floor of Metro. I couldn't wear it in Estancia even.

The CO sat Braun down next to an elderly woman who was trying to get her dog back from the dog catcher. She shook her head at him and touched his shoulder with familiarity. "Why did you do it, Jonny?"

If he had grown up in a place like Albuquerque, he'd be classified as Gifted / Special Ed. With the right meds and counseling, he'd have made it through school and maybe worked at an Albuquerque call center, placing orders for cable or phone service.

Braun's juvenile record, and a single shoplifting charge at a nearby Wal-Mart, precluded even a casino job. Since his probation forbade "any association with alcohol," he couldn't even work at the second largest employer in town—the liquor store. His only potential employment was the adult bookstore with the unfortunate name of *66 Virgins*. I never asked if that was a reference to the seventy-two virgins waiting in Paradise for all the suicide bombers.

At least the virgins didn't mind his prior conviction for indecent exposure. I did like the store's new name better than its old name — *Master Crater*.

I couldn't blame a man for developing a drug problem when he sat night after night in a video store with a bizarre name selling porn to truckers. Unfortunately, minimum wage didn't buy that many drugs, so he had to come up with a way to pay for his habit. His mistake was that he had forgotten the video camera in the store that beamed things to his boss in a remote location.

On the surveillance video of low-level transactions, a Tera Patrick video might go for an ounce of weed, Kaylani Lei for a gram of coke, a Dasiy Marie compilation for a small amount of meth. He got a little more for the sex toys. I had seen the tapes. Did the drivers wait to use their products until they got home, or did they use them while driving on the interstate? Cops talked about busting truckers for one-handed driving around here.

Braun fidgeted as more people passed by, staring at him. Could this loser know Nastia? The "courthouse" lacked a private meeting room so I would have to be creative to find out. Pursuant to the regs, I asked the guard's permission if Braun and I could talk somewhere.

"I'll have to take you to the holding cell," he said. "No funny business."

"I don't think you have to worry about that. I haven't been funny in a long time."

• • • • •

I was now inside the building's single holding cell. "Leave the door open," I asked the guard. He laughed and shut it behind me, locking me in. Braun sat down on the cell's toilet, but thankfully didn't undress.

Braun looked up and pleaded with me. "I'll testify against anyone if they'll give me a conditional discharge." A conditional discharge meant the conviction was not a felony after the guilty party completed probation.

"I'll keep that in mind."

I tried to read Braun's expressions. His fortnight in jail had sobered him up. He could handle my questioning.

"Do you know a girl named Nastia?" I asked.

He smiled. "I sold her some shoes," he said. "I called them Bettie Page shoes in the man's sizes. She had big feet for such a little girl."

"You sell shoes?"

"We're a fetish store. Most of the shoes we sell are to guys." He laughed. "Truckers like heels sometime. She wore those shoes when she was visiting a dude in jail, couple of months ago."

I lit up. This could be it.

"Was it her boyfriend?"

"I don't remember. This dude was from out of town. They just transferred him in because of overcrowding where he was. They transferred him out a few days later."

He rubbed his forehead as if it hurt. "We were in the same pod. He was like an actor or something. He was only in jail here for twenty-four hours."

"Do you remember who it was?"

He thought. "Sky High Roberts. That was the dude. From the movie *Desert Divas*."

"*Desert Demons*?"

"Yeah, something like that."

That didn't help much. I already knew Sky had a connection to this. "Were they engaged?"

He laughed. "I wouldn't call it one of those stable, long-term relationships."

"That mean Nastia was a whore and Sky was a client?"

"It means whatever you want it to mean."

"Is there anything else?" I said. "Do you have something for me?"

"Nah."

I pounded on the door.

Nothing.

• • • • •

Fifteen minutes later, when the guard finally let us out of the cell and we entered the courtroom, the judge had already called a prostitution case. A very short woman dressed in a business suit stood next to another woman in a short skirt that barely covered her ample rear end. The woman in the business suit strongly resembled the woman who ran from me at the casino. She also had big feet in her fetish heels, her Bettie Page heels, just like they sold at the *66 Virgins.*

Could she be Nastia? When did Nastia become a lawyer?

It probably wasn't her, but I couldn't be sure. I had met her too long ago, and in Crater the woman had been too far away that night to make a positive ID.

The judge directed his attention to the woman in the business suit and asked whether her client wanted to go to trial. The woman said nothing.

Finally, the woman next to her, the one in the short skirt, spoke up in anger. "Your honor, I'm the *lawyer;* the woman on my left is the defendant."

"Ma'am, you need to get an appropriate wardrobe," the judge said to the attorney, "I know this is your first day, but this is ridiculous. I want to be able to tell a lawyer from a whore."

"Your honor," she said. "I will when I can afford it."

The judge had the parties approach the bench to talk off the record. I couldn't get a good look at the defendant in the fetish heels and business suit before she was hustled away into custody, her lawyer following behind. Hopefully the lawyer was just meeting with her client and not going into custody herself.

"Where are they taking female prisoners?" I asked a guard.

"Depends on where there's room. Every female facility in the state is overcrowded these days. And hell, she's just going to be booked and released once her pimp posts her bond. She'll vanish into the night."

So I couldn't find the woman even if I wanted to. The lawyer didn't return. Was she going to jail, too?

"Who were they?" I asked the guard.

"I don't know," the guard. "Both of them were just passing through."

I checked the docket for the day. I didn't recognize the name of either the lawyer or the client. I crossed referenced them on my phone's Internet with every other listing on nmcourts.com. Nothing there, either. That could be a computer error, or perhaps Nastia was a made-up name after all.

• • • • •

Braun's hearing took a matter of minutes, a relief after the circus back in Metro. We pled out, got his conditional discharge. The guard let him change into street clothes in the holding cell and he quickly emerged outside the courtroom a free man.

We stood outside in the incredible wind. The refinery now looked like a Martian colony in the reddish soil. I looked for the Crater here in Crater County, but felt like I was already too deep inside it to see the walls around me.

Braun's mother and girlfriend came over and hugged him, once the deputy took the cuffs off him. Both women hugged me as well for a weird four-way hug.

"You owe me one," I said.

"I can still get you a vibrating plaster cast of—" he was about to name a porn star.

Unless he could somehow produce the legendary Asia Carrera herself, in person, circa 1998, I wasn't interested. I just smiled. "I'll think of something. Was that Nastia up before us?"

"I don't know," he said. "I wasn't paying attention. All those whores look the same after a while."

"Do you have anything for me?"

"Hold on a second," he said. He reached into his pants, and pulled out an envelope. The envelope was marked "Attorney Client Privileged."

"Did you leave this for me?" he asked. "Someone dropped it off earlier. I don't know who, though."

"No, I had nothing to do with that," I said. "Can I see it?'

I opened the envelope. The letter inside read: "Whatever you do, don't go see Sky Roberts."

• • • • •

I headed out of Old Town Crater. For one moment the sun shone perfectly. Even the mobile homes and boarded-up store fronts could pass for a desert Disneyland Main Street. The town didn't appear dead; but like Sleeping Beauty, it just wanted to wake up and kiss the prince.

I was the Prince of Egypt for the moment. Call me Moses, I let another one of my people go. My people, *mi gente*. Were the Jonny Braun's of the world, porn-store embezzlers, "my people" these days? God, if the dudes at the pre-environmental law club back at Brown University could see me now.

I tried to put the whole thing together as I drove toward the freeway. I pondered visiting Sky Roberts, despite Nastia's admonition. Was Nastia lying to me? Was that her in the courtroom or her back at the fight? Did I even know that the faxes were coming from Nastia, or from someone out to send me on a wild goose chase? Or in New Mexico that would be a wild roadrunner chase, I suppose.

Hmmm. MDC was on the way back to Albuquerque, just off

I-40. Then again, lawyers aren't supposed to interview defendants who are represented by counsel.

But that was more of a suggestion than a commandment, right? If the founding fathers had wanted people to have a right *against* self-incrimination, and the right *to* counsel, they would have put it right there in the original constitution. Well, they waited until the Bill of Rights, in the Fifth Amendment to be precise. And in the Sixth Amendment, too.

How far would I go?

THE SEEDY SIDE OF SESAME STREET

A FEW MILES DOWN THE freeway, my car developed a mind of its own and veered toward the Paseo de Volcan exit, the way to MDC. Paseo de Volcan, street of the volcano, or was it really *Paseo de Inferno,* the highway to hell?

I found myself at the jail entrance right at six o'clock sharp. It was too late to enter the pods, but the jail held video meetings for families until eight. Perhaps they'd let me do a video meeting with Sky. I would just be a blurry presence on the screen to him, and he would probably confuse me with someone else.

• • • • •

Pick-up trucks packed the parking lot, many of them with a stick-on reflector seal of a young imp pissing on various words like *La Migra* and the Albuquerque police department. This time I remembered to keep my phone in the car.

Inside, Double V sat at the receptionist desk, her blond buzz cut showing streaks of gray in the unforgiving florescent lights. She talked back to an angry family of twenty or so. She kept her cool, even though her pregnancy stretched her uniform so much it looked like an alien wanted to emerge for dinner.

"Didn't expect to see you back," I said.

"The State don't give no mental-health time," she said. "Least I'm out here in the lobby where I'm safe, with the 'loved ones.'"

Safety was relative. The line of loved ones snaked out the door, and the snake tried to bite its own head. Inside, inmates could be locked-down, segregated by gangs. Here, rival families sat in the same sweaty lobby together. No one patted them down.

Many "jail widows" waited in line, showing a lot of cleavage. Double V greeted a woman in hot pants and bra. "Who you seeing tonight, Rosie?"

"That depends," she said. "Is Dave back from the jail in Los Lunas yet?"

MDC might as well put a stripper's pole in the lobby, although they might want to reinforce it as it would need to take on a whole lot of Rosie. The Rosies of the world stuck with their men through thick and thin—jail, probation, probation violation and then prison.

Why couldn't I have someone who loved me like a jail widow? My crimes in relationships were relatively minor. One woman broke up with me for narcissism: I talked about myself too much. Dealing in narcissism, I told myself, is not as bad as dealing in narcotics.

"So who are you here to see?" Double V asked me.

"I'm kinda here unofficially," I said. "I'll wait my turn."

Several of the jail widows had their boyfriends' names tattooed on the backs of their necks. A scuffle ensued when Rosie and another widow shared the same man's tattoo.

"I had him first," Rosie said.

"Well he's mine now," said the other.

Double V played Solomon as the two women stood in front of the reception desk. She decided which widow got to see the man first. She went with Rosie, who had the bigger tattoo of his name.

No one had my name tattooed on her neck. Jen sure didn't. God knows where Nastia had tattooed her *lyobov's* name.

• • • • •

I choked up a bit standing with the children, the jail orphans. These kids could be extras on *Sesame Street*. My parents were still mad at me for not reproducing. "We're not getting any younger," my mother kept reminding me. "We need a legacy."

My God, if you had trouble conceiving, you should get convicted of a felony. Just staring at a woman during a jail visit would impregnate her. Every criminal was somebody's parent or somebody's child.

The line finally died down by seven forty-five. Fifteen minutes left, time to do or die. "So can I see Sky Roberts?"

"He's in the in infirmary," Double V said.

"Is he okay?"

"Well, it's for his own protection," she said. She started to push a sign-in form towards me.

"Do I have to sign in?" I asked. "Like I said, I am sort of here . . . unofficially."

She smiled. "I said I owed you one. Consider this the one."

INMOST CAVE

DOUBLE V CLICKED ME BACK to the main hallway. During the day, the hallway teemed with activity—inmates, guards, and people in plainclothes who worked for the administration. The corridor was dark except for the ghostly green emergency lights. Our footsteps echoed through the halls.

"I've never been to the jail infirmary," I said.

"Well you're in for a treat. Have you got your shots?"

"Shots?" I asked.

"You never know what you'll catch in there."

"Then I'll sue the ass off this place."

"Three words," she said. "Whenever a lawyer comes in here voluntarily, those three words are 'assumption of risk.' Especially if you don't sign the register."

We walked a hundred yards through the dark corridor before she clicked the door for the infirmary. "This is as far as I can go with you." She left me in front of the unit's sally port. "Ready to assume more risk?"

I stood there for a moment. "I don't know."

"I can take you back," she said. "It is kinda late, and you ain't supposed to be here, we both know that."

Nastia had warned me against seeing Sky, but this was about Dew, this was about Luna, and most importantly, this was about Jen. I took a deep breath. Time to go in. She closed the door behind me. I stuck in the sally port for a moment. The stench of vomit overpowered me; the ammonia made it worse.

I desperately wanted to press the button and leave. God, imagine life plus twenty years of this.

The lights inside were a darker shade of green, like an S&M club in East Berlin might have been during the cold war. Once I adjusted to the lights I saw into the biggest CO guard I had ever seen. In this light, he resembled the Incredible Hulk.

"I need to see Sky Roberts," I said.

Hulk didn't really care this late at night, but he managed to ask "You sure you're allowed to be here?"

"They wouldn't let me back here if I wasn't." I flashed my bar card.

"I know you," Hulk nodded. No one ever tried to break into jail but he frisked me just to be sure. I didn't even bring a pen in with me. "Sky's the last cell."

"Will you bring him out?"

"You get to go see him, up close and personal."

• • • • •

I passed two cells with amputees. The man in the third cell could be a leper. His yellow eyes cut right through me. A few of the inmate patients moaned in pain.

"I'll kill you if don't shut up," the leper shouted to the person next to him. The inmate yelled at me. "You're my lawyer, right?"

"Yeah," I said. "Dontae, right?" I had represented him on God knows what a few months ago. "What happened to you?"

"You don't want to know."

He was right. I didn't.

In his cell at the end of the hall, Sky wore a "High Risk Inmate" red jumpsuit, but he looked way too thin and sickly to be a risk to anyone other than himself. I couldn't actually go into cell; I had to stand outside in the darkened hallway. The entire wing smelled like piss and puke and blood. After tapping on the window, Sky finally acknowledged my presence.

"You're not my lawyer," he said. He tried to place me in the fragmented databank of his brain. "You're that asshole from the case back in that small town," he said at last. "I hate you, right?"

He wasn't sure whether he hated me or not? I had one instant to convince Sky to stay with me in this dark room.

"Sky, you're right, I'm not your attorney. You don't have to talk to me." I had the barest fig leaf of legality.

"So what the fuck then?"

I took a deep breath of the disinfected air. "A child has been kidnapped. I think it has something to do with *Desert Demons*."

Sky's body started shaking. He wasn't just in here for his protection; he was doing serious detox.

"And?"

"And a dancer named Nastia visited you when you were in Crater County Detention Center couple of months ago. She might know something. Do you know anything about her?"

"I know a lot of dancers."

He hadn't kicked me out yet, so I couldn't resist. "Did you know a waitress named Pink? Wore a pink wig, dressed like a comic book character?"

He laughed a knowing laugh.

Had he fucked Jen?

"Nastia danced for me a few weeks ago," he said. "At the Zone. I invited them both back, that girl Pink too, the waitress."

I clenched a fist with rage.

"That bitch blew me off, said she was a waitress and never crossed the line."

"So did Nastia come?'

"Yeah, she *came* all right. Many times. She was with me when I got the DWI."

"Was she your girlfriend?"

"Which one?"

"Nastia, the one who says she's an Eskimo? Talks with a Russian accent?"

Sky laughed. "Yeah right, I'm gonna date a midget Eskimo stripper in New Mexico. Even if she does back flips on the pole."

"Did she ever mention her true love? Her *lyobov*?"

Sky stared at his reflection in the bulletproof glass. "Yeah, she kept talking about someone, but I didn't pay attention. Why do you care about midget Eskimo strippers with Russian accents?"

The infirmary lights flickered for a second. Behind me, an inmate vomited up the day's meals.

"Hurry up in there," Hulk shouted from down the hall. "Or I'll lock you in with him."

"Why was Luna's child kidnapped?"

"Dude, I got nothing to do with that. I'm sure the big boys is pissed that I'm locked up and production is going to halt. The bonding companies backing the movie are gonna lose everything if we shut down."

"Who, specifically, would be pissed?"

He laughed again. "You're not much of a detective, are you?"

"What do you mean?"

"Roman Romero, the exec producer, but he's in Mexico."

"Roman Romero? There's international money in this?"

"Not just him," Sky said. "There's a big Arab dude, Ahmad Assed. He's like a pharaoh, some shit like that."

"Wow. It is big."

Sky tensed up. "You don't fuck with guys like that. They can get to you anywhere, even in here."

That realization caused another round of shakes; perhaps this Roman Romero controlled Sky's body by remote control or voodoo doll.

"They would have to have somebody local to pull this off. Do you have any idea who that would be?"

He thought for a moment. He knew the name. But his shakes got bad. Real bad.

"So who are you again? Can you guarantee me immunity and get me into a witness protection program that is so good that I can still act and also have protections so no one can even fart in my general direction. Can you do that?"

"I'm nobody. I can't guarantee that."

"Then I got nothing to say to nobody." He pressed an intercom button. "CO, this ain't my lawyer. Don't let him see me again."

"I'm sorry," I said. "There's been a misunderstanding."

Hulk came over to me. He was angry. "You're not really supposed to be here, are you?"

I said nothing.

He jiggled the cuffs attached to his belt. He could lock me up before counting to three.

"I heard how you saved Double V. I'll say you were here visiting Dontae. I'll forget that this shit happened."

• • • • •

I walked alone down the corridor. Thankfully, Double V let me out as quickly as possible. "Don't ask me for another favor," she said.

In my car, my phone blinked, indicating two texts from a private number.

I read the first text. "Not me at Crater County."

I scrolled down to the next text. "Told u not to see Sky, but u got guts. I like guts!"

Somebody liked me at least.

• • • • •

That night I surfed the web. Roman Romero had indeed been arrested in Mexico on extortion charges there, he had also threatened a judge, another crime. Still, he had an alibi, too. He was in jail in Mexico and had been for the last month.

Ahmad Assed ran one of the Emirates, and he presiding over their three-week film festival even now. What was an "emir" anyway? Was that better than a sheikh? I couldn't go after him either. Jail wasn't always an alibi for drug lords or drug emirs. I still suspected the man. It would not be that hard to order a kidnapping from jail or an Emirate. Even Sky had been able to get a message to the outside world via the wrestler. Jail communication worked faster than the Internet.

Washington already had the FBI scouring everything. He probably knew about Roman Romero and the Emir. That was over my pay grade, and probably over his as well.

Someone else knew the location of Luna's child and I would find that person.

Unless that person found me first.

WEDNESDAY
SONG: "My True Love" by Trevor McShane

ATOMIC FLASHBACK

I AWOKE AT DAWN WEDNESDAY morning. Talk about the highway to hell and back. Alamogordo and Las Cruces, and then up to Albuquerque, the Bermuda triangle of driving except it was all beach and no ocean. Alamogordo was a big small town; Las Cruces was a small big town, according to the census bureau. That was a distinction without a difference.

I found a pair of nice black dress shoes in my closet, no need to look like a total slob today. Then I donned an orange radioactive tie to go with a boring gray suit, as I would pass by the Trinity bomb site.

I needed to be in Alamogordo's Otero County District Court 209 miles away, at ten o'clock sharp, ready to rock, so I left before dawn. I had the Rio Grande on my left most of the way, so I could pretend I was in civilization. Eighty miles south, in a little village called San Antonio, I turned east on Route 380 and headed into the outback.

Twenty minutes later, over a barren ridge and back down into the desert, I passed Stallion Gate, the turnoff for the Trinity Site, where the first atom bomb exploded in 1945. I had visited there on one of the two days of the year it was open last October. The memory hit me harder than a neutron bomb.

Jen had envisioned an atomic picnic, and invited Luna and me. "Maybe we'll get bitten by radioactive spiders and turn into superheroes for real." Luna brought along Dew and Rose came along for the ride. He mentioned something about scouting locations.

The site was closed now. Probably just as well, the wind felt radioactive. I pulled off the road, just to absorb the impact of the past. The memory still had a half-life.

• • • • •

That October day was still hot for this late in the fall. Luna drove her minivan off the exit to Stallion Gate, south from 380. Rose sat in the front seat. In the back seat, Jen sat behind Luna, her arm around then four-year-old Dew. Dew wore a little Laser Geishas baseball hat. I sat behind Rose, and stared at the desert.

"We're almost there," Luna said as we came to a check point. "Radioactive land. It's like a post-apocalyptic Disneyland "

"Will we see Godzilla?" Dew asked. "Like in the cartoon?"

"I hope not," Luna said.

"Look Dew, a horny toad," Jen said, pointing to a toad crossing the road.

I laughed. "Wouldn't the radiation mutate an ordinary horny toad into a—"

"Don't even go there," Luna said. "My daughter is four, even if she already reads at a ten-year-old level."

Rose went on about his last film. Luna was obviously charmed by the man. His world was so glamorous. He even invited Luna to come with him to Cannes in a few weeks.

"Can I come too?" I asked. "Oh wait, I have a burglary trial coming up in Carrizozo."

Jen leaned toward me and touched my arm. "I'd rather go to

Carrizozo than Cannes," she whispered. "I think what you do is cool."

"What do I do?" I asked.

"You save people," she said. "Maybe you can save me someday."

We parked in the crowded lot. The Trinity site felt biblical, but it was hardly something out of Revelation. I expected to see three kings riding on donkeys bearing frankincense and myrrh. Instead, I saw tourists with faded military tattoos on their flabby arms. A few had bumper stickers proclaiming the need for "More nukes, less kooks!"

The "kooks" consisted of a few protesters holding signs that read, "Never again!"

Dew kept talking about monsters; apparently Robo-Godzilla was cooler than the real Godzilla.

"Have you been letting her watch monster movies again when you're babysitting, Jen?"

"Just the Geisha cartoons," Jen said. "She loves them.

The women did a weird ritual. "Laser Geisha Pink," said Jen.

"Laser Geisha Blue," said Luna.

"Laser Geisha *Lavender,*" Dew piped in.

"There isn't a Laser Geisha Lavender," said Luna.

"There is now!" Dew shouted.

When we walked the quarter mile to the site, Dew's face slowly fell when no horny toad monsters emerged from the desert. There wasn't even a crater here, just a stone obelisk that stood not much taller than a European NBA center.

Even the trinitite, the little remnants of the blast, were disappointing —just little greenish rocks.

Dew frowned. "Where's Godzilla?"

"Sorry," Luna said. "I told Godzilla to go to his room since you were coming."

Dew smiled. "Tell him to come anyway. I want to see him."

"Maybe Godzilla's invisible," Jen said, "and only comes after the naughty little girls."

As if on cue, a sudden burst of wind blew Dew's hat into the air.

"Just kidding," Jen said "Auntie Jen will protect you from Invisible Godzilla."

Dew laughed and wandered around the site. She picked up a few trinitite rocks, but Luna, ever the mother, made her put them back. It was illegal to take the rocks from the site.

Maybe it was the radiation, but Jen gave me a look, a real look. That night on the sand dunes was just a one-night stand, right? Perhaps not.

"Let's walk for a bit," Jen said.

We excused ourselves and wandered around the rocky field, picking up a few remaining nuggets of trinitite, to catch and release. I picked up a greenish rock. The radiation was supposed to be miniscule, but it still felt tingly in my hand.

Jen smiled at me. She was so beautiful, so helpless, yet so strong. I looked at Luna, Dew, and Rose down by the obelisk. They were out of my league. No, the radiation didn't do the tingling. Jen took the trinitite from me and our hands locked for a second, the trinitite felt magical.

"For luck," she said, suddenly kissing me.

Just like Trevor McShane's song! *My true love*, indeed.

I suddenly felt it, like a burst of gamma rays coming from my heart. "I love you," I said. "You keep saying you're the cheap Korean knock-off of Luna, well you're more than that to me. I really love you." I felt like Princess Leia in *Star Wars* talking to Han Solo.

"I know," she said, aping Han's blasé response.

"Don't throw that line from *Star Wars* at me. I'm serious."

Jen threw the trinitite up in the air, as if flipping a coin. The trinitite spun in the wind, twirling end over end. She grabbed it and pretended to read its rocky entrails. "I love you too," she said.

"Are you sure?"

She laughed. "I really do love you," she said. "My true love. Luna was my only friend, and now she's got her own world. My daughter is disabled and my mom blames me for my bad genes. In the few weeks since that night in the dunes, I realized how much you mean to me. You treat me with respect. No other man has ever done that; I was just a piece of meat to them. I know you'll protect me."

"Of course."

She threw the trinitite at me.

I bobbled it in my left hand, before grabbing it in my right.

"Can you make a ring out of trinitite?" I asked.

"A ring?"

"Maybe it's just being here, at the end of the earth. But seeing you here I know I want to protect you. I don't know you that well, but I want to learn. And I want to take the rest of my life to do it. Jen, will you marry me?"

She took the rock out of her hand, and threw it up in the air once more. This time she let it fall to the ground. The rock split in half.

"Sure," she said. "But let's call it engaged to being engaged."

"We better let the rock sit there," I said. "It's against the law to take that stuff."

Just then, Dew hurried to us as fast as her short legs could carry her. "Watch me, Auntie Jen."

Dew saw the broken rock, grabbed a piece and hurried down to the obelisk. Then she raced around it as fast as she could.

"What is she doing?" I asked.

"I'm turning back time," Dew said.

Luna blocked her path and grabbed her. "Super-collider."

"You can't hold me," Dew said. She ran around again, then again. She finally stopped, out of breath.

We all sat there for a few moments. I told a few funny stories about monsters. My family once owned a piece of the Empire State Building and we had to get King Kong insurance, even though it was a pre-existing condition.

"Is there a Queen Kong, a Prince Kong or a Princess Kong?" Dew asked.

"There is now," I said. "I now crown you Princess Kong."

She gave me the trinitite. "Hold this for me."

Stealing trinitite was illegal, but I wanted to savor this moment forever so I stuffed it in my pocket.

That was the last I saw of Dew. Jen's electrons would escape to L.A. in a few weeks and Luna would disappear into her own crater with Rose.

• • • • •

Back in the present I opened my glove compartment and found a fragment of trinitite. What was their radioactive half-life? Was it anything close to the radioactive half-life of love?

CARIZOZO KID

I RESUMED DRIVING EAST ON 380 over a ridge and into the Valley of Fires. Ironically, the Valley of Fires State Park, a natural formation with twisted black rocks, looked far more radioactive than the Trinity site.

I sped up to avoid any potential Lava Zombies.

My bladder felt like it had lava inside as well, bubbling lava. I needed to stop chugging Starbucks' Double Espresso cans. Unfortunately, urinating outside in the park would be a Federal offense.

I stopped in Carrizozo, the only town within miles. This town was bigger than a hamlet. Would that make it a *King Lear?*

My prostate felt like a bomb about to burst. Unfortunately for me, someone had claimed the only bathroom at the gas station. I pounded for a few moments, to no avail. Then I ran to the competing gas station across the street.

"Out of order."

I bolted across the street again, hoping to find a clean bathroom in a local restaurant. Unfortunately, three obese rednecks waited in front of me, munching beef jerky. Figuring five minutes for each, and that was fifteen minutes more.

Perhaps I could sneak behind the restaurant, but a vigilant state trooper stood by his vehicle at the intersection, radar gun in hand. Could a radar gun spot someone peeing?

State cops charged peeing in public as indecent exposure, as opposed to littering. That's what got a client locked up once and he did four years in the joint. Well, technically he was on probation for an attempted murder.

If busted for indecent exposure in Carrizozo, my charge would be on the Internet forever. My life would be over. Would I have to register as an indecent offender? I'd have to take over Braun's job at the adult bookstore in Crater.

Another greasy spoon lay another block down. I calculated it would take less time to run there, as opposed to running back to the car, fiddling with my keys, starting and then driving and parking, so I ran, hoping to avoid breaking the five-mile an hour speed limit.

Inside, I hurried past the staff to the rest room.

"Patrons only!" a fat waitress yelled "You gotta order something."

"Get me a chicken salad sandwich," I said.

"Okay," she said. "It will take a few minutes."

"But hold the chicken, the salad and the sandwich."

Before she could protest, I plopped five dollars on the counter.

"You gotta take the key," she said. "Make sure you lock it when you finish."

●　●　●　●　●

After I finished, I hurried back to the rest stop just as Rose left the bathroom. "What are you doing down here?" I asked.

"Scouting locations," he said.

"You're still doing movies, even after the *Desert Demons* fiasco?"

"Who said anything about movies?"

He left without another word. This was the end of the earth.

Well, you could literally see the end of the earth from here. Was he spotting hide-outs for Dew?

I contemplated calling Washington, but what could I say? That Rose was an asshole?

• • • • •

I returned to the original gas station, which was now empty of course. I filled up with gas, and then picked up a bottle of cherry cider that was on sale in the quick-mart. This part of the country got bombed by its own government, but the lingering radiation resulted in the best cherry cider in the world. It was like mutant cherry cider—sweet and tart in just the right proportion. If the Lava Zombies did come for me, I'd offer them a pitcher of the stuff and hopefully that would satisfy their blood lust.

The young clerk twitched in her polyester uniform. Either she suffered from lingering radiation or she subsisted on a diet of hot dogs and cherry cider. And yet, she had the fresh-faced look of a Hollywood starlet waiting to be discovered. She was also voluptuous enough for *Playboy's* Convenience Store Cuties.

She smiled at me warmly. "I know you." Her name tag said Haydn. Haydn was too pretty to be marooned here in lava land.

"How?"

"You're that lawyer," Haydn said. She had several science fiction magazines open, and seemed to be drawing her own graphic novel. She sure didn't belong in this particular galaxy, but it's not like she could get a job at Dreamworks all the way out here. "You're representing my pops today in court down in Alamogordo."

"Okay, right. How much for the cider?"

"I've got it." She reached into her own pocket to pay for the cherry cider. "Just save my pops."

"I'll do what I can," I said.

"That's all you can do," she said. "I'm sure he's just another criminal to you, but he's my pops, and I do love him. Don't forget that. Don't ever forget that."

"I'll do my best." She was right. Every criminal was somebody's kid, and quite often somebody's parent as well. Maybe prison made them more fertile. What did I have—penal envy?

In my haste to get back on the road, I spilled cider on my tie, making a cherry bloodstain near the bottom.

• • • • •

The fifty-mile stretch from Carizozo to Alamogordo was desert, the small oasis of Tularosa, and then desert again. Fighter planes flew overhead heading toward the White Sands Missile Range. If someone bombed this place, how would anyone know? Alamogordo held thirty thousand hardy souls. Scraggly palm trees graced the main street; these palms would no doubt survive anything short of the Apocalypse.

Inside the squat adobe courthouse, I searched for my client on a bench filled with old men who could all be laid off from the last cattle drive. My client sat near the end of the line, I mean, at the end of the bench. The girl's father was an old white cowboy, Ethan Edwards, but he went by the moniker of the Carrizozo Kid. He once raised cattle in Carrizozo but had switched to cooking meth. He looked like John Wayne on his deathbed, even though he was barely fifty.

The Carrizozo Kid remained out of custody, so he couldn't be Nastia's *lyobov*, right? He couldn't have anything to do with the kidnapping this far out in the boonies. Hell, I was probably on Nastia's shit list anyway, and flying solo from here on in.

The Kid had lived a rough life, like Benjamin Button toward

the end, or was it the beginning? Meth was a hard habit to quit. I'm sure the prosecutor would bring up every single dirty urine analyses (UA).

We talked about his drug problem. I had a job to do, regardless of my pre-occupation. His poor daughter up in Carrizozo had just stared at me like I was her father's guardian angel.

It wasn't about the clients; sometimes I did it for the families.

How can you defend someone's who's guilty?

Because he's got a pretty daughter named Haydn who gave me free cherry cider.

The Kid shook from withdrawal. I needed to convince him to sign the plea and get into the drug court program and my work here was done.

"Can't we take it to trial?" he asked.

His mobile home had caught on fire from the chemicals, so they could search without a warrant due to the "community caretaker" exception. That meant a cop could enter a burning house without a warrant. The cops then took the Kid's burning clothes and found the drugs in a baggie halfway up his rectum. I sure didn't want to give the judge my client's initial explanation; that the drugs ended up there by accident.

"We can take it to trial," I said. "However, this plea gets you into treatment next week. If we take it to trial and lose, the judge will be pissed for wasting his time. If we take it to trial and win, well, you're going to go out and party and probably get arrested again."

"Give me a minute," he said. "You really care about guys like me, right? Even though you're my lawyer."

"I'm not really *just* a lawyer; I'd like to think I was your friend." I stifled a smile as I said that.

"I need a friend." He signed the form after another minute. The whole hearing took thirty seconds, max.

"You saved my life."

"Just doing my job."

"No, really," he said. "If there's ever anything I can do to help," he said.

"Maybe," I said. "By the way, does the name Nastia mean anything to you?"

He laughed. "She bought meth from me a few times. They filmed a couple of scenes over at White Sands and she was a movie groupie."

I wondered if Nastia got a credit on the set: crew slut.

"Did she say anything?"

"I don't want to say anything more. You got attorney client privilege. Well, I got dealer-client privilege."

"But I just saved you."

"Yeah, but I still gotta do two years of the drug court program. You didn't do enough."

What else did I have to do?

IT'S NOT EASY BEING WHITE

I CHECKED MY TURQUOISE WATCH when I left the courtroom. It wasn't even eleven yet and my Las Cruces hearing was set at one in the afternoon, sixty miles away. This Cruces pre-trial hearing would be less stressful than Alamogordo. We hadn't received any discovery yet so I would just ask for another pre-trial in another month, a two minute hearing max.

I drove west across Route 70 at the speed limit. No need to tempt fate underneath the fighter planes from Holloman Air Force Base, or the cruise missiles from White Sands Missile Range. Yes, there was a White Sands "National Monument" adjacent to the White Sands "Missile Range." Hopefully no one confused the two and decided to have a picnic on a target site for the Predator drones to bomb.

The military could easily take speeders out with a cruise missile if they wanted. I debated visiting the monument for the first time; it might be years before my next chance. This was God's country. Perhaps I needed to commune with God, or at least with the really cool scenery prominently featured in the first *Transformers* movie.

This would also be the perfect place to stash a body. I sure hoped Rose wasn't here to do that.

Did I have time? I calculated time versus distance to figure speed to find I had thirty minutes to visit a national monument. I once spent seven minutes in the Jefferson Memorial and only five minutes on top of the Washington Monument. White Sands would take thirty minutes, twenty-five if necessary.

I passed a sign announcing the official jurisdiction of the White Sands Missile Range. The US government could now legally bomb me. My car might as well have a bull's-eye on top, but then again, what else was new?

Thankfully, the missile warning light didn't flash, so no bombing for the next thirty minutes at least. On the other hand, the crises kept coming. Dew was still missing. Jen's killer was still at large. Perhaps, by taking a break I'd find the answer within myself, or at least find inner peace.

Whatever. . . .

Driving west on Highway 70, my left brain wanted to stop, and my right brain wanted to keep going. My thirty minutes at the monument wouldn't affect anything either way. If I didn't go, I'd get to Las Cruces with way too much time to spare. Then what? I'd wait at McDonalds for half an hour instead of seeing a wonder of the world.

Thirty miles in, I almost missed the turnoff for the monument. The sand was gray, rather than white. I lowered my expectations; there was no black and white in life anyway, just shades of gray.

I stopped at the guard post, paid a small fee. A two-lane road carried me north through the desert. The road aimed directly for an apparent iceberg rising from the tan desert. I went full speed ahead, just like the Titanic.

The speed limit on the windy entrance road was forty-five, but I punched it to seventy. No planes above me, and there was no place down below for a cop to hide.

The road veered sharply to the left before I hit the iceberg . . . well, before the sand berg. Wasn't Sandberg was a famous poet? White dunes twenty feet high cropped up on either side. A few minutes later, the pavement ended and a white wonderland began.

I was transported back to biblical times. Could it take forty years in the desert to escape this wilderness before the Promised Land? I could visualize Moses breaking the Ten Commandments in front of the Israelites in the first picnic area.

I kept driving until the road dead ended in a trailhead parking lot: the Alkali Trail. Alkali sounded both chemical and biblical. Thankfully, my gym clothes sat in the back with my files, so I quickly changed from lawyer to human.

• • • • •

I followed the trail away from the pavement. It wasn't a formal trail but a series of small plastic markers guided me through the shifting sands. Within five minutes, the markers were the only evidence of human life. Yes, this would be a great place to dump a body, including mine.

I stopped and stared deeper into the heart of an impenetrable whiteness. Even though the markers indicated a left turn, a fifty-foot dune stood immediately to my right, beckoning me.

Why do men climb sand dunes?

Because they're there.

I took a running start. After hitting the first bit of sand, momentum propelled me upward. My shoes were filled with sand by the time I reached the summit. The whole ascent had taken a few minutes max, but my heart had never pumped so hard.

I needed to catch my breath. Slowly air came down from the bottom of the Alkali Trail and finally made it to the back of my brain. I opened my eyes and stared at the white sands as they kissed the bluest sky.

"Just like heaven," Robert Smith of the Cure sang in my head.

Would the bush next to me to start burn and begin talking in the late Charlton Heston's voice?

"Hey, Charlton, *que paso?*"

The bush didn't reply. It didn't even smolder.

My phone rang, of course. Private number.

"Where are you?" Nastia asked. "You have court in Las Cruces, *da?*"

I could practically see her white face there in the sand. "I'll be there," I said.

"It's very serious."

I didn't want to face reality outside the dreamscape. "I need to know something," I said. "Before I go any further."

"*Da?*"

"Why me?" I asked. "You've probably lap-danced for other lawyers. You've sucked off half the movie crews in the state. I'm sure you've fucked all the Federal, State and Tribal law enforcement."

"Hey, I've done what I've had to do to survive. You can't judge me, you don't know me. I've never fit in anywhere. I'm always alone."

In the white sands, I saw a vision of my half-breed Eskimo, excuse me *Inupiat*. She wouldn't belong in her world over there. She wouldn't have any connection to the Native people here. She probably had learning disabilities like ADD, substance abuse problems, daddy issues and no self-esteem, unless people handed her dollar bills.

"You're right," I said. "I can't judge you. I don't know you. But still, why call me? Why would your stupid, *lyobov* or true love or whatever, possibly think I can save a little girl when the cops and FBI can't?"

"Because I see something in you that you don't see in yourself," she said.

"You don't even know me."

"No, but I know people who know you. Everybody knows you. My world, *our* world, is a small one and word gets around, *da?*"

"Why won't you tell me the name of this person?"

"It's not time yet. You've *almost* proved yourself to me, but you haven't proved yourself to my *lyobov*."

"Is this a test?" White clouds rolled over the horizon. "Are you some kind of a guardian angel, like Clarence in *It's a Wonderful Life*, and I'm your pet project so you can get your wings?"

"I'll never get my wings." She laughed. "I'm just a girl on the run from really, really bad people. A girl who got in way over her head. If the wrong people see me, I'm dead, *da?*"

"Seriously?"

The clouds came closer. Jets rumbled off in the distance. The German Air Force did training exercises here as well. Were they still called the *Luftwaffe?*

"Seriously," she replied. "No one believes me. Nobody believes me except you."

"I don't totally believe you." More jets flew overhead. Curse you Red Baron. "I don't have much time. Why do you care about this little girl?"

"It's my only chance at redemption," she said. "My only chance of getting my life back, of getting my soul back, is saving Luna's daughter."

"Do you have an immunity deal with the Feds?"

"Something like that," she said. "It's complicated. I lost my own daughter years ago. This is a kind of make-good. A do-over."

Had she killed her own child by accident? By neglect? Or worse, by murder? Had the authorities told her they would drop the charges in one death, if she prevented another? I sure wouldn't be able to find out here in white sands.

"But you didn't answer my question: why me?" I asked. "Don't give me this bullshit about seeing into my heart while you danced on my lap."

"No. In practical terms it's not that complicated. You have the conflict contract. You travel more than any attorney in New Mexico. You know Luna; you're in her inner circle, so you want to help her. You know film people in L.A. No one else has the connections you do to all walks of life. You're the only one who can help us."

"Us?" I said. "Who's us? Who's this true love, this *lyobov* you keep talking about?"

"My *lyobov* is someone you've already met, but someone you don't really know yet."

I had already met all my clients at their arraignments, but I didn't really know any of them. My gut instinct made him someone yet to come this week, in the two more days to go, not counting this afternoon at Cruces.

A sonic boom went off. Above, a jet just broke the sound barrier. Time for me to fly myself.

"Nastia?" I yelled into the phone. "Nastia?"

The words were absorbed into the white sands. She was gone.

I left the trinitite there, a sacrifice. Then I really prayed. For Luna, and for Dew, for Jen's soul and for my own. Then I descended the dune and made it back to the trail. The markers were harder to find on the way back.

The jet circled overhead, and began heading west in the direction of Las Cruces. Was someone up there watching me?

CRUCES, BABY, CRUCES

EVEN WITH THE PHONE CALL and brief wardrobe change, only thirty-three minutes passed in White Sands. Still, I hurried through the rest of Route 70 hoping to outrace any missiles. Ascending the rugged San Augustin Pass, the car passed the exit for the Missile Range Headquarters.

On the other side of San Augustin Pass, the highway descended into the steep Mesilla Valley, with the Rio Grande at its base. The city of Las Cruces proper sat ten miles ahead, but the highway filled with subdivision after subdivision cropping up in rough desert. Who lived out here, rocket scientists?

No, more like rocket mechanics.

The subdivisions held nice little Spanish villas, but the open range littered itself with mobile homes, and honky-tonks. A few of the bars were already open this early in the day. I hoped the rocket scientists didn't grab one for the road *before* their morning shift.

The road was a straight shot into town; so the car just rolled forward on its own. I picked up the file, Tyler Something or Other—Ag Battery on a peace officer—and read as I rolled downhill. This should be as easy as the Carizozo Kid, in, out, nobody gets hurt. Pre-trials were the easiest hearings known to man.

Would Tyler have a connection to Nastia?

I turned to my page of notes while holding the wheel steady. Tyler was a jock from Cruces High who had gone on to play offensive lineman at UNM. In his mug-shot, I called him Tyler Durden because with his spiky hair he looked like Brad Pitt in *Fight Club*. I'd known a lot of jocks like Tyler in high school; everybody did. I'd hated most of them, but every once in awhile a few were cool, like the older brother I never had.

Tyler had quit football and quit school after a torn ACL in spring training. Unfortunately, he found himself in a verbal altercation with his girlfriend. She apparently called him the worst thing you could call an athlete: a loser. He never touched her, but a neighbor called the cops because of the noise.

Tyler said the cop grabbed him for no reason, much like a linebacker jumping off-sides. Offensive linemen were creatures of habit. You come at them and they push you back until someone blows a whistle. Unfortunately, either the steroids or the push-ups made Tyler's pushes harder than those of the average man.

Still no big deal. But wasn't I supposed to file something on this case? Jen mentioned I had missed something. Oh well, too late now. I'd just wing it.

I put the file down at the Las Cruces city limits, where the highway transformed into Main Street. Las Cruces could be the missing link between small-town Alamogordo and big-city Albuquerque. Main Street meandered a bit as it headed southward, until it hit the meager downtown. There wasn't much of a skyline, but the few new buildings brightened an otherwise crumbling block.

The courthouse lay north of the downtown. It was one story, sprawling and fairly modern, with discrete traditional Spanish touches—a perfect fit for the jurisdiction.

Unlike Albuquerque, the parking here was free. Still, this wasn't a rural wonderland; the courthouse had metal detectors in front. After passing through the detectors, I arrived in the cramped courtroom with a few moments to spare. The Assistant District Attorney, a tough woman with short hair, handed me a piece of paper. "Notice of Intent to Amend Criminal Complaint to First Degree Murder."

First degree murder? Wasn't this just a battery on a peace officer? When did you get crucified for shoving a cop, even a cop in Cruces?

I scanned the gallery; Tyler should be sitting out there. But no, he sat with the inmates in the jury box. The law had picked him up already. He struggled to hold back tears as his family waved at him.

"What's going on?" I asked him, the only inmate with blond hair in the box. He outweighed all the other defendants, and yet when one inmate accidentally nudged him, he choked back tears. Some game face.

"You're so dead on the inside," his neighbor snarled.

"The cop died," Tyler said. "Apparently the cop's head hit a mirror, and shards of glass migrated into his brain. That's what the report said, 'migrated.'"

I vaguely remembered hearing about that, but the other side hadn't bothered to send me the discovery. Or had they? What had Jen said about it? My filing was haphazard at best.

He whimpered, "I was all wasted. I just pushed him. It was just like a bar fight."

"Not any more."

"Can I still get probation, like you said?"

"Not with a dead cop," I said. "What else do you know about this guy?"

"He was this rookie, first day on the job. He married an NMSU cheerleader. She just gave birth to twins. Once he died and that hit the papers the whole town went bat shit. You didn't hear about this?"

"I haven't been reading the Las Cruces papers lately," I said. "A lot's been going on in Albuquerque."

His neighbor in the next seat laughed. "White boy, you're looking at a life sentence, but don't worry, your life won't last that long."

Tyler had definitely killed the wrong guy.

"Unless it's white boy day," the man continued. "And it definitely ain't white boy day today."

Someone touched me on the shoulder. "Synthia Armijo," she said. "Can we talk?"

Ms. Armijo, the prosecutor, had *Death from Above* tattooed on her arm, indicating a military background. Her nickname was "Army Ho," but she was certainly no ho. She took me to the edge of the gallery. She pointed to three rows of people who wore black t-shirts sporting the victim's angelic face and the words "In Loving Memory." If someone murdered me, would anyone have a loving memory?

"As you can see, this is a sensitive case," she said. "On both sides."

Across the aisle, Tyler's family sat with his football buddies. The entire Lobo offensive line had journeyed down for the hearing, not a good thing in Aggie country. They all wore t-shirts with number 42, Tyler's number.

Good old Number 42 didn't deserve to spend his life in prison for one errant block. I figured he owed about two years to the State, loss of down, and then he could get four more downs to get on with his life.

Perhaps eventually Tyler could coach in a place like Carrizozo, or Crater even. A few years out, a few years clean, Tyler could be coaching the boys' football team and taking them to State—a great redemption story I could take to Hollywood someday. It's *We Are Marshall* meets *Hoosiers*.

• • • • •

Armijo handed me a form. "You can just stipulate and we don't have to have a hearing. It might get emotional, and that would be unfortunate for all concerned."

In the gallery behind me, fortune certainly didn't smile on anyone. Each side exchanged curses.

"He's not going to get life without parole," she said, "but I have to put it on the table to satisfy the lust of the crowd here."

In the jury box Tyler covered his face so his offensive line wouldn't see him cry. "I haven't cried since I got cut from varsity, sophomore year."

"Let's just get through the hearing," I said.

The judge called the case. "Let's win one for the Gipper," I whispered to Tyler when he sat with me at the table.

He smiled. "I took History of Football at UNM. I know that quote. Ronald Reagan played the Gipper, right?"

I scribbled furiously while Armijo explained all the reasons why Tyler deserved to face a murder rap, even though time had expired. (The officer died after the ninety-day deadline to file the charge.) Armijo mentioned in passing that there was a lawsuit by the family against the hospital for negligence, and said there might be an off chance that the death occurred because of negligence and not because of Tyler's shove.

What the hell?

She hadn't provided me with that information of course. If not for White Sands, I would have arrived twenty minutes earlier and could have been more prepared for this. God, I felt guilty.

"Save me, man," Tyler said.

"I'll try." What else could I say? Nastia had said she saw something in me that I didn't see in myself. Well, Tyler's life was in God's hands. It sure wasn't in mine.

As the prosecutor sat down, I knew there was only one thing to do.

Instead of playing *Fight Club*, it might be time to play "Wimp Club." Sort of.

"Your Honor," I said after a long pause. "I'm not supposed to be here right now."

That was a line from the movie *Clerks*, but neither the judge nor the prosecutor would know the independent film from the late twentieth century. I had never received notice of the State's motion and this felt more like an ambush than an argument.

"We sent the notice a while back."

"Well, your honor, I can honestly say I never got it."

Well, I might have received the notice and threw it away during one of my binge cleaning episodes. "Your honor, I've been doing this without a secretary; I don't have the staff or organizational skills to handle a case of this magnitude. I should have subpoenaed somebody from the hospital to testify about the alleged negligence, but I had no idea of this development. This is ineffective assistance of counsel on my part."

The other lawyers in the room gasped. No lawyer ever said he was bad, especially in front of a client, in front of other lawyers, and most especially in front of a judge. That was asking for a disciplinary complaint.

"Mr. Shepard has a good reputation," Armijo said. "He is one of the best lawyers in the state. I'm sure he can handle a case like this. He did that murder down in Aguilar County. And he represented that mentally ill woman who was accused of killing the Governor's wife."

"I've indeed handled cases all over the state," I said after a pause. "But I have never done a murder trial under the contract. I'm not murder qualified. The State knew, or should have known, this. The murder in Aguilar was a long time ago. It was a juvenile case and I had all the resources of the public defender department. And as for my last murder case, that never went to trial. I would have lost it, if it had. I have too much on my plate. . . ."

Since when? Since Jen died? No, I hadn't been much of a lawyer since Jen left me the first time. I probably threw out the notice. I was the worst lawyer in the world.

"Mr. Shepard isn't ineffective *per se,*" Armijo protested again.

We continued for a few minutes, our roles reversed. She kept saying I was good; I countered how *bad* I was.

"Someone from the hospital should be here to talk about how the officer really died," I said. "But most important, Tyler is *not* supposed to be here. There are rules that must be followed."

Back in the day, I would have been more academic, considering my Ivy League background. The ivy in my past had long since been supplanted by New Mexico green chile. The more I talked about how I couldn't give Tyler the defense he deserved, I played Clark Kent less. Instead, I played Jimmy Olsen, or worse, Lois Lane.

"Tyler deserves better," I said in conclusion. "Our constitution says he has a right to effective assistance of counsel, and I haven't given it to him."

The judge stared at me. Tyler stared at me. Armijo showed no emotion; she expected to win.

"What's going to happen now?" Tyler asked.

"I don't know," I whispered back. "Only God does."

The judge was the closest one in the building to having God-like powers. "Mr. Shepard is quite correct," he said. "I know this decision will make me unpopular in this room, but the State had their chance. They knew the officer was critically ill. They could have given notice of their intent, and then double-checked the receipt of the motion so the Public Defender Department could get a *qualified* attorney."

"It's not my job to make sure he does *his* job," Armijo said.

"It is when you're trying to put a man in prison for the next sixty years using my tax dollars," the judge said. "I don't want to get reversed on appeal. I am deeply concerned that Mr. Shepard is here defending someone on a life or death matter. He has indeed provided ineffective assistance of counsel by losing the pleading, even if the pleading wasn't sent in a timely manner to begin with."

I laughed. This was a technicality on top of a technicality. If I had been a better lawyer, and responded in a timely fashion to their un-timely motion, the State would have an easier time frying Tyler.

"What does that mean?" the victim's wife yelled from the gallery.

"Ma'am, normally I'd hold you in contempt, but I understand the depth of your emotion. Ladies and Gentlemen, I'm going to *deny* the motion of the state to amend the charge to first degree murder at this late date."

The victim's family started cursing, and the offensive line cheered as if Tyler had just intercepted a pass and run it back for a touchdown.

"You go, Tyler!" someone yelled.

"Order! Order!"

The deputies stood in the aisle, ready to sack the first person who moved.

The judge didn't want me to savor my moment. "But son, you're still facing felony charges. I will alert the public defender department that you need a *qualified* lawyer this time."

Tyler froze every muscle. At twenty-two the rest of your life was a long time. Life meant death. He finally nudged me. "See if you can get me out. They'll kill me in jail."

"Your honor, I have an obligation to be a zealous advocate,

to be a qualified and *effective* advocate for my client and request that he be released. Maybe his family can put up a property bond."

I then went through a litany of every good thing about Tyler. He didn't even know he had done so much good in his twenty or so years on earth.

The judge played with his gavel for a second. "I'll let him out on a million dollars unsecured appearance bond."

Even if every UNM alumnus chipped in, no way was Tyler posting a million dollars unsecured appearance bond. What was an appearance bond anyhow? They did things differently down here.

Surprisingly, Tyler smiled. "Thanks man."

●　●　●　●　●

I didn't want to leave just yet; it was dangerous out there. Hopefully the audience would realize I was just doing my job. Tyler moved very slowly and deliberately. This was the time-out before the last play of the game, perhaps the last play of his life. A few moments later Tyler came back into the courtroom. He wore his Lobos jersey, the jersey of a free man. Maybe it was white boy day after all.

"What?"

"Appearance bond, dude. Don't you get it?"

"I'm not sure."

"They do that down here. It's cool. If I don't show up for court I pay the million dollars, but I don't have to put anything up front."

I had never heard of an appearance bond before. I was actually a better lawyer without knowing it, effective by being ineffective.

Tyler smiled at me. He would have given me a hug, but he was not a hugging guy unless he was in the End Zone.

Speaking of End Zones . . . "Do you know a dancer named Nastia up at the End Zone in Albuquerque?"

"Nasty Nastia," he said with a wink.

I wanted to protest— She's my friend, she's not nasty. Instead I asked —"Do you have a message for me from her?"

He laughed a nervous laugh. "I don't got no message for nobody until I know how the case is gonna shake out."

I didn't know how to interpret that. Either he didn't know anything, or he knew something and didn't want to tell me.

He laughed again. "Can you promise me that you can save me?"

"I can't promise that I can save anybody. Even myself."

"Then I got nothing to say to you." He got up to leave. "But thanks for getting me out."

He turned his back and I grabbed him by the shoulder. "I can promise to try," I said. "But I will need your help."

"Let me think about it."

YADA YADA JORNADA

I SAT IN THE COURTROOM alone for yet another ten minutes to let the tension die down. I heard a commotion came from outside and hurried to the window to see Tyler's football buddy push a member of the cop's family, as if blitzing the quarterback. The other guy probably played offensive line thirty pounds ago; he held his ground and pushed back. This was *Fight Club* for real.

I glanced at the small clock in the rear of the courtroom. Time to get moving. I dreaded the drive to Albuquerque; the drive from Alamogordo was bad enough. My phone rang. It had been "on" all along, at the maximum setting. If it had rung during a murder hearing, I'd be locked in county jail on contempt for sure.

"Dan, it's Judge Cruz." She hesitated for a moment. "Luna."

"Anything?" I asked. I didn't know what to call her in response.

"Please come by tonight. I'm going to need all the moral support I can get. We're having an informal wake for Jen."

"A wake?" I said. "Do Koreans have wakes?"

"She's half-Korean. Well, the Koreans are the Irish of Asia," she said. "I just need some support. With Jen gone, I need all my friends."

"I'll be there."

⟡ • • • •

I was so glad to be considered a moral supporter and a friend that I didn't pay attention while leaving the courthouse and bumped into an obese man in a black shirt bearing the dead cop's face.

"Watch where you're going, asshole," he said.

"That's him," another black shirt yelled. The black shirts soon surrounded me. This was a country rock crowd, many of them had been groupies of the band Lynyrd Skynyrd, and I had trespassed into their sweet home.

Security stayed inside the building, watching with disdain. My client had killed a cop. I was on my own. Even the face on the t-shirt mad-dogged me.

The obese man pushed me; he had muscle behind the fat. "How the fuck can you represent the man who killed my brother?"

"He's got a presumption of innocence. His guilt has to be proved beyond a reasonable doubt."

"You really believe that shit?" the obese man asked. "Why don't I push your head through a fucking mirror and see if you still believe in reasonable motherfucking doubt."

"I reasonably doubt that you'll fucking live," said the widow.

Security remained inside. Tyler's football buddies observed the events, but remained a safe distance away on the other side of the parking lot. They didn't owe me anything . . . yet. When I said ineffective, that burnt them. Sure, I had saved his life, but Tyler still faced prison.

The Lynyrd Skynyrd crowd surrounded me three deep. They could kill me just as easily as the inmates at the jail. I certainly couldn't make it to my car so I turned to face the angriest jury of all time.

"I fight for Tyler because he is a human being," I said. "Just like you, just like me. If your brother the cop had fired first and killed Tyler, or let's say by mistake had killed Tyler's girl, you better believe you want someone like me standing up for him and making sure there isn't a lynch mob coming after him. Because we don't really know what happened that night. If you kill me, you sure as hell want a lawyer who will be your zealous fucking advocate and make sure the lynch mob doesn't come after you."

For one moment, I had them. *Gimme three steps,* I sang to myself, quoting Skynyrd. *Gimme three steps mister, and you'll never see me no more.* I remembered too late that the singer was long dead.

"If we kill you, ain't gonna be no lynch mob coming after us," one said.

Before they could come closer, someone threw a smoke bomb. Then another. Everyone started coughing and covering their eyes.

Through the smoke I heard a woman's voice.

"Dan, this way."

"Nastia?"

The accent wasn't Russian. A hand reached out and pulled me out of the smoke. The woman wore a hoodie over her head and a bandanna over her face.

I opened my car door. "Go," she said, her accent back "I'll be all right, *da?*"

I drove away through the smoke. Maybe she was my guardian angel after all.

• • • • •

When the smoke started, security finally exited the building. Nastia was nowhere to be seen. Was she ever there at all?

• • • • •

I didn't inhale until the freeway, and didn't take exhale until crossing the Dona Ana county line near the small village of Hatch and was safely up the ankle of my final leg of the triangle.

The ancient route to the north earned the name *Jornada de Muerto* back in the conquistador days. I drove up the Jornada at warp speed. Small white wooden crosses lined both sides of the road. How long had they been there?

I passed Truth or Consequences, which had been named after the old TV show. I was a big fan of Truth. Consequences I didn't care for so much.

My favorite classic rock station blared U2. Bono sounded like he sat right next to me as he told me that he still hadn't found what he was looking for.

I arrived in Albuquerque at four-thirty, just before rush hour and quickly showered at the Bosque Apartments. Driving slowly up Central Avenue I hadn't found what I was looking for, but I parked anyway, next to a sign reading: PLEASE NO, PANHANDLING, PISSING OR PERVERSION. No, Albuquerque wasn't Disneyland.

I ended up buying sushi.

WAKE TOURIST

I STOPPED OUTSIDE OF LUNA'S apartment complex, the converted asylum. Perhaps the building should return to its old role of housing the mentally ill. *Sign me up.* Missing Jen certainly pushed me in that direction.

In Luna's living room, several folk clustered around the dinner table. Nurse Song stood in a corner with a tall Korean teenager, Susie Song, the famous up-and-coming golfer. Susie revealed herself as Jen's first cousin.

"Jen always told such great stories," Susie said. "I always hoped we would have a great adventure together some day."

A Latina joined them, Luna's younger and prettier clone. We'd met before when she was a waitress, but she re-introduced herself as Jen's other half sister, Selena. All three women had the same father but different mothers, a tangled family tree to say the least.

"Where's your father now?" I asked. Jen never talked about him.

"Prison," Selena said with a frown.

"Ouch," I said.

"I've got a feeling there are plenty of stories left to tell about our family," Selena said, a little coldly, "with or without Jen."

• • • • •

Once again I felt like the outermost person on Luna's inner circle, the thirteenth person in the room. This was like the Last Supper, with sushi.

It wasn't a joyous occasion, but everyone chattered sociably, talking about March Madness and pretending to be upbeat about the Lobos chances. I realized this party wasn't about Jen, or even about Dew. It was about Luna. She still wore her black dress, now slightly wrinkled, as if she hadn't changed since the kidnapping. Luna constantly reached out to touch the people around her, as if she dreaded being alone.

I stared at Luna. Her hair was nearly totally gray. "I haven't eaten since they took Dew," she said. "I'm disappearing before my eyes."

I didn't know what to say. Gabriel Rose sat down next to Luna and she held his hand tightly.

"Thanks to all of you," Luna said. "I still have faith that we will find Dew before I have to—"

Have to what? Luna had stopped a two hundred million dollar production in the name of justice. What would happen when the kidnappers started sending back body parts?

Luna's phone rang, interrupting Rose's latest advance. She looked at the display on the phone, "Unknown Number."

Washington took the phone and the call. We all waited breathlessly.

Nurse Song signaled for us to join in prayer. We all bowed our heads for a few moments. I wished I prayed more often.

"Amen," Washington said before picking up the phone.

A mechanical voice came on. "You know what to do," the voice said.

Knew what to do? Apparently I had missed a lot while I was on the road.

"Transfer the money now!" the voice commanded.

Washington watched for the proper codes to come. He typed a few keys and said at last, "I'm sending ten million American dollars now."

Washington looked intently at the screen of his phone, which looked like something out of James Bond, but on a budget. He cursed the phone, then hit another button with his thumb.

This was not a man who stopped to pray at White Sands when things got hairy. He certainly didn't have a designated depression spot on the *Jornada*. He hit a few more keys and stared intently at the little screen. He hid the screen from the rest of us; I couldn't see the images there.

I looked away from Washington. Behind him, a picture of someone who must be Luna's dad taking a picture of a three-year-old Luna hung on the wall. Her father was a doctor who'd been caught in a pharmaceutical scandal. He was from México, but it was doubtful that either the American or Mexican government knew where all his financial bodies were buried.

It all made sense now. Luna had this amazing loft on a judicial salary, Luna came from dirty money and that dirty money would pay the dirty ransom.

I flashed back to every credit card transaction in my life. What was the official psychiatric term for credit card anxiety?

Washington turned his phone so everyone could read the screen. It displayed a bank website. "Transaction Unsuccessful" The screen announced. "Insufficient funds."

Insufficient Funds?

Insufficient funds for a ransom? Either Luna (or her father) didn't have the money in the account, or there had been mistake in the electronics.

"What just happened?" Luna asked. "What the hell just happened?"

The phone rang again.

Washington frowned. "Everyone who is not immediate family get out of here!"

That meant me. Even Rose got the hell out of there.

"If there's anything I can do . . ." I said.

"Just go," Luna said. "All of you. I think I need to be alone right now."

I kept waiting for word from Nastia. Hopefully she knew something. If not, Dew was dead, and Jen had died in vain. So much for Luna's faith in justice, her faith in me.

And I still had to go to Santa Fe tomorrow.

THURSDAY
SONG: "Here's to All Who Sing" by Trevor McShane

NEW MEXICAN GIGOLO

I DIDN'T SLEEP THAT NIGHT. Although the spring equinox began at midnight, winter still wanted to go out like a lion instead of a lamb. The lion took a bite out of me and chewed me up. I shivered, even after piling on more blankets.

Ophelia, that crazy old girlfriend had done something called "Siberian Trancing" during her tough times, which was some kind of weird singing with your eyes closed. Jen had even done it once.

"Here's to all who sing," I mumbled the words to an old McShane song.

I tried to trance myself to a safe, warm place: white sand and blue skies, but then the wind howled, trying to break down my thin adobe walls and pluck me back to jail. Lord, please tell me what I'm supposed to do!

I'm a just a little conflict-contract attorney on the edge of this story, like Rosencrantz and Guildenstern in *Hamlet*. They were the bit players who died off stage, and yet still inspired Tom Stoppard's play *Rosencrantz and Gildenstern Are Dead*. If I was Rosencrantz, Guildenstern was already dead.

• • • • •

My eyes finally closed at five-fifty in the morning. I slept blissfully for ten minutes until the phone rang promptly at six. I picked up the phone, didn't even bother to say hello.

"The little girl's still alive," the voice on the other end said. "Still alive! There's hope, *da?*"

"Nastia?"

She didn't identify herself. She didn't have to. "It's all about Santa Fe. The movie people, *da?*"

"I think so, too," I said. "But why didn't the money go through?"

"Maybe they wanted more," she said. "I'm not a banking expert. They could have worried the line could be traced and deliberately didn't want an electronic transfer. Or maybe this isn't about money."

"So what am I supposed to do?"

"I'll try to get word to you today," she said. "But my *lyobov* hasn't figured everything out, yet. My *lyobov* doesn't believe in you, yet."

"What do I have to do?"

Silence from the other end. Two more days. Hopefully, Dew would survive the week.

I tried to go back to sleep for another hour before the sun finally rose. Screw this early to bed, early to rise trend.

No breakfast in the fridge except for a can of Starbucks Double Shot Espresso Light. I chugged it, checked my calendar again, while staring at Nastia's picture in her gymnast outfit. "Who are you?"

An image formed of a pale, little gymnast on the run, hiding out on her dog sled while being chased by the polar bears of the world. The difference between her and Jen was that Nastia was a survivor—in all senses of the word.

Jen had always disappeared at the first sign of trouble, especially in her relationships. How many men had there been before me? How many men had she had in L.A.?

Nastia had her *lyobov*. She'd stick with her dude through endless winter nights. With me, Jen bolted for dry land once the ice between us got a little thin. I desperately wished someone would love me like Nastia loved her *lyobov*.

I stared at my closet before picking my nicest suit for the day, a navy blue number from the Palm Springs Armani outlet. I almost went with my rattlesnake cowboy boots, but it wasn't time yet. Under a towel, I found my nice black shoes that were actually made of leather.

My one turquoise Armani tie matched my watch. It cost more than the suit; it actually cost more than what the state paid me for the case. But today was Santa Fe after all, the home of Santa Fe style, which never went . . . out of style.

Unfortunately, my car didn't start in the freezing cold, but I could still make the seven thirty-five train up to Santa Fe which arrived at nine. Plenty of time.

I took the Central Avenue bus to the Alvarado Transit Center downtown. The transit center was a gray imitation of a Spanish mission, and the train had a red and yellow roadrunner gracing its sides. I barely caught the Express before the metal doors slammed shut. I was lucky to find the last seat available on the upper level.

Northbound, the train passed through the worst part of town—more like New Jersey than New Mexico with its oil tanks, barbed wire and mysterious warehouses. How many bodies were buried in the brackish drainage ditches?

I started humming lines from a Grateful Dead song: *"Driving that train, high on Rogaine, Casey Jones you better watch your speed. Trouble ahead, trouble behind, and you know that notion just crossed my mind."*

In Japan a few years ago, I rode the *Shinkansen,* the bullet train. This was the world's slowest bullet, barely going ten miles an hour through the warehouse district. The *Shinkansen* had a beautiful hostess in a cute little uniform who smiled as we passed Mt. Fuji. The fat conductor who took my credit card for the ticket here certainly didn't resemble the cute geishas on the *Shinkansen.*

Twenty miles north, after Casey Jones passed Bernalillo High School with an announcement about entering Spartan Country, the conductor warned that we had crossed onto an Indian reservation, and no photography was allowed.-

Thankfully, the train picked up speed, quickly leaving the mobile homes and factories behind. Spartan Country indeed, we passed rural scenes right out of *National Geographic.* The Rio Grande made the valley greener down here, yet the dry hills still held virgin snow.

The villages on the reservation mixed modern pre-fab boxes adjacent to crumbling adobe structures. Each pueblo had brown missions from the Spanish days, an uneasy reminder of the past.

"Ask not for whom the bell tolls," I said out loud for no particular reason, as we heard bells. "It tolls for thee."

"Do you always talk to yourself?" a woman asked from the next seat. She was deep into a paperback called *La Bajada Lawyer.*

Who the hell would write a book called *La Bajada Lawyer*? That translated to "The Descent Lawyer." La Bajada Hill was actually the hill that separated Santa Fe County from the Albuquerque metropolitan area.

Off to the side, I saw a cow skull; it looked just like a Georgia O'Keeffe painting.

My phone rang. Unknown number.

"Dan Shepard, this is the magistrate in Moriarty, are you ready for your hearing?"

What hearing?????

"I have misplaced my files. Which defendant?"

"You."

I had forgotten my damn speeding ticket case for speeding through the canyon. It was a sixty-five in a forty-five because I sped up before the construction zone had ended, which made it even worse. Was I supposed to be in Moriarty right now? That was a hundred miles away and I didn't have a car.

A magistrate could issue a warrant just like a judge and leave word with the Santa Fe authorities to lock my ass up. I had already seen Luna lock a lawyer up on Monday. The train conductor had arrest powers as well.

Casey Jones then took us directly below La Bajada Hill, before making a side assault up the eastern flank. The train strained up the steep grade, the spiritual divide between Albuquerque and Santa Fe.

My heart raced faster with every foot of elevation. Now I knew how my clients felt. Jen was right; a lawyer who defended himself had a fool for a client or a fool for a lawyer.

"I'm heading up to Santa Fe right now. This is a phone hearing, right?"

"You submitted the pleading, but you didn't get the officer's signature," the magistrate said. "I haven't signed it yet, so technically at this moment, you *are* required to physically be here in my courtroom."

Luna had already locked up one lawyer this week. Magistrates locked up lawyers all the time. I thought about this magistrate. He had a cattle farm south of town and joked he liked punching lawyers as much as punching cattle.

I wished I had a real lawyer right now so I could ask, "What's going to happen?""

The magistrate did not respond until we hit the summit and Casey Jones took us into a barren field. I could now see the white

Sangre de Christo Mountains in the distance. The highest peak, Santa Fe Mountain, wasn't quite a perfect cone like Mt. Fuji, but in desert here, it would have to do. For a moment we had left civilization behind.

"However," the magistrate said. "I just talked with the officer and he's willing to stipulate to this being a phone hearing, and also dismiss the case if you don't violate for the next ninety days, if is that agreeable to you."

"Of course."

"Thank you, Mr. Shepard. See you in court in person next time."

"If there's still a next time." I let out a deep breath as Casey began a steep descent. *La Bajada* indeed. We crossed under the middle of the freeway as if we were in the big city. Heading into Santa Fe, we passed the Penitentiary of New Mexico on our right.

• • • • •

Over an hour after we left, the train crawled into the outskirts of Santa Fe. This bullet ran out of steam near adobe homes and cinderblock warehouses. I checked my watch. Casey Jones certainly wasn't high on cocaine, any more. Damn, this train went slow for an express.

Casey stopped at South Capitol, a bland government office park that could indeed be back in New Jersey, a nice part at least. The train waited for people to get off. The state workers didn't seem to be in any particular hurry to get to work.

The train practically walked into downtown Santa Fe. It felt like the Santa Fe of old here, lots of two story adobe buildings, and magnificent views of the Sangre de Christos.

At nine-fifteen, Casey Jones pulled us into the small Santa Fe depot in the midst of downtown. The depot stood next to the film office, which was located in a converted movie theater. No time to check that out this early in the morning. I smiled. Santa Fe always looked like one giant movie set.

• • • • •

Not much time. I ran down Guadalupe Street, gasping for breath. The seven thousand foot elevation affected me worse than I expected. Still, Santa Fe courts usually ran on Santa Fe time. Because we were closer to the sun up here did the altitude affect the physics of justice?

The new adobe courthouse fit right into the ancient city. Inside the second-floor courtroom, the guard told me that my client, Cody Coca, sat in the back room. "Your boy's getting agitated," the guard said. "So I sent him back there for his own protection."

Agitated didn't sound good. I turned off my phone; I didn't want to agitate him further.

When I got to the holding room, I saw that Cody wore his blue jail clothes, but he must have used a magical dye to make the blue more intense to match his eyes. He carried himself like an actor *playing* a criminal rather than the real thing.

"We match," he said, noting my blue suit.

"I knew you'd be wearing blue today."

Cody had once bragged how most of his partying had been with the high-end folk in Santa Fe. "I'm kinda like a gigolo," he said back then. "Thousand bucks and I can be your friend—a true boyfriend experience."

"If you're such a hot shit gigolo, how did you qualify for the public defender? Where did all the money go?"

He pointed to his nose. "Up here," he said.

"Why are we here today?" I asked.

"They ended up dropping the tampering. I peed dirty, but they're going with trafficking."

"That's it?" I rifled through his file. "They're charging you with a second degree felony. That's nine years! You sure they didn't find you with any stuff?"

"No way man, I just peed dirty," he said. "I took one line at a party. I had to be polite. They can just give me a month, right?"

I read his indictment. "They're giving you the *bitch*. The habitual offender enhancement on both new felonies—one for the possession and one for the trafficking."

"If I go to prison, I'll be someone's bitch in no time," he said. "And not in a good way."

Bitch, bitch, bitch. I could hear the inmates in my head.

"How can they do that?"

"I guess when you had it up your nose you possessed it. And when you peed it out, they figured you were trying to sell it."

"But I only had a month left."

I tried to do the math. It wasn't just nine years, it was around twelve altogether with all the enhancements, all the bitches. When did peeing become trafficking?

Cody stared at me with intensely blue eyes. "We gotta talk when you get me out of here. I will most definitely make it worth your while. If you know what I mean."

He smiled with intent. He knew something all right. Maybe he knew Nastia. Other than Tyler down in Las Cruces, he was the only client in her league.

We kept talking about his legal issues; I needed a "white horse" case, a case that would ride to the rescue to save poor Cody Coca. He had connections in jail and had managed to stay safe the two weeks he'd been in.

"Do I have time to go outside and look up a case?" I asked the clerk.

"Just be back as quickly as possible," she said. "The judge has a murder case this afternoon."

• • • • •

I tried to access legal websites on my phone's slow browser. No luck. The court's research computers were down, and without any access codes up here I hoofed it to the Supreme Court library, passing new-age tourists, artists, and the homeless.

The New Mexico Supreme Court building resembled an old Spanish fort in colonial days. Native Americans sold jewelry near the little park on the side. Tourists probably thought the Supreme Court was just another museum.

Inside the airy court library, the computers were off for the duration. Nothing in New Mexico worked these days. I researched the cases manually, using the dusty hard cover *New Mexico Digests* like Harry Potter perusing ancient spells. I finally discovered the venerable case of *State versus Halsey*, 883 P2d 1.

It might as well be Voldemort's *Avada Kedavra* curse itself! Yes!

In the decision, the New Mexico Supreme Court, right here in this very building, held that mere consumption of drugs was not *possession* of drugs, and most certainly not *trafficking* of drugs. Those few words would change the next few years of Cody Coca's life.

I recognized the name of the lawyer who had argued successfully for the defense. Didn't he write those unrealistic legal thrillers? I took a deep breath, made two copies, and then hurried back to the courthouse, nearly tripping over a Navajo vendor selling trinkets.

"You break, you buy," she said.

When I picked up the trinkets, I hadn't broken anything,

thank God. I didn't need any more bad luck on a day like today.

I passed through the metal detector without beeping, and hurried into the courtroom just as the judge remanded the final trafficker for the day into state custody for the next ten years.

The judge was an elderly Hispanic man who didn't take kindly to outsiders like me. With his long beard, he could pass for Professor Dumbledore.

I didn't have time to even open my briefcase before joining Cody Coca at the podium where I cited the case by memory. I then opened the briefcase and handed the judge actual copies. They were damp with my sweat, and a little crumpled. The judge handled the crumpled papers like soiled toilet paper, quickly tossing them aside.

"Most lawyers don't bother to do research any more," he said.

"I'm not most lawyers, your honor," I said.

The judge smiled. "I'll dismiss the new case with prejudice," he said at last. "His probation is almost over, so I'll give him credit for time served."

"Credit for time served?" Cody asked.

"He's free to go tonight," the judge said.

"Thank God" Cody said out loud in a voice that sounded Californian. "I *so* want to be out of jail."

"Mr. Shepard," the judge said as he fingered the gavel. "I suggest you expedite the paperwork and get it back to me so I can sign off on it immediately. This will get your client on his merry way."

I didn't like the way he said "merry," but I didn't want to protest. Cody and I went back to the holding cell. He wanted to hug me, but a guard stopped him.

"I knew you'd come through for me," Cody said. "As soon as I get out, we gotta talk."

What the hell did he mean by that? Maybe he was Nastia's *lyobov*. He might know about the kidnapping.

But before he could say anything more, the guard took him away. "The quicker I get him back to jail, the quicker he will get out," the guard said. "You know the jail runs on Santa Fe time, too."

I expedited my ass over to a cyber cafe on Guadalupe Street to get the thing done. I had to type out an Order of Release, an Order of Dismissal, and finally an Amended Judgment and Sentence. I also had to figure out how to print on a magical printer that seemed to require some spells of its own. It took five tries.

Finally successful, I ran through the adobe streets back to the courthouse to get the papers signed by the judge. I outran a few joggers on the way back. Unfortunately, once inside the courthouse, with the copies in something approaching numerical order, the judge was gone.

"He's doing jury selection on a murder trial," the clerk said.

"Should I wait?"

"The court closes at five, you know that. Just wait until tomorrow."

"Look, I'm having the worst week ever."

"Not as bad as this defendant. He's going down hard."

"Help a brother out here. I think my client knows the location of a kidnapped child. He will only tell the information to me, if and only if I can get him out tonight. If he sits in jail, he won't tell me anything, and the poor little girl could die. It's a matter of life and death."

My spiel worked. She e-mailed the judge then frowned as she stared at the screen. "Okay. Go on inside and get it signed during a lull."

I hurried down the hall to the courtroom. A guard frowned at me and said, "Don't run in court."

Inside, famed cowboy attorney Mitch Garry questioned a potential juror about fairness. I snuck into the courtroom and handed the paperwork to the bailiff. Twelve angry men in the jury box stared at my disheveled self. The judge read the pages, re-ordered them, then re-ordered them again. He frowned.

Maybe it was the altitude. Not enough air had made it to my lungs or to my brain during my little jaunt. I fainted, crumpling toward the floor.

• • • • •

I woke moments later, but it could have been an hour. Apparently the defendant himself grabbed me before my head hit the railing.

"Are you all right?" the judge asked.

"I don't know."

The judge shook his head. "This is not worth dying for," he said, as he signed the paper.

I looked at Mitch with his first-degree murder client. He was a real lawyer. What the hell was I?

"It is worth dying for if it's done right," I said.

After taking time to catch my breath, I walked briskly out of the courtroom. The papers were filed. It had finally warmed up. It was the first day of spring.

So what to do until Coca got out?

SUFFRAGETTE CITY

AT LEAST MY PHONE WAITED until I left the courtroom before ringing. It was. Allen Koenigsburg, my agent's assistant, who confirmed my meeting for this Monday in Beverly Hills.

"We've set up a meeting with a writer-producer who is interested in adapting your book into a script," he said when I called.

"I have a script. Do you want me to bring it?"

Allen laughed. "We're better off with *his* script," he said. "Dan, you've gotta understand we absolutely love your ideas, but you have a problem with execution."

"Execution?"

"It's not about your writing. It's all about whose name is on the script. You just don't have the name yet."

• • • • •

Using the browser on my phone, I booked a flight online with a return that night. The only available flight was through Las Vegas. I had spent thirty minutes in White Sands. Why not an hour in Vegas?

I felt like a jet setter with ADD. Talk about conflicting emotions. Despite my chance at success and stardom I still couldn't be happy until I solved this damn mystery.

Time to check out the film connection. I didn't need Nastia to tell me what to do.

• • • • •

The New Mexico Film Office lay back by the depot, in a converted adobe movie theater. Hollywood conquered by the Spanish. I walked up the stairs, the movie posters practically teleported me to the west coast. The movies were random, with no connection except they were all filmed locally. *Terminator Salvation* had the biggest poster, *Transformers* a close second. I didn't remember a few others like *In the Valley of Elah, Swing Vote,* and *No Country for Old Men.*

The receptionist, a young woman named Amber, wore the latest styles as if she had teleported in directly from Beverly Hills. Her eyes were bloodshot and looked as if she hadn't slept in days, living on reds, Vitamin C and cocaine.

Amber had a piercing stare that scanned my body as quickly as a hit producer rejecting a bad script after the first "Fade in."

"Can I help you?"

"Need some information on a movie being filmed here," I said. "I'm an attorney."

She rolled her bloodshot watery eyes. "Not without a court order," she said. "Are you with the FBI?"

"Not even," I said. When did I start talking like that?

Amber returned her gaze to her computer screen, clearly dismissing me. "Didn't think so. Well, even the FBI has to get a court order. Good day."

She actually said that with an English accent. I couldn't tell whether it was real or fake.

Maybe the FBI didn't know the sordid details of movie deals. Court orders were tough when it came to government agencies. Everyone wanted to protect their turf, and the film office was a major player in the New Mexico economy. They didn't want to roll over to anyone.

"If you don't have the appropriate paperwork, I'll have to ask you to leave. Again, I must say good day."

Her phone rang. "Hello Gabriel, good to hear from you again."

Gabriel. Was she talking to Gabriel Rose, Luna's boyfriend? A security officer came up the stairs.

I hurried outside, and watched another train arrive across the street in the depot. Should I just go home on the four: thirty?

No, not yet.

The spring sun felt good on my skin. On a bench, a homeless couple mumbled to each other.

"You talk about the alien artifacts," said one. "And then I'll cut in and say how we can get Lindsay Lohan attached once she passes the medical exam and the clearance."

Everybody's in show biz. Had these folks managed to get a deal?

How do I get back inside? There's got to be a way. *Think*!

Who owed me one in Santa Fe?

After checking my phone's long "contact list," I called an old friend, Sarah Cady. She ran a local company, Suffragette Cleaning, and she had contracts to clean many State buildings. Her company name came from a distant descendant, the famous suffragette. I helped a good number of her employees on a regular basis through my contracts; a sex offender in Santa Rosa cleaned toilets and apparently he did a great job. The suffragette owed me one. How many people owed me things these days?

"Do you guys clean the state film office?" I asked.

"Every day," she laughed. "It's the messiest office we do."

"I need a favor. Could I join the team? Just for one night. You won't have to pay me, and I'm pretty handy with a mop."

I didn't mention the only time I saw a mop was in jail.

"I can lose my contract for even an appearance of impropriety, and in Santa Fe everyone is guilty of something."

I wouldn't give up. "Remember the janitor who stole the painting from the museum?"

"He hung a Georgia O'Keeffe in his bathroom of his mobile home," she said. "He liked the way it 'tied the whole room together.' The dude had no idea it was worth several million. So?"

"I kept him out of prison. You still have that contract. So can I play janitor?"

"Why?"

"It's better if you don't know."

I stared at the homeless couple rehearsing their pitch one more time.

"Sure, you can play janitor," she said at last. "Just don't steal any paintings and put them in your mobile home. I see you as a method actor, so at least try to help out with the cleaning for real. I have a special crew for the film office. I think you'll love these guys. You'll fit right in."

● ● ● ● ●

With more time to kill, I wandered around a few bookstores. Sure enough, an author was doing a signing at one. Don't you know that you never sign on Thursdays?

I laughed. "Dude, don't even ask me if I want to read your stupid book."

I immediately regretted my words. What the hell? The book was in English and didn't have that many typos. I bought a copy and had him sign it for me.

It was never a good idea to piss off an author.

● ● ● ● ●

Sarah Cady's cleaning crew pulled up to the film office in the Suffragette Cleaning van promptly at five. The suffragettes didn't run on Santa Fe time. They were all from Latin America and their hair was dyed blond and cut in the latest styles.

"We're all actresses, models and writers," one woman said. She was a dead ringer for Gwyneth Paltrow back when she won an Academy Award for *Shakespeare in Love*.

"A Suffragette was 'discovered' two months ago and got cast in a movie, so we all signed up for this job," Gwyneth said. "I want to be in something set in the gang world, a musical Hispanic version of *Romeo and Juliet*."

I didn't tell her about *West Side Story*.

The crew chief, Quixote, could pass for a tweedy college professor in his early forties. With his coke-bottle glasses, he looked like he had spent much of his life tilting at windmills like his namesake. Indeed, he revealed he taught creative writing in Mexico, but the professors were on yet another extended strike. "We strike more than we work, so I earn more money cleaning buildings than I do teaching grad students," he said.

Quixote claimed someone stole half the episodes of *Law and Order* from him during the show's long run. "I'm the 'go to' guy for punching up their Hispanic characters, but they don't ever pay me guild minimum."

"You should take that up with the Writer's Guild."

"You can't be an illegal alien and be in the Writer's Guild," he said. "Although, I'm perfectly legal now of course."

"Of course," I said. "We're all perfectly legal here."

He had a spare shirt and ID that said Quixote II. "You're not the first person to be the second Quixote," he said with a smile. "The last guy was a 'lost boy' from the Sudan. He fit right in."

I felt like a lost boy these days. "I love you guys already."

"Just hook me up with your agent sometime," he said.

"It's a deal."

The crew tidied themselves up as if getting ready for an audition. "It's show time," Quixote said.

I took a deep breath of thin air as we passed under the marquee of the office.

"This is for you, Dew," I said to myself, "and for you, Jen."

I still had to prove myself to Nastia's damn *lyobov,* especially if it was Cody Coca. Yeah, it was show time all right.

• • • • •

I followed Quixote into the film office holding a vacuum cleaner as if it was an Uzi. Amber didn't even acknowledge us. She read a script with one bloodshot eye and watched the latest dailies on her i-Pod with the other.

"Don't worry," Quixote said. "She won't see or hear us."

How many times had I ignored the people cleaning my building? Well, actually I didn't ignore them because they usually told me about their cases.

I helped the crew dust as we bantered about my upcoming meeting with the Morris Williams Agency. Gwyneth slipped me her headshots.

"The quality of mercy is not strained," she began, Portia's monologue from *The Merchant of Venice.*

"Quality or not," I interrupted. "I can't help you, unless you test positive for coke or get busted for stealing."

"I'll keep that in mind."

After snooping around the back of the complex, I finally found a massive unlocked file room that contained files for *Desert Demons.* The production company had provided a list of shooting locations in the top document. In addition to the refinery, they used a major set-up at the old Penitentiary of New Mexico. The historic site was first used as a soundstage for the Adam Sandler remake of *The Longest Yard*.

The producers listed their shooting schedule. In subsequent correspondence they required electrical hook ups for the additional cells in the back. Due to security concerns, storage space at the prison set was limited. The State allowed them to store equipment within the facility in the unoccupied cell blocks, even the ones in the back. The storage was strictly limited to the "historic facility" as the remaining units surrounding the old pen still functioned as a working prison. On the map, the historic prison sat in front, the satellite facilities separated by a half-mile or so of high desert scrub.

Hopefully the actors wouldn't run into the inmates. I'd hate to be a gaffer moving lighting through a deserted old prison.

I found another contract deep within the bowels of the file. Romero was not a personal signatory, but his company attached itself to the project. Another company, "Ahmad Assed Investments," plopped down a major chunk of change as well. I knew all that already.

I didn't know that the State of New Mexico guaranteed one hundred million dollars of State money, one hundred freaking million dollars. This film was the biggest project in New Mexico history; it had already lost tens of millions of dollars. New Mexico would definitely want to protect its investment and would call in the loan on the first sign of trouble. Something more must be going on here.

I heard footsteps and froze as Amber walked by on the way to the bathroom. If she recognized me, everything could explode in my face.

Quixote came to the rescue. He hurried to her and grabbed her hand. "I did stand-up in Acapulco," he said. "I'd love to show you my reel."

Amber frowned. "I say *no* for a living. Why do you keep trying?"

"What else can I do?" said Quixote. "It's the American dream. Even if I'm not American."

Amber smiled for a moment. She was a dreamer too, of course, and Quixote had a charm about him. He really should be a stand-up comic somewhere.

Quixote, sensing an advantage, then told a joke that made Amber smile for the first time. Then he said, "I have something else you might be interested in."

"What do you have that I could possibly be interested in?" she asked.

He gave her a disk. "It's coverage of the script you're reading, Senorita."

She giggled. *"Gracias."* They went back to the front of the building.

I returned to the task and quickly found more addendums to the contract in the next file. The movie was way over budget; Sky was only one delay in a string of them. In order to get financing from the State of New Mexico, Gabriel Rose had personally put up ten-million dollars plus his ranch in Santa Fe as collateral. Bad move.

The film office had sent a demand letter indicating that the State wanted an additional bond, since with Sky Roberts in jail the movie would not be completed. The demand letter wanted ten million dollars and they wanted it now. Ten million dollars was a lot of money. Ten million dollars was worth kidnapping for. Ladies and Gentleman we have a prime suspect: Gabriel Rose, who just so happened to call this very office today.

Could Rose really be extorting Luna while caressing her at the same time? Why not? It was nothing personal, it was all strictly business, strictly *show* business.

Who had knowledge of the inner workings of the industry? Cody Coca, assuming he paid attention while he was snorting his life away. I checked my turquoise watch. Cody should be out soon.

Footsteps came down the hall, and I resumed sweeping as Amber entered. "Can you help move some furniture, *por favor?*"

"*Sí.*"

When we finished cleaning, I thanked my new friends. "I owe you guys one," I said.

"No, we owe you," Quixote said. "You're better than our usual guy with a mop. He's an existentialist playwright who tried to convince me I didn't exist. That existentialism shit doesn't work on a clogged toilet."

• • • • •

I took a cab to the jail to meet Cody. I hoped he would give me the magic words that would solve the mystery. Finally.

The Santa Fe County Detention Center sat across the street from the Penitentiary of New Mexico, like the Pen's wimpier brother.

Over at the Pen vicious floodlights revealed the several facilities, ranging from supermax to veritable penal country clubs for the model prisoners and warden's pets. It could pass for Oxford; each facility was like its own college and separated by a few hundred yards of desert.

In the front, on the other side of the entrance, I could see the historic facility, sometimes called "Old Main," as if it was the first building of an Ivy League college. Since the brutal riots in 1980, Old Main had been closed and then turned into a movie set. In Adam Sandler's remake of *The Longest Yard,* the Pen had played Arizona. Who was the Pen playing now for *Desert Demons*?

There wasn't a lights out at the movie set at Old Main as shooting could go on all night. The producers wanted to finish all the second unit stuff that didn't require Sky. If Luna relented and let him out, hopefully they could get back on schedule.

• • • • •

I sat with the Santa Fe Jail widows inside the SFCDC lobby. The lobby was shabbier than MDC, even though the crowd dressed as for an opera opening. This was Santa Fe, after all. One difference, I sat next to two jail *widowers* who were wearing black overcoats and red scarves

"When is Cody Coca getting out?" I made the receptionist double-check that the release order had been filed and a certified copy faxed. The receptionist was even ruder than Amber, as if this was a Canyon road gallery and not a correctional facility.

"Why are you so anxious?" the receptionist asked. "It's not like *you're* the one in jail."

"Sometimes I'm not so sure I'm not."

• • • • •

"Lobby's closed." An hour later, a guard ordered us to wait outside in the cold. By now I was an honorary jail widower. It may have been spring during the day, but at night at this altitude, winter had returned with a vengeance.

An artist widower talked about the latest "mixed media / performance art" show set for tomorrow at a gallery with the bizarre name of *Manygoats, Manymedia.* Unfortunately, the incarcerated artist had taken several items of mixed media without permission of their rightful owners. The items included toilets, tricycles, and an old Chevrolet Impala that he somehow used in his interpretive dance of the Pueblo revolt.

Luckily the artist would bond out tonight—in time for the show tomorrow.

Cody finally came out right before midnight. He wore his street clothes—tight jeans, a leather vest, no shirt—in the cold high-desert night. He didn't shiver so maybe he went out this way all the time. He was so overjoyed to see me, he gave me a hug.

A tight hug.

"I know the kidnapping has something to do with the movie," I said. "I think Gabriel Rose is involved. You know him?"

"Met him at a party once. He gave me an eye, maybe."

"What can you tell me?"

"What are you talking about?"

"Aren't you a friend of Nastia's?"

"Who?"

His eyes were blank. Cops called it nystagmus. He really didn't know anything. I shook my head. "Well, what did you want to talk to me about?"

He laughed. "I thought you were cool—for a lawyer. Why don't you come over to my place? Now that I'm off probation I can get us some coke and we can party all night, if you know what I mean."

"But you said you knew about show business," I said, dismayed. "I'm sorry, but I don't swing that way."

"I want you to be my *agent*," he said. "Don't flatter yourself."

FRIDAY
SONG: "Three Places at the Same Time" by Trevor McShane
THE PRONOUN GAME

THE TRAINS DIDN'T RUN THAT late, so I caught a ride home with another jail widower. His girlfriend had violated probation by stealing a roll of toilet paper out of the gallery. The gallery had pressed charges, the lowest valued art theft on record.

"You got a girlfriend?" he asked.

"I don't know."

• • • • •

As I showered the next morning, my mind tried to put it together. Had Nastia been lying to me? She promised somebody would know something *this* week. Today was Friday; I had only three clients left, all in Albuquerque.

I made a quick mental list of my cases for the past week, other than the small possibility of Tyler in Las Cruces; none of them could be a Nastia *lyobov*. No one on today's list seemed a likely candidate either.

I steeled myself for a tough day, three courtrooms at the same time in two different buildings. *Three places at the same time*, McShane had sung. Yeah, but he didn't have to risk contempt.

Why couldn't Scotty beam me from court to court to court? I

stared at my infamous rattlesnake boots. Yes. This was the last day of the week, the last day to find Nastia's *lyobov,* right? Time to be the rattlesnake lawyer, yet again, even if the boots barely fit me anymore.

I prayed my car would start. Thankfully, God let the engine turn over. Spring had arrived this morning, so the earth and engines turned a little bit faster. The snow melted and flowers bloomed. If you don't like the weather in New Mexico, wait a minute. It's bound to change.

Albuquerque. After all this shit I was back in Albuquerque. I remembered the line actor Ricky Jay said in the movie *Boogie Nights* when describing a bad porno movie. *"It is what it is."*

Albuquerque was what it was, all right.

I parked in the big structure adjacent to Metro, all the way on the fourth floor, the last space on the roof. Today would be a docket from hell.

I checked my turquoise watch. Gentlemen start your engines, time for the *race judicata.* First lap would be metro. The elevator was broken so I descended the stairs in those damn stiff boots. Rattlesnakes didn't do well on stairs.

Inside Metro, the guard mentioned that Luna's leave of absence might become permanent. The Chief Judge had reported her to the Judicial Review Board for unprofessional conduct. Luna needed to return to the bench . . . or else.

Another guard intently read the newspaper instead of watching for criminals. CRUZ OUT OF CONTROL! ran the headline. In smaller type, under Luna's picture, was a quote from the Chief Judge of Metro: "She took an oath!"

"Right now we're in a judicial emergency," the editorial stated. "All of Metro's *pro tem* judges are gone, due to budget cuts. Cases will be dismissed; justice will be denied if Judge Luna Cruz is not on the bench doing the job she took an oath to do."

Luna obviously hadn't told the press about the kidnapping. Why? She had put her career on the line. Despite the tone of the article, the author admitted Luna was getting to be a better judge, after an initial period of adjustment. But it was too little, too late.

The editorial went a step further, blaming attorneys like me. "If defense attorneys keep delaying, perhaps they should sit in jail next to their clients."

• • • • •

Defendants packed Luna's courtroom; a few paced in the hallway. A male and female cop wagered on whether Luna would actually show today.

I noticed the self-appointed "court monitors," sitting in the back. They took notes on the proceedings. "We're gonna publish them online," one elderly blue haired woman said to her neighbor. "We're gonna rip the blindfold off Lady Justice."

My client from MDC, Alejandro, sat in a small chair against the wall. He wore the MDC jumpsuit and his ankles chained, but his hands were free. Although an accused armed robber, he was in court today on a "failure to keep dog leashed" charge, a violation of the municipal code. Ironically, he had already posted bond on the armed-robbery case, but the no-bond hold on the dog case kept him locked up. He had a suspended sentence on a previous case, so he could get nine years from this real life dog shit case before he even went to trial on the other one.

I hoped they'd dismiss the dog case, but the Animal Control Officer's nickname was "Miss No Dismiss."

I begged the ADA, an anorexic woman with the unfortunate name of Feather Fawcett, to put the case to sleep. Officer Miss No Dismiss argued loudly against cutting Alejandro even the smallest break. "He must respect my authority!" Miss No Dismiss shouted to Feather, sounding like a female version of *South Park's* Eric Cartman.

I'd made no progress with Feather when Alejandro motioned me to approach. "If they find me innocent of letting my dog run free, can they still charge me with the armed robbery?"

"Yes," I said. "The reason this is so important is because of the suspended sentence on the earlier case."

Alejandro was the only inmate within earshot. "By the way, do you know someone named Nastia?" I asked.

"Everyone knows Nastia," he said. "The Eskimo stripper?"

My heart skipped a beat. Unfortunately, the CO brought another inmate over and sat him down next to Alejandro and Alejandro shook his head. "Can't talk now," he said. "I do gotta tell you something when we got a chance."

I checked my turquoise watch. Time for lap two. I needed to run to District or face contempt from the judges over there. Then again, Luna could hold me in contempt here in Metro. Contempt was contempt. A Metro judge could send a lawyer to jail for missing a traffic case while he handled a murder case in District.

After the editorial, Luna must know she skated on thin judicial ice, especially with the blue haired monitor sitting right there in her courtroom. I would violate her Hotel California rule. *"You can check out any time you want, but you can never leave."*

"Feather, I need a favor," I asked. I almost said "Favor, I need a feather," but I caught myself.

"I don't know," she said. "I'm not in the favor business. Or the feather business either."

"I have to go to Judge Whitemer's courtroom, and then to Judge Pasteur across the street in District. I'll be right back, but you know how things are over there. Can you tell the judge I had to go? In a perfect world, District takes precedence over Metro."

"This isn't a perfect world," she said. She paused for a moment, and shut her eyes. "Did you say Judge Whitemer? That's where Angelina is assigned."

She sighed. I knew Angelina, an ADA rumored to be bisexual. Feather's heart beat through her sweater. She had a crush on Angelina, along with everyone else of both genders. Clients begged me to have their cases transferred to Judge Whitemer, just so Angelina could prosecute them.

"I can put in a good word for you with Angelina," I said. "I can play Miles Standish, or Cyrano, or whoever."

"You got the nose for Cyrano," she said with a smile. "If you do that I'll help you out over here, and keep Judge Looney Toons off your ass until you get back. Deal?"

"Deal," I replied and shook her bony hand.

• • • • •

I waited to cross six busy lanes of Lomas Boulevard to the District Court side. An officer here handed out jaywalking tickets like speeding tickets at the Indianapolis 500 so I was always careful. Seriously. Ever since a prominent attorney had been plowed down by an errant driver, cops began cracking down. Or else the city just wanted a quick thirty -dollar fine added to the treasury during these troubled times.

When the walk signal appeared, I ran as fast as my rattlesnake boots would carry me to the entrance.

"If you go fast enough, you don't beep," a guard said when I passed through the metal detector. "Something about the excited electrons."

Unfortunately, the elevator light indicated it was stuck on the seventh floor. When it stayed there for another minute, I ran up the stairs in desperation.

In the courtroom, Frank Cortez sat in the jury box with the

other inmates. A big guy, his gut poked through the buttons of his jump suit. With his beard and matted long hair, he claimed direct descent from the ancient conqueror. He sure smelled like one.

His tattooed arms detailed the Spanish conquest.

"Your arms could be in a museum," I said.

"They were photographed for *Ink* magazine," he said. "My back got the centerfold."

"So about this plea," I said, not wanting to imagine the centerfold. "Seven years."

"Seven years is too long but I'll take it if it's credit time served. I've been in two months already, man. Remember, when I turned myself in, even though I was dirty but you said I would be all right."

The worst words a lawyer can hear from a client are "but you said."

Frank was correct— I had said he would be all right. I owed him one. "I'll see what I can do. By the way, is Nastia your girl-friend?"

What was I thinking? I couldn't see Nastia with the illustrated man.

"You said everything would be all right."

Before he could say those damn words, "but," "you" and "said" one more time, Judge Whitemer entered. He was a distinguished gentleman with a bow tie, who could write witty theater columns for the *National Review*. The judge had retired over a year ago and continued on the District court bench *pro bono*.

"I hope justice means something to you all," he famously said during his "retirement" speech. "It certainly means a lot to me."

Judge Whitemer faced the inmates sitting in the jury box. "I want to start by advising you of your rights." He gave the longest advisement of rights of any judge in the state. My God, I didn't realize that we had so many rights left in the Constitution.

I had time to spare as he droned on. I wandered over to Angelina, who sat at the prosecutor's table hunched over a *Sports Illustrated*. She wore a black business suit that showed as much leg as the canons of professional ethics would allow. The Court of Appeals had banned her from wearing her red outfit for oral arguments. A big fan of the LPGA tour, she eagerly scanned an article about Susie Song, Jen's cousin, the famous golfer.

"Susie Song is so hot," Angelina said. "She's going to play here in a men's tournament this year instead of the LPGA one that same weekend."

I smiled. "She needs to make up her mind which tour she wants to play on."

Angelina smiled. "Maybe she can play both, if she's winning."

I sensed why both men and women lusted after Angelina; she resembled Angelina Jolie with her lips and tattoos. I wanted to negotiate a plea on Frank Cortez, but I knew I had to deal with the Feather issue first. Or was that the first issue feather?

"Hey," I said. "I know someone who likes you."

"What is this? *High School Musical*?" She closed the Susie Song article tightly, as if I caught her reading a *Playboy*.

Maybe she really did play on her own team.

I smiled at her. "Well, kinda." Time to play it cool. "That person wants to keep it on the *down low* since that person works in the judicial system. Are you seeing someone?"

She frowned. "I just got out of a long-term relationship." She paused. "Do you really know *someone* who might be interested in me?"

She played the pronoun game and kept it vague. She distinctly said someone and not *a man*.

Judge Whitemer was discussing every possible outcome of a trial, what could occur, and how twelve—not ten or eleven—people had to find someone guilty.

Angelina smiled at me. "Well, I could be interested, if it's the right *person*."

Bingo. Again, she used *person* and not *man*.

"I think I might know the right person," I said, "and this person really, really likes you."

"Well, if this *person* and I have common interests, like law for example, I might be. . . *interested.*"

I laughed. "By the way, could you knock off three years on the plea on Cortez over there? He's already been in for two months, so could you give him credit for time served?"

"He's not the person with the crush on me, is he?"

We stared at the fat man and the history of Custer's last stand at Little Big Horn on his arm. I felt like Custer all right.

"Not even," I said. "This person is a big time lawyer. But first things first, we have to deal with Mr. Cortez."

"Why should I care about Cortez? I've got all the explorers today, by the way. Cortez. Coronado on shoplifting. Pizzaro on larceny. I've even got Ponce de Leon on criminal sexual penetration on the fountain of youth."

Time for some performance art. I gave a stirring speech on Mr. Cortez's behalf. "He's been profiled in a national magazine," I said. "He was even a centerfold."

"A centerfold?"

"Well his *back* was."

"Just give me one good thing to hold my hat on," she said. "Walmart will hire anyone."

"He came to court even though he knew he would test dirty," I said. "The dude had faith in me that I could get him out."

"Faith is something these days." She thumbed down Cortez's record, then followed the history of the conquests on both his arms.

"He trusted me and I promised him everything would be okay."

"Never make promises you can't keep."

She stared at the file. "I'll cut you a break."

"Don't you mean cut him a break?"

"I'm doing this for *you*. Not him."

I hurried back to Cortez, and explained the plea included credit for time served.

He nodded. "Cool, dude, you're the best."

Judge Whitemer was now explaining their rights under laws currently under consideration, laws that might not ever get passed. Judge Whitemer calmly told them that even if that particular law passed in the next legislative session, the defendants would still be waiving their rights.

Angelina smiled at last. "I've heard some good things about this *person* who might like me."

She must have figured out it was Feather, but before I could go back to meet the object of her desire it was time for lap three. Benally in Judge Pasteur.

• • • • •

I hurried down to Judge Pasteur on floor six , learning on the fly how to run in boots without tripping. In Judge Pasteur's courtroom, the ADA wore red and green. She handed me a misdemeanor plea. "Merry Christmas," she said. "The alleged victim is in jail in Hawaii, and the state is too cheap to transport him."

Benally faced only ninety days unsupervised probation. Since this wasn't a felony, he would still be able to keep his job at a casino. If convicted, armed robbery was a second-degree felony, nine years with 85 percent good time. That meant he would only credit for four days a month, while other inmates got credit for fifteen. At best, I expected two third-degree felonies, cap of six, out in three.

I walked to the gallery and searched for him. Unfortunately, he wasn't there. A guard told me he was in the back. I asked him for permission to go to the holding cell, and he reluctantly agreed. I had never been back there before and nearly gagged. A dozen or so inmates stood in an area the size of a single back in MDC.

"Is Benally back there?" I asked the crowd.

He was in the back and literally had to push his way to the front. Any pretense of confidentiality was gone, but I had to talk to him right now. The other inmates pushed against the bars. For a moment, the bars creaked under the stress of the bodies.

"Could you give us some space?" I said.

They backed up an inch, max.

"Dude," I whispered. "They're dropping the armed robbery *and* the aggravated battery. They're even dropping the attempted murder. No felony. You get to keep your job, your guns, and your vote. All you have to do is plead to the pot."

"Could you explain that again? Why do I have to plead to pot? I'm innocent."

I explained it to him again, thoroughly, and then explained it yet again. In the back the inmates chattered amongst themselves on the merits of his case.

"But I *did* do the armed robbery inside," Benally said. He didn't care whether the inmates heard him. "I held the guy up. I said I was going to kill him. The gun wasn't loaded."

"Doesn't matter."

He gave me a long explanation of needing money to save his old orphanage back on the rez. He wanted me to subpoena the orphans to testify on his behalf.

"Dude, I don't care about the orphans. The alleged victim is doing time in Hilo, Hawaii. The DA can't afford to transport him. That's why they're dropping this down to the misdemeanor.

However, if the dude gets released within the next six months, they can take it to trial and you will lose. You will get nine years. That's why you should plead to the pot and get out today."

"I didn't know about no pot," he said. "I don't do nothing. This was for the kids; maybe you can tell the judge I did the armed robbery for the kids."

"Armed robbery is nine years. Attempted murder is another nine years. Pot is a misdemeanor with ninety *days* probation. What do you want to do?"

He asked, "I get out today?"

"Yep. If you plead to the possession of pot."

"I told you I didn't know about no pot," he said. "They must have been smoking it while I was inside the store doing the robbery and telling the clerk I wanted to kill him."

"Please don't say that too loud," I said.

The guard came back. "They're ready for you." He made the other inmates back up as he opened the door and let Benally come out. For one moment, the inmates could have easily rushed me and the guard, but they stayed inside.

The guard looked at me when he closed the bars. "How can you defend these scum?"

"They're not scum, they're people."

• • • • •

"Are you ready?" the judge asked when we got to the courtroom.

"Sure."

The judge did an advisement of rights, once again. He asked Benally why he wanted to plead to "one count of possession of marijuana."

"But I didn't know about no pot."

Silence in the courtroom.

"That's not good enough," the judge said. "The State is dropping second degree felony counts of attempted murder, armed robbery, and kidnapping if you will plead guilty to one *misdemeanor* count of possession of marijuana. Please tell us how you came to possess marijuana," he said.

I stared anxiously. Benally had to make the admission. He shook his head. "I told you I didn't have no pot."

"What?" the judge asked.

"I didn't know it was in the car," he said.

"Mr. Shepard, I think you had better talk to your client," the judge said. "I'll recall when you're ready."

I had to get back to Metro before Judge Looney Toons held me in contempt.

"I'll be right back," I said, leaving before being excused.

• • • • •

I didn't just jay walk, I jay-*ran*, boots and all, across Lomas Boulevard. My boots actually rattled in pain as I made it to the opposite curb. Thankfully, the cop was busy busting someone else and stood, pre-occupied, writing a citation.

Luna took the bench with a vengeance. The female cop handed the male cop her paycheck, and signed the back.

A picture of George Washington hung behind Luna. He looked frozen and deathly white as if he had just come out of the Delaware. Did George just wink at me? Luna had that same air of death. Why was she even here? It must be because Luna believed strongly in honesty and in justice. Those assholes tried to intimidate her, kidnapped her child, but Luna wouldn't relent.

"Hang in there, your honor," I whispered when she took a recess. "I'm very proud of the way you're handling yourself."

"Well, you're the *only* one," she said, shaking her head.

Time to capitalize on what little clout I had. "Your honor, could we call Alejandro's case? I have two pending cases over in District."

She pointed to the line of attorneys. "I have to go right down the docket, name by name. I'm sorry. I'm under a lot of—"

She paused. Was she going to say "pressure" or "stress?" Instead, she nodded toward the freelance court monitors with their notebooks, jotting down our *ex parte* communication. "Let's just say I have to follow procedures to the letter. And every other lawyer here has to be somewhere else."

"I've got a fraud case in Federal Court," one lawyer shouted.

"I've got a death penalty case in Deming," said another.

Luna frowned and motioned me to approach. "Just because you slept with my sister doesn't mean you get to skip in line," she whispered.

That hurt. My clients were just as guilty as their clients. In fact most of my clients were guiltier. I nodded at Alejandro. "I've got to talk to you, man," he shouted from the gallery. "It's really important."

No time. No time.

The answer was right over there, but first I had to handle two other hearings at the same time. Why couldn't I clone myself, damn it?

"I will let you leave," she said at last. "That is, if you can get the District Attorney's permission."

I nodded and leaned over to Feather. "Angelina could like you. She said she likes lawyers."

Feather smiled. "He has my permission," she said without hesitation.

"Thank you," I said on my way out the door. "So what do you want to me to do as Cyrano?"

"Tell her there's a special DJ on Friday at O'Keeffe's Place." Feather said. "DJ Danger Dyke."

Apparently O'Keeffe's Place was the name of the hottest club, and was presumably named after the artist.

"Sure," I said. "Cool, I'll tell her that. I would write a love sonnet on her behalf, I was you; but a DJ umm . . . Danger . . . ummm . . . sounds good. Thanks for holding my place."

"I can't hold it forever."

I tried to make eye contact with Luna on the way out, but she focused on a contentious he said / she said case involving a speeding ticket. Unfortunately, the "he said" was the highly decorated officer who had just won the bet. "She said" was a prostitute on a revoked license.

Surprisingly, the cop did not properly "calibrate" his radar, so Luna dismissed the case. The court monitors mumbled in amazement.

• • • • •

The jaywalking cop eyed me warily, so I waited cautiously until the white crossing light appeared. Thank God Albuquerque stood a good two thousand feet lower than Santa Fe. As I sprinted across the street my lungs thanked me for the extra air, especially when I ran up the seven flights of stairs again. My ACL buckled under the impact of up each stair.

Inside the court, Judge Whitemer repeated the advisement of rights that he had given only a half an hour before. "Mr. Shepard is an excellent attorney," he said, slowly and deliberately. "I've personally seen him do cross-examinations of witnesses and get them to recant their testimony. He does an excellent closing argument. Mr. Cortez, are you absolutely, positively, sure you want to plea?"

Cortez rattled his hand-cuffs. "Can we win this one?" he whispered to me.

I glanced down at the file. Ten eyewitnesses. I could get two, maybe three max to recant. I couldn't get ten to recant. I was good; I wasn't that good. I had a moment of panic. What to do? No, as a lawyer, I had to do what's best for my client. If we lost this one he'd be locked up for good. Even the best football teams have to punt.

"No, we can't," I said. "We can't win. I don't want to play with your life."

This wasn't the story of Cortez's case. This was the story of *my* life.

Cortez shook his head. He tried to hold the cuffs still as he faced the judge.

"Your honor, I did it," he said. "I plead guilty."

The judge then tossed me a bone. "If Mr. Shepard advises you take a deal, it must be a good one. Are you satisfied with his representation?"

I stiffened. Was he? Did he get satisfaction? *I can't get no satisfaction.* Why did this mean so much to me?

Cortez smiled. "Your Honor, I gotta admit, he's been there for me. He's the only lawyer I've had in all my felonies who ever cared."

My pulse quickened again, this time with joy. This whole thing would be over in minutes.

The judge reminded Cortez that he would have a few more years of parole. "When you finish up in five years, make sure you check in at the parole office up in Santa Fe to get a release by three p.m."

"I gotta check in now?" Cortez asked, confused. "I thought I needed to wait five years."

I felt like I had spent five years in court on this plea alone.

"That's correct," said the judge. "In *five years*, when you finish, make sure you get there by three p.m. And they don't have parking. I always recommend parking in the block on the other side of plaza. There's free parking there."

My God, I couldn't even remember where I parked from an hour ago There was no chance Cortez would remember the free lot in five years.

We somehow made it through the hearing alive.

"Thank you so much," Cortez said. "Hopefully I can get a furlough to get a lap dance from my girlfriend at the Ends Zone."

"By the way, what's your girlfriend's name?" I asked, my heart beating faster.

"Destiny," he said. "Why?"

One down.

• • • • •

I dashed back to Angelina. "So would you be willing to meet this person at O'Keeffe's on Friday. There's a special DJ." I didn't want to say the name.

"I'd love to meet this *person*," she said. "I love this whole Cyrano and Roxanne thing. It's so very literary."

Actually it was a Roxanne and Roxanne thing. I tried to hurry out the door, Cortez's entire family waited outside like a conquering army, ready to pillage.

"I'm so confused," his mother said. "Is he getting probation or prison?"

She started crying, before I could escape. Just because her son was a criminal, didn't mean that she didn't love him. I patiently explained what five years meant in light of fifty percent good time and credit for time served that did not get good time, then explained it again. She did not have to go to the probation office today at three.

"God bless you," she said.

· · · · ·

I hurried down to the sixth floor for Benally's plea. Perfect timing.

Judge Pasteur smiled with relief as he tapped his watch. "Ready?"

"Just a minute, your honor."

As we talked in the jury box, Benally stayed adamant about the pot. "You can't make me lie," he said. "That's like *purchasing* yourself."

How to break this impasse? They'd max him if we took this to trial, hell they could keep him in jail for another six months as they searched for the witness. I had a brainstorm. We would do an *Alford* plea. An Alford plea essentially stated that although a client maintained his innocence, the state could prove the case beyond a reasonable doubt. *Alford* had occurred in North Carolina, but New Mexico courts followed the rule. An Alford plea made sense where the client's alibi for smoking a joint was an armed robbery of a convenience store.

Maybe my life was one big *Alford* plea. I was innocent, but God could prove me guilty of something.

We hurried through the plea and I intoned the magic words that my client steadfastly maintained his innocence, but agreed that the State could prove his case beyond a reasonable doubt. All Benally had to say was, "Yes, Your Honor" a few times.

When it was over, Benally hugged me. "I'm free," he said.

He literally jumped up and down. "Thank you. I'm never gonna drink again."

"You're crushing me."

He finally let go.

"By the way," I asked him. "Do you know Nastia?"

"Who?"

Two down. One to go.

• • • • •

When I arrived in Luna's courtroom, I took a deep breath. This was it. It all came down to Alejandro. That made a strange kind of sense; he was there when this whole adventure began. He had mentioned the girlfriend back in G-7. He knew about the kidnapping. Nastia had said it wasn't him, but her credibility was shot these days.

Before I could talk to him, Feather approached me. "Did you see Angelina?"

"She'll meet you at O'Keeffe's."

Feather smiled. She approached the judge. "Your Honor, I'd like to help you lighten your docket. The State will be dismissing the case of *State versus Alejandro Limkin* with prejudice. We'll remove the hold, so he'll be free to go."

Luna was about to bang her gavel when her clerk pointed to a line on the file. "He still has a warrant fee he needs to pay."

Alejandro stared at me with his big brown eyes. He didn't have a hundred bucks, and he could stay in jail pending final payment. I'd better save him before he opened his mouth.

"Your honor," I said. "I'll personally pay the hundred-dollar fee. Assuming they take credit cards downstairs at the customer service window."

Luna nodded. "They do indeed. I had to pay a fine there myself once."

She banged the gavel. "Once the fine is paid, he's free to go."

Alejandro sat back down. He would get out after all. MDC chucked them out a lot quicker than Santa Fe. MDC even transported the inmates to the bus station. A liquor store there catered to newly released inmates, but that was another story.

Alejandro took a deep breath of freedom. "I owe you, dude."

Luna smiled at me, likely her first for the week. "Mr. Shepard, thank you for helping me *lighten* my docket."

"Your Honor, I hope I can be of assistance to you in the future."

The guard escorted Alejandro toward the door and I asked him to let me meet with Alejandro in the back room. In that brief moment of privacy, we talked in the small entryway before he joined the other prisoners.

"So Alejandro, you were there in MDC when I heard about the kidnapping. Who did you call?"

"My girlfriend."

"Nastia?" I asked triumphantly.

"Not that slut. My girl's a waitress. Her name is Mia."

I remembered Mia, the existential waitress. Okay, that still works. He tells Mia-the-waitress about the kidnapping. Mia tells Nastia. Nastia calls her boyfriend and then calls me.

For a moment, I wondered if Mia had played Nastia. No, I distinctly remembered Mia and her voice. She didn't call me.

"Do you know where Luna's child is?"

"Why would I know that?"

So much for Alejandro.

He grabbed my arm before I could get away. "By the way, I'm a suspect in another case. Do you know what's going to happen with that?"

I did not turn around after I escaped his grasp. Still, I had given my word so I paid Alejandro's fine down below.

A hundred bucks shot to hell.

A whole week shot to hell.

It hadn't been any of my clients after all.

• • • • •

I walked to the top of the garage, my eyes taking in all of Albuquerque. The sun illuminated the granite of the Sandia Crest to the east, and the dormant volcanoes to the west. Albuquerque could be the bad Bedford Falls in *It's a Wonderful Life.*

I contemplated jumping the hundred feet down to the asphalt of Fourth Street. The fall might not be enough to kill me, but then again, I didn't know what would happen, did I?

What did I have to live for anymore? I wouldn't be a hero after all. I was the George Bailey of law. Some kind of wonderful life. I didn't help nice people buy homes; I helped the mother-fucking scum of the earth. Life would be better if they just stayed the fuck in jail where they belonged.

Where the fuck was Clarence, anyhow?

As if on cue my phone rang. Private number.

"Dan, it's Nastia," she said.

"You've been lying to me the entire time."

"It was the only way, as I try to figure this out."

"I don't want to talk to you," I said. "I can't believe anything you say!"

"You don't understand." She started crying. "I'm just one little woman on the run. I'm making this all up as I go along. I'm doing all I can. I've got to save Dew. I've got to. It's my only hope. Please help me."

"*So what's going to happen?*" I yelled. God, I was as bad as my clients.

Nothing came from the other end. Nastia was as clueless as I was.

I hung up and stared at the ledge.

The phone rang again. Jesus, can't a guy contemplate suicide in peace? Another private number.

"Hello?"

"Dan, it's me, Angelina." It took me a moment to remember the DA. "Why don't we make it a romantic evening, and you can pick me up in person on Friday."

Wow. I had failed at finding Nastia. I had failed at helping my clients. I had even failed at being a matchmaker.

"I'm sorry, Angelina." I said. "While I'm very flattered, I'm currently involved with someone else."

Someone dead.

I hung up.

Still staring at the ledge I felt emptiness. Why did I have to be such a dick to Nastia? I imagined my little gymnast doing splits. Poor girl. She was right; she was just one person on the run, trying to figure it all out. Worse, she was a whore, a drug dealer, and possibly even a spy. She made Jen look like an angel.

But then, Jen always ran away from life. Nastia was taking incredible risks in talking to me. When she saved me down in Cruces, she put her life in jeopardy. Would Jen ever do something like that?

I remembered the empty feeling I got after I rejected Jen when she called me at the jail. I had been an asshole. That same horrible feeling washed over me again.

Was I falling in love with Nastia now? Of course not. She was just a rebound from Jen. I was projecting this whole guardian angel thing on a woman I barely knew.

Yet, why the hell did I want to meet her so badly? Because if I met her, if I found her *lyobov*, I saved Dew. I still had something worth living for.

I walked away from the ledge.

Part III

Saturday
SONG: "Albuquerque" (reprise) by Trevor McShane

PREGNANT SHARK

JEN'S MEMORIAL SERVICE WAS SCHEDULED for Saturday morning in the Botanic Gardens; part of the city's famed Bio Park that lined the edge of the Rio, Albuquerque's attempt at big-time culture. It almost worked.

I lived across Central Avenue from the Bio Park and dodged traffic by hoofing it. I went with jeans, a black rugby shirt and sneakers. Jen wouldn't care about my outfit, would she?

On the other side of the street, I passed the small aquarium that was adjacent to the Botanic Gardens. I called it a "seven-minute aquarium," because that's the duration of my usual visit.

I had last come here nearly six months ago.

Jen insisted on staying for a full hour in the small aquarium. She especially loved the "touch pond," and about molested a poor starfish. She also loved the jellyfish exhibit.

"Wouldn't it be great to just be able to float through life?" she said. "Getting carried along by the current?"

Even as a jellyfish, I'd still have to float to two different places at the same time.

The aquarium had a restaurant on the other side of the massive shark tank. Once we sat down inside the café, I couldn't take my eyes off a very pregnant shark. The shark had a baby bump and waddled through the tank as the other sharks gave it a wide berth. Maybe they were frightened that the offspring would come after them.

Did sharks lay eggs or actually gave birth to little sharks? There was a tiny piece of paper on our table that told about the pregnant shark, which had apparently become a tourist attraction. The gestation period was eleven months, and occasionally some unborn sharks ate weaker sharks in the womb. I thought of MDC.

How did sharks fuck anyway? The paper didn't say. Was there such a thing as shark foreplay? Could the pregnant shark sue her significant other for spousal support?

Jen didn't glance at the pregnant shark as it swam just inches on the other side of the glass. "I was thinking about the jellyfish," she said, "and how they say good bye."

I dreaded her next statement so instead stayed focused on the shark. Did the aquarium give the mama shark a fresh seal for a baby shower?

Jen went on about her "issues" and "feelings," and the many bad things in her life. "Perhaps it's time for me to float away for a while, and see where the current takes me."

She had me at good-bye.

The shark winked at me. Could it see me through the glass? Was I food or did it wonder about me?

Woody Allen once said, "A relationship is like a shark, it has to constantly keep moving in order to survive."

We were dead sharks all right. The next day Jen sent me a text that she intended to move to L.A., and I shouldn't call her again. Sharks said good-bye by biting each other.

Jen might have told me so much that day. Why was I so obsessed with that damn shark instead of the real woman in front of me?

Today Luna mentioned that Jen had prepared a will. Jen had always said that her days on this earth were numbered and apparently was prepared. In her will, Jen specified that her memorial service should take place in the *Sasebo Japanese Garden*, a section of the Botanic Gardens named after Albuquerque's sister city in Sasebo, Japan. Even though Korea and Japan didn't always get along, a service in a Japanese garden sounded like a great "last look," as O-Ren Ishii stated before dying in a big sword fight in *Kill Bill.*

We still had to pay the nominal entry fee to get into the Botanic Gardens, even for the memorial service. The cashier pointed out that admission allowed entrance to the zoo, the aquarium, and the children's railroad.

Washington put a firm hand on my shoulder. "I'll pay for him," he said. "Don't tell Luna about this."

I felt three years old under his grip. "You're totally useless, you know that?" Washington asked.

"If there's anything I can do to help?"

Washington searched his brain, and then nodded. "What are you doing Monday?"

"I'm going to L.A. for my script meetings."

"You might not be useless after all," he said.

• • • • •

I walked quickly to the magnificent Japanese garden at the far edge of the park. The garden boasted a nice little lake; wooden bridges, rock sculptures, and a waterfall. This would be a fitting last look for Laser Geisha Pink.

As we sat down, Luna announced an hour delay from the dais. She was alone and Gabriel Rose was nowhere to be seen. God, I hoped she'd dumped him.

How to kill time before a funeral? I contemplating returning the aquarium and petting the baby shark. My admission to the entire park was paid for. It had been a few months, how big would the baby be now?

I teared up, and then bawled for real. I was crying over a fucking baby shark. No, I was crying over everything—not just Jen, but Denise, Luna, Dew and all the lost sharks in my life.

Bleary-eyed, I wandered around the Botanic Gardens. Even this early in the spring flowers bloomed cautiously, testing out the whole rebirth thing. Cherry blossoms threw caution to the wind and showed their pink. *Memoirs of a Geisha,* indeed. That had been filmed in Long Beach, but if the tax incentives were right they could film *Memoirs of a Laser Geisha,* right here in the gardens.

Jen would have loved it here. Pink blossoms floated past me in the wind like escaped jellyfish. On the other side of the park the butterfly pavilion hadn't opened yet. Ray Bradbury wrote a story about changing the timeline by crushing a butterfly in the past. I would crush ten thousand butterflies to bring back Jen.

On my way back, I passed two glass greenhouses shaped like pyramids. Perhaps Jen could be buried in one of the greenhouses like a modern-day Cleopatra. One of them housed a desert landscape; another had been re-designed to reflect a part of Asia.

A ray of sunlight hit the Asian pyramid. Jen's entire life was lived in a glass house. Her whole life she had thrown stones, and they had come back to haunt her.

I returned to the Japanese garden as U.S. Marshals brought in one last person, a male prisoner in his seventies. He sat in the front row reserved for family. Nurse Song, Susie and Denise sat alongside the prisoner, with Jen's other half-sister, Selena. Denise didn't move a muscle; she either had a moment of Zen or the right dose of meds.

Luna gave the man a hug, and wiped away a tear. She then she sat by herself on the dais. Pony-tailed men finally brought in the casket. They were Navajos with black suits and turquoise bolo ties. Jen had died on the reservation, after all, and her body was still the subject of an ongoing investigation.

I prayed for a closed casket. It was all a lie, right? Jen was really still alive and would jump out and say boo! Unfortunately, the pall bearers opened the casket. Jen was definitely dead. The mortician must have worked hard to get rid of the visible signs of her death. No one went up. Denise didn't even flinch.

• • • • •

Luna first called on a Korean minister. He said a few words in English and then in Korean. Even the Korean syllables reminded me of Jen. I felt guilty for even thinking about Nastia.

Luna rose again and walked slowly to the podium. "I can tell you the story of how I first met Jen. I had just been voted out as District Attorney and was leaving Crater County for good. I broke into my father's clinic to get an old picture. Those of you who've been to my apartment have seen it, the picture of him taking my temperature."

The old man put his cuffed hand to his face to wipe off tears.

"What you don't know is that the clinic still contained lots of unguarded medications that were left behind. For one brief moment I thought of ending it all."

No one took their eyes off Luna.

"Then Nurse Song drove up to the clinic and introduced me to her daughter. Jen needed help. Once I talked with Jen, and agreed to help her out, I finally had a reason for living again. Jen Song, my half-sister, my *sister*, saved my life."

Luna told us that her greatest regret was that Jen would never achieve her potential. Jen had so much to offer. She pointed to the cherry blossoms in the distance and said pink was Jen's favorite color. I started to cry again.

"I wonder if I still have a reason to go on living. . . ."

That's when Luna's phone rang. Very loudly. Her ring tone was "*I fought the law and the law won.*" The version by The Clash.

She froze. The electronic interruption was the equivalent of the Enola Gay atom-bombing a geisha house. Washington rushed to the podium, grabbed Luna's phone and took it away.

"Could you call back?" he said into the phone.

Apparently they couldn't. He ran out of the garden.

Luna shook her head. "I don't know what else to say. Jen never knew how to say good-bye."

• • • • •

At the end of the memorial service, Luna and Washington hustled off to one of the greenhouse pyramids where they argued heatedly about something. Washington talked on the phone again, and then relayed a message to Luna. She nodded.

I hung out by the little lake. All the water here interconnected, perhaps flowing into the shark tank. I skipped a few stones and watched the concentric circles, hoping that somehow they led to something.

Just at my absolute moment of Zen, the phone rang. "It's me," Nastia said.

"Are you here?"

"I'm nearby."

"I'm sorry for yelling at you."

"I don't blame you. I don't have all the answers, *da?*"

"Does anybody? So are you going to tell me something useful for a change?"

"You're going to have to figure it out yourself. If someone asks you to do something, do it. And one more thing. I lied about lying. You already know my *lyobov*. My *lyobov* will help you save the day."

"Should I even bother asking?"

She laughed. "You'll know when the time is right, *da?* You're getting closer."

Washington tapped me on the shoulder. "Dan, come inside. I think you can help us."

I hung up and looked at the big man. "Yeah?'

"Who was that?"

"Nobody."

"You said you were going to L.A. on Monday, right?"

"Yes."

"We just spoke with the kidnappers. You know about our ummm . . . transactional problems. They want to be paid in cash."

"What does this have to do with me?"

"Well, they know you're going to Los Angeles."

"How do they know that?"

Long pause. "I told them. Hope you didn't mind. They want the money to come with someone who's not a cop and is relatively harmless."

"Relatively harmless?" That sounded like one of the books in the *Hitchhiker's Guide to the Galaxy* series. "You want *me* to be the bag man?

I never really knew whether a bag man carried the money, got the money, or put it in the bag.

"You'll be perfectly safe. You'll carry a briefcase and leave it at the drop off point. Once you give them the money, they'll release Luna's child."

Or the kidnappers would kill me right there for no reason at all. I was an attorney, not a bag man, whatever that was. The bag man always got killed. Wasn't that a reggae song, *"I Shot the Bag Man?"*

I didn't want to be a bag man. "I'm very busy in the morning. What time?"

"We'll try to work it into your schedule," Washington said.

I felt like a total dick. I saw Luna off in the distance. What could I say?

"Of course, I'll do it. When do I pick up the money?"

"Don't call us," he said. "We'll call you."

"Isn't it a weird coincidence that I just happen to be going to the same place as the kidnappers?"

"Who said it was a coincidence?"

I sure didn't like the sound of that.

SUNDAY/MONDAY
Song: "The Eagle Flies" (reprise) by Trevor McShane

ORANGE ALERT

I DIDN'T HEAR ANYTHING ON Sunday. I mourned Jen, cried a bit, and watched *anime* cartoons in her honor. Hopefully the kidnappers would return Dew before *Sixty Minutes* and the whole thing would be over. Luna would get her life back. They couldn't really be serious about using me as a bag man, could they?

I took a brisk morning run in the Bosque, despite my aching heart and worse knees. The Rio Grande flowed to my right. I ran faster and faster, racing the driftwood flowing down the river. The driftwood flowed faster in the open water, but occasionally pieces caught on snags and eddies.

• • • • •

No word by Monday morning. I hummed a McShane song, "The Eagle Flies." Well, the eagle was flying, but just for one day. I only packed two scripts in a ratty briefcase. I didn't even bring a toothbrush. I practiced my pitch. I was in the ballpark, but I had to keep throwing fast balls to get out of the bull pen.

How many lawyers had delusions about being writers? Every Public Defender in L.A. probably had a script of his own.

Allen had told me they liked *Legal Coyote*, a "coming-of-age" story about a lawyer in rural New Mexico. I also had a "fish-out-of-water" story that just happened to star a lawyer in rural New Mexico.

Okay, I didn't have much range.

I still hadn't heard anything from Agent Washington. Hopefully, he wouldn't want to come along for the meetings at Morris Williams. I hated two people in a room during a pitch. Still, a guy with a gun and a badge could certainly close the deal.

I went with black shirt, black jacket, and the nice black shoes. I wouldn't be the rattlesnake lawyer in Hollywood, just another dude with a dream. Sinatra once called writers "schmucks with Underwoods." At least I had a word processor, but I was still a schmuck with spell-check.

● ● ● ● ●

I arrived at the Albuquerque Sunport early. It was my favorite airport in the world: big enough for all the amenities, but small enough to be manageable.

After parking on the top level, I tried to practice my pitches again but "It's not just a coming of age story, but something totally new," soon became "I won't release the briefcase until I see the girl." That's what bag men were supposed to say.

I boarded the shuttle with a family traveling to L.A. to see Disneyland. "Are you going to L.A. for business or pleasure?" the mother asked, pretending that she cared.

"Business." I said. I had already sweated through my jacket, and it was still early.

"You're sweating," the little girl said.

"I know."

By the time I reached the security checkpoint I still hadn't heard anything. I had deliberately avoided wearing a belt, but I still beeped like crazy. I sure couldn't brag about always clearing metal detectors in court. A very big TSA agent motioned me into a room, a special room. "Come with us, sir," he said ominously.

He just took me to a back room, bare walls except for a picture of the president. Inside, the terror suspects out-numbered the chairs, so I stood. A few seats down, an Arab man wore a sweat suit and seemed to be praying to himself.

In front of me, a long-haired college kid wore a black t-shirt that read, ANARCHY IN THE USA! under a blood-red image of someone peeing on a flag. He muttered "freedom of speech, freedom of speech," over and over to himself, possibly trying to convince the picture of the President staring down at him. Unfortunately, the kid's fly was still open.

"Don't touch that!" a guard whispered when the kid reached for his fly. "We still got to take a picture."

Finally the TSA agent called me into another room down a long hall that reminded me of the barrenness of FBI "space." I didn't know whether to be happy or sad when Washington greeted me.

"Sorry, I'm running late," he said. "Are you still up for this?"

What do I say to that? I had a brief image in my mind of being gunned down.

"Well?" he asked again.

"I guess so," I said at last.

Washington nonchalantly handed me a briefcase filled with money. It was ratty, identical to the briefcase that held my scripts.

I had never worn a wire in my life. I wondered if there were some Pavlovian shocks integrated into the system. Washington made me sign an elaborate release form. I would be responsible for the ten million in cash.

"I suggest that you don't lose it," he said.

"Where did the money come from?" I asked.

"Let's just say Luna's family can be very resourceful in a pinch. In fact, they were a lot more resourceful than we ever imagined."

Resourceful? Luna's father, the handcuffed man at the funeral, had probably given the Feds a secret off-shore account. Dew was his granddaughter after all. The briefcase was lighter than I expected. How much did ten million weigh?

"So where do I take it?" I asked.

"We don't know yet," he said. "Somewhere in Beverly Hills. That's all we know."

"Should I call them?"

"*Don't* call them!"

"They'll call me," I said. "I get it."

"I suggest you leave your phone on."

He grabbed my phone out of my pocket. He took it apart and added a small chip.

"Are you going to listen to my calls?"

"What do you think?"

"How will I know who they are?"

"If you hear an electronically disguised voice, chances are it's a kidnapper."

"Is there anything I should say to indicate that I'm in trouble? Like a code word or something?"

He laughed at me. "They would kill you before we could get anywhere close to you. Do you understand?"

I gulped.

"Just act normal. And make sure you give them the right briefcase."

I shook. "I don't think you understand. I never act normal. I don't know what normal is."

"Hurry, we can only hold your flight for another minute."

I had to go to the bathroom of course, and peed next to a man in a suit. He was probably another agent observing me to ensure I didn't flush the case or use the cash to wipe myself.

I put both of my briefcases down next to me and accidentally hit the briefcase with the shake. I hoped the urine didn't somehow make it onto the money. Would the kidnappers kill someone for peeing on their money? My clients did aggravated assaults for less. I worried about handing them the wrong briefcase. My scripts would have to be worth ten-million dollars to save my ass from the FBI.

I was good, but I wasn't that good.

My sweating grew worse.

I barely made the final boarding group on the Southwest flight. It's never a good thing when they hold a plane for you and everybody on board knows they will be late because of you. Everyone looked down at my two briefcases.

"Which one is the bomb?" the little girl asked.

A full flight, I had to wedge between an obese couple. The fat man's girth spilled into my space.

The kids from the shuttle sat in the row ahead. The girl kept looking back at me, and that made me sweat even more. "What's in that case?" she asked.

"Nothing!" I said, way too quickly. "Well, screenplays."

"No *that* case," she said, pointing to the other case. "What's in that case?"

"A little girl," I said. "But she'll be free once we get to L.A." She shut up.

• • • • •

I changed flights in Vegas. Back at a low altitude, I felt a spring in my step, well, a spring in my lungs, but you know what I mean. As I hurried down C Concourse, suspicious characters darted out from behind every slot machine. Was everyone looking at me?

My God, I had a briefcase filled with millions of dollars, and I'm in Las Vegas. If I put it all down, I could double my money and be set for life. Viva Las Vegas!

Did they have a roulette wheel here?

What did Cowboy say? Always bet on red?

Then again, more likely than not I'd get really, really dead. I went right to plane and took the first available seat, even though it was in the middle, and buckled my seatbelt securely.

EX LAX

I ARRIVED AT L.A.X., AND hurried down the concourse of Terminal One, and then exited into the sea of carbon monoxide of the arrivals area. I was glad I didn't need to hit the crowded baggage claim. That would be reserved for bags with even bigger ransoms. Everyone talked on cell phones, of course their phones were way more advanced than mine.

My phone rang as I hit the noisy cab area, so I had to hurry back in. A client needed a furlough from prison. "Remember when you got me a four hour furlough to visit my sick girlfriend?"

"That must have been nine months ago." I said.

"Well, I got her pregnant last furlough; she's about to give birth. Can you get me a furlough to be in the delivery room?"

I didn't know whether to laugh or cry.

• • • • •

I was second in line at the rental counter. Would the FBI reimburse me? The kidnappers sure wouldn't, and I didn't want to push it with Morris Williams. What type of car does a bag-man rent? I needed something big. My briefcases wouldn't look right in the backseat of the usual compact Geo.

With only a day in L.A., I bit the bullet and went with the upgrade: a Porsche. Image is everything when you're the bagman. No one takes money from a bag man in a Geo.

"Do you want insurance?" the clerk asked as she furiously typed on her keyboard.

"Does it cover accidental death?" I asked.

"That's extra."

"How about if it isn't an accident?"

"We do cover acts of God."

Unfortunately, my first credit card was declined. I could use the money from the briefcase to pay for the car, but that would be a federal crime. Would the kidnappers kill the kid if I shorted them a hundred bucks?

No need to risk it. I found a new credit card. It took a moment to open the account by phone, but everything worked out.

"Are you sure you are all right?" the clerk asked. "You look like you're going to faint."

"I'm fine."

• • • • •

Despite the morning craziness, I was forty minutes ahead of schedule for my morning meeting at the Morris Williams Agency. I prayed for traffic so I could waltz in fashionably late and say traffic was a bitch, but no such luck. My phone rang constantly. My criminal clients kept asking about their cases. I took their calls. I could check out of the Hotel New Mexico, but I could never leave.

I parked the car in the underground lot across the street from the agency. Rumbling came from all directions.

"Is that an earthquake?" I asked the valet as he gave me a ticket.

"It's a Hummer," the valet said, as the vehicle emerged from the depths of hell. "Why are you so jumpy, *ese*? You are writer here for a meeting?"

"Yeah."

"I can always tell you writers. Actors keep their cool, but writers look like they're about to have a heart attack. Like you."

"How about kidnappers?" I asked. "See any of them around?"

He shook his head. "None that I know of. I did get a big tip yesterday. Maybe it was ransom money."

"I'll keep that in mind."

Actually meeting with a Hollywood producer was the least of my worries. I laughed. Maybe I should be the bag-man more often.

I glanced at the rate sign on the wall. This was the most expensive parking lot in the world, more than motels on Central in Albuquerque and those joints threw in a bed. They wouldn't pay for my rental, but maybe the kidnappers would validate my parking.

I found a bathroom in the parking garage. What famous asses had sat on those toilets and peed in these urinals? Many famous writers probably had diarrhea, just like me. I went to the mirror, took off my shirt and washed myself. I stunk.

A junior agent came in and stared at me. "Are you supposed to be here?"

"I have a meeting with Saul Podell," I said. "I'm Dan Shepard, with an 'A.' I wrote a novel."

"A novel?" He laughed. "It's all about blogs. Novels are so out this year."

I crossed El Camino, took a deep breath, and entered the black glass building. Did the sheer gravity of the building collapse stars and convert them into energy? They wouldn't get that much energy out of me.

The lobby décor looked like the FBI space without the bulletproof glass. The head receptionist greeted me in a warm

French accent. I flashed my bar card from force of habit, and told her I was an attorney.

She smiled. "Who are you here to see?"

"Allen Koenigsburg in Saul Podell's office."

She made a quick call and then smiled warmly. "He'll be right with you."

I was so used to metal detectors that I expected one of the young men to hurry over and wand me, but they continued to answer phones in a corner of the lobby. Looking out the window I saw Gabriel Rose emerge from the parking garage in a shiny convertible. He honked impatiently at a few lagging pedestrians. I looked closer. It was him all right, chatting away on his hands-free phone. He honked one more time before he sped away.

My phone rang and I jumped. Was it Rose? No, it was the mother of a client.

"Four years, out in two. It would be up to the judge to decide." Our connection was bad, and I spoke a little louder than I had wanted. The words "four years" echoed across the lobby.

I sat in a circle of plush chairs. Like Rose, everyone in Hollywood could be the new and improved version of me. Their skin was cleaner, their hair shinier, their clothes fit just a bit better. Lord knows how much they spent to get that way.

A few of the actors who were also waiting in the lobby smelled much worse than expected with a strong odor of alcohol and bloodshot, watery eyes. Luckily, these people usually got rehab instead of jail time for their sins

A pretty woman in black clutched her own briefcase as she sat next to me. She looked like Anne Hathaway in the *Devil wears Prada*. This woman looked like she actually wore Prada.

"I couldn't help but follow your conversation," she said. "They're optioning you for four years? That's an amazing deal. Is it pay or play?"

"Kinda," I said. "It's a new deal I developed: a *pay-or-plea* deal."

"Are you an agent?" she asked. "A producer?"

"In a way," I said. "I like to think of myself as a producer of morality tales."

She could be an actress playing a writer, or perhaps a writer researching a script by dressing as a young actress. To her, if I was *in* this lobby, I had to be someone important.

"Are you bringing them a new project?"

"I have ten-million dollars in this briefcase."

She smiled. "Well, financing is always the first step."

● ● ● ● ●

The circle replaced itself with more stars, starlets, and producers. They all nodded at me. For all they knew, I belonged here. I nodded back. Another producer sat with me. He didn't even look at me while he talked on the phone. He recited every cliché about passive-aggressive deal-making, and kept saying "You're killing me, you're killing me."

After an eternity, Allen Koenigsburg emerged from the elevator and introduced himself. If Rose was the successful version of me; Koenigsburg was Rose at twenty-five. He was a younger version of me in an alternate universe. He even had a trendy goatee like the "evil" Spock on the old *Star Trek*. He wore a suit and tie, the upgraded version of my court outfit in Santa Fe. How could he afford to dress like that on an assistant's salary?

Allen escorted me into a cramped elevator, even smaller than a jail sally-port. He frowned. "What's with the two briefcases?"

"I have a lot of material," I said.

"I don't think you'll get to it all today."

He had a bulge under his pant leg. "You have an ankle bracelet," I said. I can spot them from a mile away.

His face reddened. "You're the only person who's noticed it."

"Do they know?"

"I hope not." He might have been me in an alternative universe, but never going to jail made him a lot wimpier than me.

"I'll keep that in mind," I said. "Does this place represent anyone in *Desert Demons*?"

"That's one of the biggest shoots ever. Everyone in town has a piece. We've got the writer, and a lot of below-the-line people."

"I'll keep that in mind, too."

Allen walked me through a maze of cubicles to Saul Podell's office. It looked more like a telemarketing firm than the most powerful agency in the world. For a power player in Beverly Hills, Saul's office was smaller than my office as a public defender in a small town. I even had a better view of the mountains out my window.

Saul didn't look like a Hollywood player. He could pass for an insurance agent in his gray suit and red tie. My scripts were just big health-insurance policies to him. If my work was good, he got to keep his job during the next shake-up.

Saul introduced me to the producer whose name I didn't catch. I was too nervous. That producer looked barely twenty-two. Jonny Braun, the guy who worked in the sex shop in Crater, could be his twin, right down to the ADD.

"What have you got?" the producer asked, not even bothering to introduce himself. He looked at me with disdain, much like Braun looked at someone asking for a fetish video.

"It's like the old series *Northern Exposure*, but with a lawyer in New Mexico rather than a doctor in Alaska." I told how my book was about my true-life experiences as a public defender in a small town.

The ADD-addled producer frowned and pretended to speed-read the script. "Where's it set again? Mexico?"

"New Mexico." I couldn't help but be cute. "We're the new and improved Mexico."

"New Mexico? I got your New Mexico right here." He grabbed his crotch. "Do you have any idea how the whole *Desert Demons* fiasco is screwing all of our clients?"

"I've heard."

"Why do you write about lawyers?"

"I'm a criminal defense lawyer. I'm still practicing."

I knew what was coming next. "Lawyers are out," he said.

"Story is always in," I said. "Character is always in."

"One thing I never get is how you can defend someone you know is guilty."

"It's weird, but I once sent in a script and a producer said it wasn't compelling and the characters seemed clichéd and stupid. By amazing coincidence, a lot of my clients are not particularly compelling, and in fact *are* clichéd and stupid."

The producer didn't smile. "Couldn't we make him a small-town guy who comes to the big city to be a prosecutor?"

"I don't know. My book is about a small-town defense lawyer. That's what I was. That's what I know. I guess I could set it in Arizona. I kinda know Arizona. As long as there's an honorable defense attorney in there somewhere, we can make the main focus be on the prosecutor."

"We could make it in Texas."

"Texas could work," I said. "I've thought about Marfa."

"Marfa?"

"It's this small town, kinda near the border in West Texas. It's famous for the mysterious Marfa lights."

"The Marfa lights?" He stared blankly. "I was thinking more like Houston or Dallas."

"Houston? Houston is a city of like five million people. I've only been there once. I don't know Houston at all. I don't think you get it. Houston is not exactly sagebrush country. Same with Dallas."

"You heard of the Dallas *Cowboys*?" the producer asked.

"I don't think any of them are actively involved in the ranching industry."

The producer frowned as he scanned the back cover of my book. "And he's a defense attorney? A public defender? Could you make him a rich private attorney? Or maybe a prosecutor?"

I felt nauseated. If my blood was tested I'd be way beyond the legal limit for caffeine. "Again, I don't know what it's like to be a prosecutor. I try to find one good thing about every client. The lawyer's journey is the realization that criminals are people too."

The producer frowned, as if I had just returned soiled pornography to a video store. "But criminals *aren't* people," he said. "They're shit. You ever get robbed?"

"Yeah. A conservative is a liberal who's been mugged, but—"

"Your lawyer, he'll always defend innocent people, right? Like Matlock? Or maybe just hot chicks?"

"Well, no. His clients are usually guilty. He loses more than he wins, but he learns something along the way," I said.

"Learning something along the way is so *out* this season. If you want to send a message—"

"Use Western Union," I said. He looked shocked that I knew Samuel Goldwyn. I almost quoted him William Goldman's "Nobody knows anything," but decided to wait.

I didn't know Hollywood got this quiet. I prayed for an earthquake to end this meeting.

"Do you have anything else?" he said at last.

I looked at the briefcase. You've heard of the *Treasure of Sierra Madre*? Inside, I had *The Screenplay of Sierra Madre*, analogous to the gold mine that had tempted Humphrey Bogart in the old film. After all, I had ten million dollars in my briefcase.

No, I couldn't, just couldn't. Oh, what the hell.

"How about a judge's daughter gets kidnapped and an ordinary guy, a loser like me, is the bag-man?"

I started to hum, "I am the bag-man," to the Toons of *I Am the Walrus.*

"I'm listening," the producer said. He stared at the briefcase as I picked it up. Maybe he could really smell money.

"So the guy has millions in a briefcase, and has to deliver it somewhere or the kid is killed."

The producer smiled. "Please tell me it doesn't take place in New Mexico."

"No," I said with a smile. "The big finish takes place right here in Beverly Hills, right down the street."

He nodded. "That could work."

Just then my phone rang. I looked at the producer. "I have to take this."

"Huh?" The producer shook his head with disbelief. No one took calls during a meeting with him.

"I said I have to take this." I felt like a bad-ass. I just told a powerful agent and producer that my call was more important than this meeting.

"Yes?" I said.

"Shepard, it's time." The voice was electronically altered, like Darth Vader's collection agency. "Leave the building and walk north on El Camino Street."

"Do I take the briefcase?"

"How are we going to do an exchange if you don't take the briefcase?" Darth asked.

The caller clicked off. The producer kept considering the pitch. "How about if he's with this beautiful girl?"

I had one minute max to keep on pitching and close the sale.

Always be closing. "That could work. Could she be Indian or Es-kimo?"

"No, make her Asian. The re-sale market in China and Japan is working."

"I can see an Asian girl in it," I said. "But she gets killed at the end of Act I."

"Okay," he said. "As long as she's hot."

"She's hot. Maybe he meets a mysterious Russian chick." I cleared my throat. "Get one of those hot Russian models."

"I see it," he said. "I'm dating a Ukrainian chick, she could star in it."

I wanted to close the deal right there, but I couldn't fuck this up. "I'm sorry, but I really have to go."

I took both briefcases, and headed out the door.

Allen hurried out after me. "You asshole," he said as I waited by the elevator.

Suddenly the receptionist called him back. The producer wanted to talk to him. I kept walking. Allen motioned to me that he wanted me to call him later.

Sometimes, being an asshole is a great negotiating tool.

RANSOM RODEO

I WALKED UP EL CAMINO Street to the bustle of six lanes of Wilshire Boulevard. While I waited on the corner, swarthy drug-lord types passed me by in both directions. Everyone in Beverly Hills could pass for a kidnapper these days. They all avoided eye contact.

What was I supposed to do? My gaze darted around. My God, a real live Rolls Royce waited at the stop light. I didn't know Rolls Royce existed after the movie *Sunset Boulevard*.

The phone rang again. Private number. I picked up.

"Cross the street and head up Rodeo Drive."

Click.

I was a little slow getting across, and didn't make it before the light turned. The driver of the Rolls honked at me. "Watch where you're going, asshole!"

I hurried up Rodeo. I had been away from money for way too long. Rodeo Drive made Santa Fe seem like Crater County.

The rich are different from you and me, F. Scott Fitzgerald once wrote. Technically I *was* rich at that moment. I had millions in cash in one briefcase and maybe a million-dollar script in the other. I sure felt different.

No, F. Scott Fitzgerald could not write about me in the literary afterlife. I'd always be this sweaty guy from Albuquerque. I flashed an Eddie Murphy smile, right out of *Beverly Hills Cop*, but stopped myself. I felt far more comfortable in the jail than here. My clients there at least returned my phone calls. Here the only people who called me were kidnappers.

Sure enough, my phone rang again. "Go into the first store on your right."

Click.

I went into a high-end woman's shoe store. I could always use the heels as a weapon if necessary. Why would they choose a women's store? I stuck out like a sore thumb. My phone rang.

"Your *other* right."

Click.

Embarrassed, I nodded once to a woman who was eyeing me skeptically from behind a counter, and left.

"Now go to the men's department of the Armani store and try on suits."

• • • • •

A woman greeted me on the second floor of the Armani store. "Can I help you today, sir?" she asked icily in an English accent that was positively Royal. "My name is Victoria." Then she stared at me. "You used to work in Santa Fe for like five minutes."

Victoria had been a secretary in my old firm. She was short, but incredibly athletic. She used her nipples like accessories. I forced myself to make eye contact.

"Are you still a lawyer there?" she asked.

"Hopefully not after today," I said. "I just had a meeting at a big agency."

"Well, we've got the new Armani suits today so you can dress like you've made it."

"I haven't made it just yet," I said. I looked around, where was I supposed to go?

The place suddenly filled up with potential kidnappers: Eurotrash, well-dressed Persians, and Asians. I had to stop my xenophobia, but everyone acted suspiciously, glancing around in all directions as if they were looking for undercover cops. Did Armani have a kidnapper special for shiny kryptonite suits or designer ski masks? Needless to say, Victoria recovered her composure and snagged the new arrivals like big fish.

My phone rang.

"Don't say another word," the voice said. "Take a suit"

"Which suit?"

"The most expensive one. It doesn't matter. Change into the suit in the third changing room. Leave the briefcase when you're done."

I picked the most expensive suit and a lavender tie. Dew was Laser Geisha Lavender after all. When I sat down in the changing room, I considered dashing off with the money down the back stairs. I would look like a drug lord's *consigliore*. The Mexican border was only two hours away; perhaps I could get a job on the other side.

Washington specifically told me not to try any funny business. The FBI would kill me if the kidnappers didn't. Besides, I had to do it for Dew.

I followed the instructions to the letter and changed into the suit while staring at the briefcase. This was it. I double-checked to make sure I left the correct case, and then checked again.

"I know you're watching me," I said out loud to the mirror.

The mirror didn't reply.

• • • • •

After exiting onto the floor, I glanced back to the changing room. None of the Eurotrash people entered the room. Satisfied that I might survive the next five seconds, I finally checked myself out in the mirror. Not bad. The lavender tie reeked of star-power.

Could there be a male Laser Geisha?

Unfortunately, I had to revert to my mortal form, back to my sweaty clothes. Inside the changing room the briefcase was gone. I hadn't seen anyone go in or out.

Mission accomplished?

I said a silent prayer for Dew, and then walked outside onto the floor.

Victoria smiled. "You seem so much happier than when you had that job in Santa Fe," she said. "It's like you belong here."

"I doubt that," I said.

"What *else* can I get for you today?" she asked. "Is there anyone you'd like to buy a gift for?"

What to get Dew when and if she got out? God, I hoped she would be all right. "I'll get that lavender handkerchief."

"Cash or charge?"

It was the cheapest thing in the store, but still nearly bankrupted me. Maybe I should have taken some money out of the briefcase after all.

• • • • •

I walked south on Rodeo Drive. The money was gone, but at least I had a new handkerchief if I sneezed.

Now what?

I was just the bag-man. What do you call the bag-man after you drop off the bag? The used man? I'd better go see if I could salvage the morning.

I returned to the agency and asked the French receptionist to get Allen Koenigsburg one more time. He came down immediately.

"So have you come to your senses?"

"Let's go outside for a minute."

"I only have a minute or my boss will kill me."

We stood outside on El Camino. The only people nearby were the smokers.

"Is there anything unusual about the *Desert Demons* shoot?"

"What do you mean?" he asked. "Other than the fact that it's closing this week."

"Did they bill stuff to the movie?"

He laughed. "Dude, that's a three hundred million dollar movie. We got people billing stuff on *other* movies to *Desert Demons.*"

"Can you get me the records?"

"What are you going to do, tell my boss I'm on electronic monitoring for a DWI?" He laughed.

"I guess so." I hadn't considered blackmail, but why not? I thought of every bad thing that had happened to my clients. "Dude, I don't mean to be a dick here, but I can find your electronic monitoring tracker and make an anonymous phone call."

"So?"

"I had a guy do a nine year spread just because someone saw him with a friend doing coke. Have you ever been with someone who had drugs on them? Just being with someone like that would be enough to bust your ass. You ever been in county?"

Technically, I had saved Cody Coca from nine years for something similar, but he didn't need to know that. He looked into my eyes. He was afraid of me, but not scared enough.

"And if *Legal Coyote* goes as a series, I'll make sure you get a producer credit."

"I'll see what I can do."

• • • • •

As I went back to the underground parking lot, I realized I didn't get my parking validated.

PURGATORY ON CONCOURSE C

MORE CARS LINED THE 405 back to L.A.X. than existed in the entire state. I was homesick for New Mexico. A convertible in front of me headed for the international terminal. It looked like Rose from a distance, but then again, everyone in Hollywood looked like Rose from a distance.

Could he be fleeing with the money to Mexico?

• • • • •

After I checked in the Porsche at the rental return and took the shuttle to Terminal One, I went through another wanding, then another. At first I expected Agent Washington to appear, but I just fit a profile: a man taking a one-day trip booked on short notice. The TSA agent actually grabbed my crotch. It hurt and I limped down the corridor. Would I ever be able to get it up again? Did it matter?

In the terminal, I finally reached Washington by phone.

"Was everything all right?" I asked.

"They want more money," he said. "I think they realize the bills were marked."

"You gave them marked bills?"

"It's our latest policy directive."

I sat down before I fainted. "I saw Gabriel Rose driving around."

"We know. Let's just say he's a party of interest."

I smiled. I'd let the FBI handle it from here. Fuck Gabriel Rose.

"Can I take the bug off?"

"Go ahead," he said. "You're no longer involved. The bureau officially doesn't care about you any more."

That hurt. Hopefully they would arrest Rose and this whole thing would be over.

Once we were airborne, my heart didn't start beating normally until we were safely over the Mojave Desert. I had to do something. Anything. But what?

Behind me two women were arguing.

"So are you finally ready to tell your mother about me?" one woman asked. "I mean, we *are* married in Vermont."

"She'll freak," the other woman said. "She still hasn't figured it out when I say my lover, and my significant other."

"Aren't you sick of playing the pronoun game?"

At that moment, I figured out a possible identity for Nastia's *lyobov*. Could Nastia be playing the pronoun game, too? I certainly couldn't translate Russian, but she never said anything about gender. When she said "fiancé," she could technically mean a man or a woman.

Who had I already met who could possibly know about everything?

The FBI could arrest Rose, but they still might not be able to get to Dew in time. I realized I did know someone who could help me find her—before it was too late.

DIAL V FOR MURDER

I CALLED THE MDC MAIN reception at the airport right around six o'clock. Double V was pulling an all nighter. "I need to talk to you," I said. "About Nastia. You know her, don't you?"

"You're not supposed to know about that."

"I need to talk to you as soon as possible. I think we can find the girl. This isn't about you. It's not about me. It's about an innocent girl who might be killed for a stupid movie."

"Let's meet at the truck stop off 98th street," she said. "In the café. I get off in an hour."

• • • • •

I met Double V at the truck stop right after seven. In the moonlight you could still see the sand dunes a mile away.

Bruce Springsteen called this the *darkness at the edge of town*, a malevolent force right near by. This truck stop was on the west edge of town. It could be the last place to gas up before Flagstaff, or perhaps the last place to gas up on the highway to hell.

I drank coffee straight up; she poured a Red Bull into hers and offered me a sip.

"Are you sure you should be drinking that much caffeine?"

"My mom did meth when she was pregnant with me and I turned out fine."

"Okay."

"Don't ask me about Nastia," she said.

"Is she your . . . true love?"

"I don't know what you'd call it; she meets a lot of girls in her line of work. Let's just say our paths have crossed."

She took another sip of her concoction and grimaced.

"I don't really care about you and her," I said. "But I think you can help me find Luna's kid." I said.

"You got one freebie already. I let you go back to the infirmary to see Sky and I nearly got fired for that."

"Look V, there's weird shit going down. I think you have access to a lot of information. You're going to have your own baby soon. Don't you want to save someone else's kid?"

Double V took another sip and washed it around her mouth as if waiting for a chemical reaction. Something apparently reacted in the right way. She smiled. "All right. I'll help you. Where do we start?"

"Why don't we start calling everyone you know?"

She smiled. "You probably know some dudes on your end."

She was right. I did.

· · · · ·

It took the next eight hours, and several more coffees with Red Bulls at the café. On her phone's Internet browser she could find out a lot. As a CO, Double V had access to local jail information, plus she had access to correctional facilities all over the state. We followed a few dead ends in our calls and texts, and became as tired as the truckers coming in for a break from the highway to hell. Still, with every call, we got once step closer to Dew.

Eventually we found a gaffer who worked on the *Desert Demons* set. I never got his name. Ironically, his girlfriend had spent the night in jail in Santa Fe, and she had talked with someone, who had talked with someone. Well, you get the idea.

"Yeah, I have noticed some weird shit on the Santa Fe prison set," the gaffer said. "They've got one wing closed way in the back. I think someone in the crew's actually living back there, maybe as part of security. Nobody gets back there."

"Are they still there?"

"As far as I know," he said. "None of us working on the movie can get back there."

A long shot, but it was all we had. V had the cell number of Gulley, a front gate guard at the Santa Fe joint who had just finished his own shift. "Let me call on my phone, he won't take your call if he doesn't know you."

She dialed, and someone picked up. She quickly explained the situation.

"Don't worry," she said handing me the phone. "He's cool."

"Off the record?" he asked in a Northern New Mexico accent when I greeted him.

"Of course," I said. "Did you see anything unusual last Friday?"

"You've got to be more specific. Everything's unusual. This is both a prison *and* a movie set. I can't tell the prisoners from the actors."

"Did anything unusual come in by truck? One of the movie trucks or vans to be precise."

"Yeah, these movie guys I'd never seen before came with a van to drop off stuff on the set. One of those animal carriers. I could tell by the breathing. They said it was a guard dog or something. They had the proper paperwork."

Dew was small for her age. She could easily fit inside a big dog cage. If it was indeed Dew, I hoped she wasn't mistreated.

"Did you check inside the cage?"

"I checked the first three and nearly got my head bit off. I guess I missed the last two. I'm not gonna get my hand bit off for this shitty job. Like I said, they had the right paperwork, so it was cool. It smelled like shit."

I had an unfortunate picture. They had locked little Dew up in a dog cage and smuggled her in. Bastards.

"You guys check everything coming out, right?"

"Yeah, and I don't think any dog has come out." He counted out loud, as if going through every truck passing in and out. "Nah, nothing."

"Aren't they closing down?"

"They're gonna do one more scene Wednesday before breaking. It's the big prison riot scene where Sky was supposed to get rescued during the riot. They're hiring like million people for it."

"Don't they need Sky?"

"Nah, he's supposed to be in a cell the whole time for this one, but then again, if they don't get him out to do his part then this whole riot scene is for shit."

"You'll search everything coming off the set though, right?"

"About twenty giant trucks will come out filled with all kinds of electrical shit," he said. "Let's just say that search won't be that thorough."

I half expected him to throw another "shit" in there.

• • • • •

After I hung up, I knew.

"I've got it!"

A hell-bound trucker looked over at me. "You win the lottery or something?"

"Better," I said.

"What's going on?" V asked.

"She's there," I said. "Still there at the prison set, in one of the back cells. I just know it. Hiding in plain sight."

I hugged V. Hell, I even hugged the sweaty trucker.

"So what are you going to do about it?" V asked.

"What am I supposed to do?"

"Call the authorities."

I called Agent Washington, even though it was well after midnight. He picked up at the first ring. Guys like that don't sleep. He actually was in the city of Washington itself, briefing the bureau in person about the ransom fiasco.

"I think that Dew is at the movie set."

"And you know this *how?*" he asked in a gruff voice weakened from kissing his superiors' asses.

"A lot of rumors. People have seen unusual things going on there. I think someone's got her in one of the cells back there."

He laughed. "Do you have any proof of that?"

"I heard about some cages filled with dogs that weren't completely checked."

On the other side, I heard him hit some more keys. "I'm reading our files on the movie. Those dogs were flown in from L.A. and then transported up to Santa Fe on that Friday. They had all the proper paperwork filed with the airlines and with the Humane Society people."

"That doesn't prove anything. They could have put Dew in the truck later. You really need to check the prison."

He laughed. "After Indian reservations, there are only two things harder to search. Know what they are?"

"No, what?"

"Prisons are one. These days prisoners have more rights than real people."

"Let me guess hardest place, the second is movie sets."

"No, they're even harder. Movies have the best lawyers. That fucker Gabriel Rose will sue the Department and me personally if we go on there without a warrant. We do not want to fuck this up just as we pounce. He'll walk. And prisons. Do you know how much liability there is if you go into a prison and somebody escapes? You have to get me more. I hope you realize we are investigating the link to Ahmad Assed, the emir. We don't want you to do anything to jeopardize our investigation. I get back on Wednesday morning. Maybe we can meet later in the week."

I hung up, dejected.

V looked at me. "You better go home. There's nothing more you can do tonight."

• • • • •

Nastia called me when I got home around one in the morning. "I'm proud of you," she said. "You're almost there."

"I figured it out," I said. "Double V is your *lyobov*."

Long pause.

"*Nyet*," she said. "Or as they say in your country, *not even*."

So much for my brilliant powers of deduction. "But she said she knew you."

"A lot of people know me. The Hollywood/stripper/criminal world is basically a few intersecting circles."

"That's for sure," I said. "You told me I've already met your *lyobov*."

"Maybe," she said. "I've been hearing things. You've been making a lot of calls to a lot of people. I think you're on the right track. It's like an open secret, but no one wants to do anything. They're scared."

"Of the mob?"

"Even worse," she said. "If somebody goes back there and screws it up—"

"They'll never work in this town again."

"You're going need some outside help."

"Duh," I said.

"One more thing," she said. "If you save Dew, I think it will finally be safe for me to come out of hiding."

"I'd like to meet you."

"Don't get any ideas. I told you I'm seeing someone."

TUESDAY
Song: "Just Three Words" by Trevor McShane

THE WAITING IS THE HARDEST PART

I COULDN'T SLEEP THAT NIGHT. Would I ever sleep again?

Thankfully, as I tossed in turned, my brain worked overtime to develop a rough plan. Obviously, Washington needed more proof. I thought of calling Luna about Rose, but she'd take it as a desperate attempt from me at being an asshole. I had no proof.

There was a McShane song "Just Three Words." What the hell were those three words? Give me proof? Save the day? Get the girl?

• • • • •

First thing in the morning I called the state cops, and they wanted hard proof as well. After all, I was a defense attorney. Worse, a defense attorney with speeding tickets.

With the FBI and state cops *not* on board, I called APD and asked for Officer Tran. "I think I got a lead on the kidnapping. I think Dew's in the Santa Fe prison."

"That's sixty miles out of my jurisdiction. You should call the FBI. Or the state cops."

"That's kind of a problem," I said.

"I need a warrant."

"What does it take for you to get a warrant to go out of juris-diction?"

"Probable cause," she said. "And that the crime originated in Albuquerque."

"Well, I know from an unimpeachable source that tomorrow at around twelve noon, an Albuquerque man is plotting—plotting right here in Albuquerque—a jail break on the grounds of the Santa Fe prison. You need to arrest him at exactly twelve noon."

"And just who is this Albuquerque criminal?"

Time to put it all on the line. I had nothing on Rose. If Dew wasn't there, I would go to jail for real.

"Me," I said. "And when you write up the warrant, that's Daniel Shepard with an 'a' not an 'e.'"

• • • • •

Tran would come at noon, and I couldn't let her down. It would have to be up to me, the little conflict-contract attorney. What the hell, I tried Luna, but her phone's mechanical voice said she was unavailable to take my call.

I was on my own. Or was I?

I had friends. They just happened to be criminals. Going through my contact list on my phone, I left a message with all my clients from the past week, and with the random people who just happened to call during the week.

Thank God the casting call was for prisoners; all my clients fit the bill. I called to explain the situation. I told them about Dew. The dog cage. Everything.

They were reluctant, of course. "Why should we help you?" each asked with some minor variation. "Why should we help Judge Looney Tunes?"

"It's not about me. It's not about the judge. It's about a little girl. You guys hate people who fuck with little girls, right?"

Tyler hesitated the most. "Leaving the county would be a violation of my conditions of release," he said. "I'm not allowed to go anywhere."

"You're right; I don't want you losing your million dollar appearance bond."

I knew I needed someone on the inside, on the production staff, to make it work. I called Allen Koenigsburg.

"Allen, sorry we got off on the wrong ankle, I mean wrong foot."

He grunted a sigh. "No problem."

"Is there anyway, you can make it out here and get on the set, do Production Assistant work for the movie? You're representing half the people there. Tell your boss you need to check on things."

"I can do that," he said, "but why should I help you?"

"Remember I told you about that big project. This is your chance to bring it to your boss."

"*Desert Demons* is the biggest project ever."

"This is bigger than that. Make sure you ask your probation officer for permission to leave Los Angeles."

I spent the rest of the day working up my plan. I would get my people to be extras in the movie riot scene at the Pen. I heard from the front gate guard again. Once he started searching all the vehicles with a fine toothed comb, no one had attempted to leave.

• • • • •

Despite my efforts, by Tuesday evening I didn't have much of a posse. No one had committed.

Alejandro summed it up. "Who wants to work all day for shit money on a movie that will probably never be seen?"

"But it's show business," I said.

"Everything is show business, *ese*."

I talked to Quixote and the Suffragette City cleaning crew. They cleaned all the major state offices.

"You guys clean the prison, right?" I asked Quixote.

"We just clean the historic part. The rest of the facility is off limits without all kinds of security clearance."

"I don't' care about the rest of the prison. Do you need codes to get inside the historic Old Main?"

He laughed. "Old Main was closed in the early eighties. Back then, one key pretty much fit all. It's not a prison no more, it's a movie set, remember?"

"Perfect," I said. "I need you help." I explained the situation.

"So what's your plan to save the little girl?"

"We're playing it by ear."

"Improvising?"

"I guess so," I said. "Some of my favorite lines have been improvised."

• • • • •

Nastia called me one last time. "Keep a look out," she said. "I just confirmed with my *lyobov*. He knows it's time. You'll meet him there. You'll know him when you see him."

"So it is a *he!*"

"Just find the coolest motherfucker up there, *da?*" she said.

WEDNESDAY
Song: "My True Love" (reprise) by Trevor McShane

ANYTHING CAN HAPPEN DAY

THE CAFFEINE FINALLY WORE OFF at eight o'clock Tuesday night, and I fell fast asleep. Given all the stress, I'd actually slept fairly well and couldn't remember my dreams.

Today it was all or nothing. Death or glory. Heaven or hell and five other clichés. To get the warrant I had to tell Officer Tran to arrest me. Hopefully she would wait until the right moment. I pondered my plan while shuffling through the most bad ass clothes in my closet. What did fashionable drug lords wear these days?

They usually did not wear ties with patterns. From a pile on my floor I picked out a black t-shirt that said "World's Most Dangerous Places" with a picture of a skull wearing sunglasses. My leather jacket made me into Fonzie with glasses; well, Fonzie when he was in the advanced acting program at Yale. I did have a ripped jean t-shirt, and since it was cold this early in the spring, I brought my Brown University sweatshirt, too. Maybe my character was sentenced for insider trading or something, a different type of bag man. People did go to NM state prison for insider trading, didn't they? I'll bet none of them required the services of a New Mexico public defender contract attorney.

Fuck sneakers. I went with the rattlesnake boots.

● ● ● ● ●

As I drove up I-25, I remembered an old movie. A quote from the old *Mickey Mouse Club* show had always intrigued me— Wednesday was "Anything Can Happen Day."

I took Santa Fe exit 599 to the east, then Cerillos Road south, and headed toward the prison. A line of pick-up trucks and low-rider cars also turned toward the entrance. A few walkers even hoofed it to the gate. Were they walking from Santa Fe or Albu-querque?

I paraphrased an old Broadway cliché: "You walked in here as an aggravated batterer, baby, but you're walking out of here as a star."

● ● ● ● ●

I arrived at the prison at eight in the morning. A private se-curity guard directed all the potential extras to drive pass the prison gate and park in a big dirt lot on the outside. The produc-ers didn't spring for a shuttle for the long walk. One entrepreneur with a pick-up truck offered to drive people from the lot to the prison entrance.

"I'm playing the drunk driver in the movie," he said, a strong odor of alcohol coming with his breath. He certainly was a method actor.

As we gathered in front of the gate, I saw the crowd could pass for an audience for a heavy metal rock concert. I recognized Left and Right from the fight. I hadn't called them, but somehow the word got out.

"How did you get out this time?" Left said to Right.

"My mama is dying again up in Espanola, so my lawyer got me a furlough."

"We did time together in MDC, didn't we?" Left asked me.

"I do go there a lot," I said with a smile.

Hell, the whole gang was here: Minnie, Tyrone, Braun, Benally, the Carizozo Kid and half a dozen others. Tyler was even there with his football buddies. All of them came over and thanked me for getting them out.

"I didn't think you all were coming," I said. For one brief moment I choked up. I'm glad I had the lavender handkerchief to wipe away a single tear. Back when I was at MDC that Friday night last week, I had feared that all my clients wanted to kill me, or worse.

I looked around and did some math. If I was the rattlesnake lawyer; I had now had a posse, I looked around at my clients; they had become the rattlesnake nation!

I had not had a single trial this week, yet I had kept Minnie out of jail for at least a few moments before she re-offended. Tyrone could walk again without that damn tracking machine. Cody could try to be a star. Benally now had nine years of his life that he didn't have before. And Tyler, win or lose, Tyler would be out in time to play football while he was young enough to blitz.

Seeing them here, made me feel like Jimmy Stewart at the end of *It's a Wonderful Life*.

No, I was Clarence, the angel. I had given them a second chance to do something with their lives.

I actually had to sit down for a moment.

"Well we thought about it, it's the least we could do." Tyler said.

"But you told me that leaving the county could get you locked up?"

He laughed. "I'm doing this for you, not for me."

Alejandro was there with his girlfriend Mia, the waitress at the club. She was going to play a nurse. "Sorry about Jen," she said.

"Maybe she's in a better place."

"Hope you find Godot," she said with a smile.

"I think I already have."

Maybe I did have a wonderful life. I checked my turquoise watch. Not much time with Officer Tran coming at high noon.

If she came and didn't find anything, I was probably facing felony obstruction of justice. Maybe a ten thousand dollar cash only bond. None of these folks would have money to bail me out if she arrested me. So much for having such a wonderful life.

• • • • •

After security gave us a major frisking, and then another one for good luck, we walked to Old Main, the historic prison set. In 1980 it closed as a functioning prison and the years since had not been kind. Old Main might have sprung from Harry Potter's world; the old prison might as well be Azkaban.

I didn't know who a woman like Nastia considered the coolest motherfucker up there. Every criminal tried to look cool in his own way. Allen Koenigsburg was ostensibly there as an observer for the Agency, but since so many other people had quit once the troubles started, the director grabbed him and gave him a blue tooth. He would be the production assistant for the day.

He sure wasn't the coolest motherfucker out there, especially since he chose "distressed" jeans and polo shirt. The director gave him the thankless job of wrangling the extras with the casting director. He sweated worse than I did.

"Form a line and have your IDs ready," Allen said.

A few shuffled out of line. "We don't need no stinkin' IDs," one potential inmate said.

It took about forty-five minutes of waiting before reaching the front. A casting director smiled at all the potential background actors. "I never knew we'd get so many criminals in New Mexico."

Allen grinned. "That's why we're not filming in Canada."

The people involved in today's production were definitely the B team. Most of the real players had returned to their mansions in Malibu; the locals with money had gone to their mansions in Santa Fe.

The casting director chose almost every person in line: Minnie, Alejandro, Tyler, a couple of his buddies, Tyrone from Estancia, and Braun from Crater. They would sign a release form and take their costume, a black prison jumpsuit. Minnie and Mia got to be nurses.

"Made it," each one yelled. Where was Quixote? We needed him if my plan was going to work.

Several "actors" already sported teardrops tattooed on their face to indicate they had killed someone. I put my teardrops on with blue ink.

When I made it to the front, the casting director gave a haughty laugh, as if she had just stepped out of a Santa Fe gallery, scarf and all. "Are you here to be an inmate?"

"I guess so," I said. I may have fooled the inmates, but I didn't look tough enough to the Hollywood people. "Maybe you need dead bodies or something. I can always be a dead body."

She pointed to a rack of mannequins in the distance. "We don't have to pay the fake dead bodies."

"Those look pretty realistic," I agreed.

"More realistic than you." She shrugged. "I don't know whether we can use you. You just look too *soft*. You don't look like a real criminal, boots or no boots."

"Look, I've been in more jails than you can even dream about.

I've probably represented a thousand auto burglars alone. I've had three clients go on to kill. I've fucked the girlfriends of two clients. I am a criminal lawyer, but I am really a criminal at heart."

"We've already got enough extras to fill a coliseum."

"I'm a gladiator leading a prison revolt. I'm Maximus."

"Don't you mean Spartacus?"

"Him too. I don't know, with the boots on, I just feel like a leader."

Allen stepped in. "He can be somebody's bitch!"

They looked me over like they were buying raw meat from an unscrupulous kosher butcher. "I can see that," the casting director said.

I signed the contract and the waiver. Hey, I might be somebody's bitch, but I was a bitch in showbiz.

• • • • •

My posse didn't need changing rooms; they changed into their jumpsuits right out there in the open. It was nearing ten. Time was wasting. Only days earlier some of them had worn similar suits for real. I stripped to my underwear. I saw the other "inmates" checking me out, so I hurried into the jumpsuit.

Allen wiped sweat off his forehead. He was a long way from Beverly Hills.

When I zipped up, I felt the polyester fabric of my costume. This was certainly not a Department of Corrections regulation jumpsuit. The writing on the back of the uniforms was Arabic. Apparently we were all prisoners in a mythical Arab emirate. One inmate who could read Arabic said it said "Assed," after the show's benefactor.

Just as the casting director stood up to leave, Quixote arrived at the casting table. I wasn't the last one after all.

"Sign here and get a jumpsuit," the casting director said.

"We ready?" I asked when Quixote made it over to me.

"We ready," said Quixote.

The light hit him just right.

"You're the one," I said. "You're the coolest mother fucker up here."

It didn't quite work, but Nastia had lied about so much, who knew what she was talking about.

He laughed. "I am if you want me to be. Give me a second while I check the keys."

• • • • •

I looked at my turquoise watch as the crew adjusted the lights, and then adjusted them again, and again. I tapped on the watch face with anger. To make matters worse, cars backed halfway up to Santa Fe, all waiting to get into the gate. They contained prisoners, law enforcement and probably a large number of visitors who hoped to spot a celebrity while they were visiting Daddy at the level five facility a mile away.

Some were probably still aching to get into the movie, but had just gotten a late Santa Fe start.

Each person, each car, had to be inspected thoroughly. My spider-sense tingled. One of those vehicles could be the one to take Dew out—if she really was inside. We didn't have much time.

Finally Allen called us into a large room, the former gymnasium/mess hall near the entrance. This large room could be something out of a Spanish translation of Dickens. Allen's voice was even squeakier as he scanned all the toughs. He was out of his element. So much for him being a real criminal with an ankle bracelet.

The gigantic prison guards wore black uniforms with Arabic lettering, and were carrying futuristic weapons at their sides. Was this movie set in the future?

"They hired real prison guards," one real inmate said. "That dude works over at the Super-Max."

I made eye contact with one and he gave me a glare so penetrating that I lowered my gaze. I knew a little about the Santa Fe riots from two books, *The Devil's Butcher Shop* and *The Hate Factory*. Truly dreadful things had happened in this room. A cold wind blew through, like the ghosts of angry inmates.

This was all second unit stuff. Anton, the second-unit director nervously checked the lighting, again, as if he was still in film school at the American Film Institute. The original director, the revered Lee Donowitz of *Body Bag II* fame, had gone onto warmer climes until the issue with Sky cleared.

"No one will ever see this," I overheard him say to Allen. "But fuck it. We can all use it for our reel."

"Is this your first feature?" Allen asked him.

"Not counting porn."

Anton planned the shot with a few guys carrying hand-held cameras to get that "cinema verite look." Apparently he did that in his gonzo porn work. His cameramen did a variety of stretches, as if preparing themselves to shoot from unusual angles. No booms. Apparently the sound would be overdubbed.

Anton got up on one of the tables. I wanted him to say something inspirational, like he was Henry the V and it was St. Crispin's Day.

"You might have heard that this is a troubled production," he said.

"No shit," someone shouted from the back.

"Well, I can't guarantee that anyone will ever see this. I don't know if the director will even see it. However, this is your chance.

If it doesn't make the film I'll buy the rights back and post it all on YouTube. I want you all to go for it. Give me a real riot. And I guarantee that some day, somebody, somewhere will remember this."

He then picked up a bag and opened it to reveal an Oscar statue. "I just visited Sky and he's letting me hold onto this while he's indisposed."

The crowd laughed.

"Normally I would ask you to do it for Sky, but let's face it; we all hate Sky High Roberts. But if a guy like that can get an Oscar, why the fuck can't we all get one someday? We won't do it here, we won't do it today, but just by being here we're all on our way. And every single one of you here today will own a piece of this someday!"

The crowd was about to start laughing, but a wave of good feeling passed through them. Why not? Everybody cheered.

Quixote smiled. "Ready to do some method acting, *ese?*"

I got the word out to my buddies. "Just follow our lead," I said. Each mumbled to the guy next to him. I could be back at MDC, except this time I was on the other side. I checked my turquoise watch one last time. It was eleven.

It was weird, in a real riot I would probably be a bitch, just like the casting director had said, but here in the land of make-believe, I ran things. I had street cred. I had juice.

I had a *posse.*

Anton eyed me warily. I didn't look like the typical inmate. He might suspect something, but he really didn't care. He would not mind if there was real blood. After all, he probably would take the next flight back to the valley to shoot "gonzo porn" when this was over.

They did a few master shots of us sitting and banging on our tables, pounding on the tables, demanding our food.

When we found out we weren't getting food, we started pounding for real.

I started to get bored and didn't know what to do about it. There was no way to escape, literally or figuratively, until shooting wrapped for the day. We really were doing time.

It was achingly nice outside. "Can we have jail outside today?" I asked one of the guards.

Through an open window, I saw a van go to a service entrance. If something was going down, it was happening now.

Anton stood on top of the table again. It nearly collapsed under his weight. "Okay, we're ready to have some fun. We're going to shoot the riot scene. For real. I want this to be high energy. Don't look at the cameras. Pretend you're really rioting."

My pulse quickened. These were real criminals. At the next table over, I overheard one guy say he just got out of prison for assaulting the "baby mama" of another. I looked at the fat second-unit director, and then at Allen.

Allen whispered something to Anton, who nodded.

"We have to do this in one take, so everyone keep going until I yell cut."

One burly cameraman murmured, "Fuck it, they'll fix it in post."

Anton turned toward us when he was safely out of the way. "Ready, set, *riot!*"

People started pounding on the tables.

"Action!" We all screamed with rage against the machine. I felt one moment of absolute freedom, like it was the last day of school, and I was actually going to burn the fucker down!

School's out for the summer. School's out forever.

My posse got into the spirit of things. For one brief moment, I became the angry bitch. I blamed the justice system. I wasn't a lawyer no more; I was a criminal.

Quixote pointed to the keys and swipe cards he had with him and I signaled my posse to follow. They nodded. Then he signaled to a cameraman, a buddy of his, to follow us, too.

"Keep shooting!" Anton yelled over the din. His eyes were getting wider. The riot was far more exciting than porn. "Don't cut no matter what!"

Anton was into it now, just like Francis Ford Coppola in Vietnam filming *Apocalypse Now*. Even if the movie never got made, if this scene never made it into the movie, he'd get two minutes of prime footage, a reel that would keep him out of the porn industry forever. Shooting porn was probably easier than this. You didn't have to wrangle so many people moving so quickly. Well, not always.

"This way!" Quixote opened a door at the far side of the gym and our crew followed, still yelling. The other "inmates" followed. We were in charge.

Quixote kept swiping the key cards with every door. Old Main had been closed since 1980 and had not modified the locks from the most rudimentary electronic system.

"Slow down!" the cameraman shouted when we got to a door. "Look nasty!"

Tyler flexed a giant muscle. Braun spit. Alejandro glowered at the camera. "Nasty enough for you, *ese?*"

We all taunted the cameras. Since there was no sound, it didn't matter what we were saying.

"Fuck you!" I shouted to the camera. "Fuck society! Fuck the American system of jurisprudence!"

Well, like they said, they'd fix it in post. This method acting stuff was fun.

"Keep going!" I shouted. "All the fucking way down!"

By the second door I wasn't anyone's bitch any more. Not Clark Kent, or even Superman, I had my own Justice League of

America covering my back. Well, the super villains at least. I guess that made me Lex Luthor. Lex meant law, right?

We roared down the main hallway all the way down to Cell-block E. Quixote had one last lock to crack. Private security guards rose in front of us.

"You can't come this way!" one shouted. He drew a weapon.

"You don't want to fuck with all of us," I shouted.

I had an army of darkness! Even better, I had a camera crew.

Quixote smiled, "You're in charge, *ese.*"

I was Spartacus, or Maximus. I was the Rattlesnake Lawyer once again!

I had been waiting for this moment my entire life . . . well, the entire week.

"Open that goddamn door or we'll tear you to motherfucking pieces."

The guards flexed for one moment.

I didn't back down. "I fucking mean it. I own this mother-fucking prison. This is the rattlesnake nation."

My posse, which was growing wilder by the second, stood behind me. The guards lowered their weapons and ran like hell.

Quixote hurried to open the door, glancing toward the camera.

Then we rushed the cell block.

• • • • •

Inside, Washington held a small figure with a hood over the head. He was putting the hood on. I didn't hesitate, I went over and pulled the hood off. It was Dew.

"Cut," Anton shouted from way back in the corridor. "Did you guys get all that?"

MOTHER AND GEISHA REUNION

THE CAMERAS KEPT ROLLING AS the New Mexico State Police arrested Washington. Officer Tran brought up the rear with her own force from Albuquerque. "Should I arrest you?" she said. "Are you the bad guy?"

"No," I said with a triumphant smile. "I've got your bad guy right there."

She slapped the cuffs on Washington with gusto. "I always knew you were dirty."

"Why?" I asked him.

"Why not?" He shrugged. "I'm invoking the fifth amendment. The ain't-saying-shit clause. Maybe I can get Shepard over there to defend me."

"I do hope you get a lawyer as bad as me," I said, "and that you end up sitting in one of the real prisons down the road."

"You're not that bad," he said. "Actually, you're much better than you think."

They took him away in cuffs. He didn't say another word.

"Why would a guy like that go dirty?" I asked Tran when she returned for my initial statement.

"Usually only three reasons," she said. "Sex or money. Or drugs."

"How do you know?"

"We've been watching him for quite a while, but we didn't know where he had hidden the girl."

She explained what they knew. Luna had spurned Washington for Gabriel Rose. Then, as a Federal employee Washington faced budget cuts that had hit New Mexico hard.

"That covers the sex and money part," I said. "What about drugs?"

"Washington knew Luna had access to funds from her father, who is a former drug lord. Those funds were tied up in trust unless he pulled some strings. He played all sides against each other."

"What about the *Insufficient Funds* on the wire transfer?" I asked her.

Tran smiled. "He must have realized that the bank had increased its security, and he couldn't conceal the transfer before he transferred it to his own account. Or he just wanted more money. Washington couldn't do this alone of course, he had to rely on other people, bad people, and I think they all are going to talk."

"Why did he send me to Los Angeles?"

"Simple. Washington thought of you as stupid and expendable. He got a few million, but that wasn't enough. Besides, the bills were marked, making it hard to launder them. He hoped to get more money from Luna's family."

"Who picked up the money there?"

"He had connections in the show biz community, no doubt."

"No doubt." I smiled. "This would make a helluva story."

"No one would ever believe it."

● ● ● ● ●

Anton had left the Oscar on a table, next to a security guard. Hell, Washington should get an Oscar for acting. Washington would have won if it wasn't for us blasted kids. This was like every episode of *Scooby Do*. Well, no it wasn't. *Scooby Do* always wrapped everything up.

There was one more thing. Nastia had told me to look for the coolest motherfucker up here. I search all over the set for Quixote; I wanted to thank him for all his help. Maybe it was Quixote, maybe it wasn't. I might never know for sure.

I went over to the guard by the Oscar. "Could I hold it?"

He laughed. "I heard about you," he said.

I didn't want to ask what he had heard.

"Pick up the Oscar," he said. "You deserve it."

I picked it up and waved to all the people. They cheered. "You like me, you like me!" I said, echoing Sally Field's infamous acceptance speech.

I had a tear in my eye by the time I heard the sound of a State Trooper car. It must have gone a hundred-twenty miles an hour, making the sixty-mile trip in half an hour. It screeched to a stop and Luna ran out. For the first time, she looked like her old self.

She was Luna again, the Luna of old. She wore white and the weight of the world had been lifted off of her.

Dew saw her and dodged between the two officers who were trying to soothe her. Luna dropped to her knees, arms wide and the little girl threw herself into her mother's embrace.

"Laser Geisha Blue!" Luna said.

"Laser Geisha *Lavender*," Dew shouted.

"There isn't a Laser Geisha Lavender," Allen pointed out.

"There is now!" Luna said when she finally released the embrace. "There always will be."

Where was Laser Geisha Pink? She should be here for this moment. She should be in that hug.

I had to sit down for a moment on one of the benches. A judge had once told a client no crying in prison, but what the hell. This was a movie set right?

I didn't know whether to be happy or sad. I felt so happy for Luna, but without Jen, this was still more bitter than sweet. I soon started bawling for real and wiped it away with the handkerchief. I didn't want my posse to see me like this.

Quixote came over. "Don't worry, it's cool ese."

· · · · ·

After another long hug with Dew, Luna hurried over to thank me. "I knew you'd come through for me, Dan," she said. "I knew I had faith in something. I guess I had faith in you all along and didn't know it."

Rose got out of his car, which had followed the state car, and hugged Luna. He hadn't fled to Mexico after all. He might be dirty, but he would get the girl, not me.

Luna and Dew hugged me one more time. Then they got back in Rose's convertible. He shook my hand.

"Thanks a lot," he said. "I was wrong about you."

"I was wrong about you, too," I said. "But weren't you about to lose a couple of million if the movie wasn't finished?"

"Let's just say that Luna is worth more than ten million to me."

I'm sure he had some involvement in this, but he seemed sincere when he said it. "What about the movie?"

He laughed as he walked away. "We'll shut it down. I've got insurance. There will always be another movie."

"Not for me," I said.

I didn't want to contemplate whether or not this was an insurance scam on his part. I would never know. At least Washington was getting his just desserts.

I stood there in the New Mexico desert as the car door closed behind Luna and her child. Rose drove the car out of the prison gates. Dew stuck her head out of the side to catch the breeze.

I was so very much alone. The crowd of criminals had changed back into their regular clothes and scattered to the four winds. If I was the president of the Rattlesnake Nation, my term was ending early.

John Wayne's character must have felt like this at the end of *The Searchers*. He had found the missing girl, returned to her civilization, but civilization wanted no part of him. I didn't have such a wonderful life after all.

Something was still missing. I took one last look, expected someone to announce themselves as Nastia's *lyobov*, but no one did. Nastia's fiancé didn't want to show himself after all.

Nastia hadn't made it here either. Security was way too tight. I doubted I would ever see her again. She'd be back to her criminal boyfriend, the coolest motherfucker in the world.

"*My true love*," I sang to no one in particular.

I was just a conflict contract lawyer with delusions of being a rattlesnake.

A real prison guard came over to me. "Sir," he said. "If you don't get moving, we'll have to lock you in for the rest of the night."

EPILOGUE – FRIDAY
Song: "Albuquerque" (final reprise) by Trevor McShane

I HAD NO MEMORIES OF what transpired on Thursday. No calls from anyone—not Luna, and certainly not Nastia or her *lyobov*.

Even clients' mothers didn't call. I actually missed them asking what would happen next. For once there, didn't seem to be anything happening next. My calendar was free.

I returned to MDC, in the late Friday afternoon, just like the Friday when this all began, two weeks ago. It had only been two weeks since the kidnapping. What a two weeks.

Back to work. Back to reality. Back to hell.

The PD office called in the late afternoon. An assistant needed me to meet with a former client, a female who had stabbed someone while at a treatment facility and had been transferred to the hard-core female pod, the Maximum Bitch Unit.

The last thing I needed was another maximum bitch. I checked my turquoise watch, I could still make it to MDC before closing.

"What's the client's name?"

"I can't pronounce it," the assistant responded. "They'll know when you get there."

Double V was back on duty in the pod. She liked guarding the women, but she still kept a wary eye on them. A female shank could take out your eye just as quick as a shank from a man. Or was that a shiv?

"We got a man on the unit," she yelled as I clicked through the sally port. "You got my home girl, right?"

"I guess so."

An obese woman waddled out of her cell. My new client must have looked attractive a long time ago, but she'd clearly gone through the ringer. She had shaved her head and it had grown back in patches. She had SLUT tattooed on the back of her head. Jail food never tasted good, but apparently she had indulged in a lot of it. Women sometimes used coke and meth because they worked like a diet pill. Jenny Crank they called it. This woman had gone off the crank and mainlined on the prison's bologna sandwiches. Would that make her a Joanie Baloney?

"Hi, I'm your new lawyer," I said.

I know you," she said at last.

"What's your name? Do I know you?"

"It's Natasha, but everyone calls me *Nastia*, because I'm so nasty. Maybe I danced for you once at the Ends Zone."

Huh? *Nastia?* "You're Russian?"

"Yeah, my dad was Russian. He ran a moving business, cross country moving. Well, his brother did. I used to tell people my mom was an Eskimo, but she's really a Navajo Indian from the Crater Band. Like from fifty miles from here."

"Are you sure you're *Nastia*?" I kept staring. This was not the woman I had seen at the refinery. I barely recognized her from the club, but that was a few months and fifty pounds ago.

"I'm fucking sure that I'm me. I'm the only Nastia I know."

"Have we met?"

She smiled. "I danced for you once. But that was fifty pounds ago. God, I was so fucked up on meth so I stayed thin. I think you actually thought you had a chance with me."

"You just said your real name was Natasha. Isn't your real name Anastasia?"

"So I lied. Natasha is a boring name. Every chick in Russia is named Natasha."

"Wait, didn't you call me several times last week?"

"Call you? Dude, I been in lockdown in detox for like the last twenty-eight days. I don't call no one. They monitored me when I took a shit. I don't call no one."

She repeated herself like she was still on drugs. "I didn't call no one."

"So what is this all about?"

"The case?"

I was confused. What case was she talking about? "Yeah, I guess so. Tell me about your case."

"Some bitch mad-dogged me at chow and I was like, fuck that shit, bitch, so I shanked her ass. Now they're charging me with a new felony."

Something was definitely wrong with this picture. "Don't you have a *lyobov*?"

"You mean, like a girlfriend? Yeah, me and Double V had a thing. Everybody knows that. I was with that actor, Sky, for a while too, like back when I was hot, but that didn't work out neither. I know I gotta pick a team. And I definitely gotta stop running my mouth off."

I stared at Double V. She said she had known Nastia. That was it. I didn't press.

"Who was that girl at the casino?"

"What girl at the casino? Like I said, I been locked up in detox for like twenty-eight days until I shanked that bitch. I don't know what the fuck you're talking about. Let's just talk about my fucking case."

She didn't use the word *"da"* at all.

"You remember dancing for me at the Ends Zone?" I asked.

"I danced for lots of dudes, but yeah, I remember you. We

talked for an hour, then you gave me a big tip. I told the other girls about it, and one chick said you were a lawyer. I figured I could get some extra money from you, so I was going meet you at Starbucks, see if you would pay me to blow you or whatever."

"So why did you blow me off?"

"I got a call about another trick from my man."

"Your man?" I suddenly got excited. This was it. The magic moment.

But Nastia didn't sound magical. "Yeah, he like OD'd right after that. That's what made me freak out so bad. "

"Your man is dead?"

"Yeah, like for a couple of weeks now. He was just a pimp. What's it to you?"

What the hell was going on here?

My phone rang and Double V laughed. "Just answer it."

Private Number.

I smiled. It was the best possible time for the phone to ring.

"It's me." This time the voice wasn't disguised. "I heard you got the real Nastia as your client. I guess you figured it out, *da*? I mean –you figured it out, huh?"

"Who is this?"

"Are you ready to meet my *lyobov?*"

"He's here?"

"He's the coolest motherfucker in the whole damn state," she said. "Just meet me outside."

"Who is this?"

"You already know."

G-LOT

I HURRIED OUT OF JAIL. Doors opened up as if God himself wanted me to get out there.

Could it really be her?

Yes, it was Jen all right, alive and well standing there with Cowboy. I was so glad to see her I fell to my knees. It took a moment for my heart to slow down once I saw that left shoulder again.

"So that means your *lyovboy* is—"

"My *lyobov* is you, you idiot."

Me?

"How did you pull it off?" I asked between tears.

"Cowboy helped," she said.

He laughed. "My rez, my rules."

"Aren't you going to get in trouble?"

"Like I said, my rez, my rules." Cowboy smiled. "As long as someone doesn't really get killed, I can get away with murder. I could tell you about working with Tran who was trying to take down Washington, but you don't need to hear about that."

"That's amazing."

He got back in his pick-up truck. "I'll leave you two to sort it out. All I know is I'm the first tribal cop to bust the FBI."

• • • • •

I stared at Jen "Why did you pretend to be someone else?"

"Because they were out to get me. That's why I was trying to get out of town. I knew a lot of things, and I knew the FBI was dirty too."

"Why Nastia?"

"I didn't want to be *me* any more," she said. "She was like a dark side of me."

"I guess so."

"And besides, you said you didn't want to talk to me. I knew a lot about her. I met her a few months before, when I got back to the Ends Zone and we worked a few shifts together. One slow night she told me her life story before she got too wasted. Besides, you told me about her and went on and on. She's the hardest working woman in *HO* business. She knew everybody—from all walks of life."

"You spoke Russian?"

She pointed to a pocket Russian phrase book. "Think about it. I only used like five words."

"How did you do the shooting?" I asked.

"Movie magic," she said. "Sound effects, fake guns, the whole works. We had a few extras to help work it out."

"The dead body was a prop, right?"

"Yeah, they had a mock-up of my body already made."

"Who was the girl at the truck stop? I saw her again at the casino, and then at Crater in the courthouse."

"Just a dancer who turned tricks on the movie sets. That girl Mia, the one who talked to us in the VIP room. I knew her from the Ends Zone. I paid her a few bucks to be Nastia's stand in. She nearly ruined everything, especially when she got picked up."

"But still, why did you fake your death?'

"I was in great danger. I thought Rose was the bad guy. I knew Washington had been poking around the movie set, so I figured he was dirty, too. The way he looked at me at the FBI headquarters, the FBI could have locked me up forever. Don't ask why. Luna may be clean, but I'm not, well, not totally. I wasn't going to fake my death—until they burned my house down because they wanted me dead. That was when I called Cowboy. I didn't want to put my mom in danger. If they figured I was dead, they'd leave me alone."

"You said you lost your daughter."

"You saw my daughter. She is lost. She doesn't even know my name. She was lost to me in the womb. But this is the weird part," she said. "I went away. I broke your heart. I knew you loved Luna and I could never be her."

"So you pretended to be someone *worse*."

"I needed to see if you could like me if I wasn't a law student any more. You always said you loved me for who I could be. Well, I guess part of this was a test."

"You made yourself Nastia. She's even worse."

"No, I became Nastia because I didn't want to be me any more." She stared at me. "You don't know the half of it."

"I don't care," I said. "You're my *perestroika lyobov.*"

"What does that mean?"

"I have no idea."

Right there in the parking lot, in my car, we both wanted to make up for lost time, for lost life. I know it was "ghetto," but why not?

It was the worst possible time for my phone to ring. . . .

THE END

AUTHOR'S NOTE

I'VE SAID THIS BEFORE IN other books, I am *not* Dan Shepard. I have had a "conflict contract" and traveled all over the state, but I've certainly never crossed the lines that Dan crosses. Real conflict contract attorneys could have far more clients in a day than Dan had during a week.

All of Dan's clients are fictional; however the emotions are very real. The timeline of the books is also not perfect, and Dew grows older at a faster rate than her mother.

I began this book as an escape from a crisis and wrote a first draft during six weeks when my entire legal career was on the line. I made a vow not to look at this manuscript until a certain person died. R.I.P.

Many of the places mentioned are real—Zuzax, Estancia, Chilili, Valley of Fires, Trinity site, White Sands, and Carizozo among others. The village of Crater remains fictional, as does the Crater Band of the Navajo Nation. The people who work at the Metropolitan Detention Center are among the most dedicated correctional workers in America.

The Penitentiary of New Mexico is indeed a functioning movie set and *The Longest Yard* was filmed there. *Transformers* and *Terminator Salvation* were also filmed in New Mexico. Even the citation to the setting for the movie *Beerfest* is accurate.

Judge Luna Cruz is fictional; however there are indeed judges in New Mexico who will lock up attorneys for being late.

Thanks to all the judges in New Mexico for putting up with me.

As for Jen Song, she is fictional, but several women helped inspire her. AC, you started this obsession with Asian femme fatales. Your life could be an opera and I certainly hope it has a happy ending in Utah. To the late Jeannie Millar, one of my greatest regrets is that we will never write a script together. To Vel, you inspired Jen's ability to pick herself up from adversity. Kimberly Fisher, hopefully you can do a travelogue about the places in this book. And finally to Un Chong, I met you long after I created Jen, but Jen's heart certainly comes from you.

I began this book while my father was still alive. I rushed it because I desperately wanted to finish it before he passed on, but it wasn't to be. Dad, I wish you could be alive to read this.

ADVENTURES IN MONDERN RECORDING
(THE NEW MEXICO SESSIONS / CONFLICT CONTRACT)
BY TREVOR MCCHANE

THE EAGLE FLIES / Neville Johnson/Jesse Easter / East of Sideways Music (BMI) / Vocal: Trevor McShane / Guitars: Fred Sokolow and Jesse Easter / Drums: John Barnard / Bass: Jeff Abercrombie / Piano: John Barnard / Flute: Libbie Jo Snyder
THREE PLACES AT ONCE / Neville Johnson/Fred Sokolow / East of Sideways Music (BMI)/ Sokolow Music (BMI) / Vocal: Trevor McShane / Backing vocals: Merrily Weeber and Carole Dere / Guitars: Fred Sokolow / Drums: John Barnard / Bass: Jeff Abercrombie / Piano: John Barnard / Sax: Steve Sadd / Trumpet: Paul Litteral / Trombone: Craig Kupka / Horn arrangement by John Barnard
ALBUQUERQUE / Neville Johnson / East of Sideways Music (BMI) / Guitars: Trevor McShane and Fred Sokolow / Drums: John Barnard / Bass: Jeff Abercrombie / Piano: John Barnard / Sax: Steve Sadd
JUST THREE WORDS / Neville Johnson/Merrily Weeber/John Barnard / East of Sideways Music (BMI)/MerrilyW Publishing (BMI)/ Propensity Music (BMI) / Vocal: Trevor McShane / Guitars: Merrily Weeber and Fred Sokolow / Dobro: Fred Sokolow / Drums: John Barnard / Bass: Jeff Abercrombie / Piano: John Barnard / Violin: Sister Mary Margaret / Viola: Marvin Meadow / String arrangement by John Barnard
MESA (CROWD OF STARS) / Neville Johnson/Merrily Weeber/John Barnard / East of Sideways Music (BMI)/MerrilyW Publishing (BMI)/ Propensity Music (BMI) / Vocal: Trevor McShane / Guitars: Merrily Weeber and Fred Sokolow / Drums: John Barnard / Bass: Jeff Abercrombie / Piano: John Barnard / Sax: Steve Sadd
NO LOVE, NO HOPE / Neville Johnson/Fred Sokolow / East of Sideways Music (BMI)/Sokolow Music (BMI) / Vocal: Trevor McShane / Guitars: Fred Sokolow / Drums: John Barnard / Bass: Jeff Abercrombie / Piano: John Barnard / Flute: Libbie Jo Snyder
NEW MEXICO SUNRISE / Neville Johnson / East of Sideways Music (BMI) / Guitars: Trevor McShane and Fred Sokolow / Drums: John Barnard / Bass: Jeff Abercrombie / Piano: John Barnard / Sax: Steve Sadd
MY TRUE LOVE WILL SAVE THE DAY / Neville Johnson/Fred Sokolow / East of Sideways Music (BMI)/ Sokolow Music (BMI) / Vocal: Trevor McShane / Guitars: Fred Sokolow / Dobro: Fred Sokolow / Drums: John Barnard / Bass: Jeff Abercrombie / Piano: John Barnard
BLUE SWANEE / Neville Johnson/Jesse Easter / East of Sideways Music (BMI) / Vocal: Trevor McShane / Guitars: Fred Sokolow and Jesse Easter / Dobro: Fred Sokolow / Drums: John Barnard / Bass: Jeff Abercrombie / Piano: John Barnard
IT'S MORE THAN HEAVEN / Neville Johnson/Jesse Easter / East of Sideways Music (BMI) / Vocal: Trevor McShane / Guitars: Fred Sokolow and Jesse Easter / Drums: John Barnard / Bass: Jeff Abercrombie / Piano:John Barnard
THERE WILL NEVER BE ANOTHER ONE / Neville Johnson/Jesse Easter / East of Sideways Music (BMI) / Vocal: Trevor McShane / Guitars: Fred Sokolow and Jesse Easter / Drums: John Barnard / Bass: Jeff Abercrombie
SHE DOESN'T KNOW HOW MUCH I LOVE HER / Neville Johnson / East of Sideways Music (BMI) / Guitars: Trevor McShane and Fred Sokolow / Vocal: Trevor McShane / Drums: John Barnard / Bass: Jeff Abercrombie / Piano: John Barnard

HERE'S TO ALL WHO SING / Neville Johnson/Jack Tempchin / East of Sideways Music (BMI)/Night River Music (ASCAP) / Vocal: Trevor McShane / Guitars: Trevor McShane and Fred Sokolow / Drums: John Barnard / Bass: Jeff Abercrombie / Piano: John Barnard
DOUBLE TROUBLE / Neville Johnson/Paul Graham/Kevin Hunter / East of Sideways Music (BMI)/Wilder Than Music (BMI)/Astroglide Music (BMI) / Produced by Paul Graham / Recorded and Mixed by Paul Graham PapaGenius! Studio, Henson Recording Studios, Hollywood, California / Vocal: Trevor McShane / Backing Vocals: Merrily Weeber, Trevor McShane / Drums: Jeff Rothschild / Bass: Paul Bushnell / Guitars: Paul Graham, Paul Bushnell / Guitar Solo: Paul Graham / B3 Organ: Patrick Leonard / Organ Solo: Patrick Leonard

Double Trouble P Neville Johnson and Paul Graham 2010; all other songs P Neville Johnson. Learn more at www.TrevorMcShane.com.

Special thanks to: Cindy Johnson for always being there for Trevor; Jonathan Miller for writing a great book and inspiring these songs; Stephen Short for doing a superior job with enthusiasm, grace, taste and humor; John Barnard for doing his best to make this the best it could be; Jeff Abercrombie for being an excellent host at Thud Studios II and a superb musician overall; Matt Brownlie for his skill and patience; Chase Curry for his many excellent artistic suggestions and collaborative spirit; and Bernie Becker, the mastering master, for always doing a great job and supporting Trevor. Tony Rancich, who owns the Sonic Ranch, is a very special, kind and interesting person who was very gracious to us, and we will be back to do more recordings at this very special enclave. Major shout out to Paul Graham: "Double Trouble" rocks! Lisa Wysocky, muchas gracias for editing and designing the cover artwork for the book and CD, and handling the business of manufacturing. Finally, thanks to all tthe players and singers: we could not do this without you and look what we did. What a great team you are—what fun it has been! he players and singers: we could not do this without you and look what we did. What a great team you are—what fun it has been!

THE EAGLE FLIES (Johnson/Easter)
There's a whisper in the wind
There are murmurs everyone can hear
 There's a sense that surrounds us
There's a feeling everywhere
There is hope, there is light
And the eagle flies

There's a reason we are optimistic
It has to do with who and what we are
Where we come from and where we've been
And what we've fought for
An inner strength and faith
We hear the cry on high
And so the eagle flies
 It's no longer black and white
Not about who's wrong or right
Just an understanding that
In this world we're all together

On the same road ahead
To a better destination
And so the eagle flies

THREE PLACES AT ONCE (Johnson/Sokolow)
How can I be three places at one?
Seems like somebody is chasing me
When I am searching for my someone
Everybody needs somebody to need
To love, to hold them closer
To tell them it will be all right
When the sun is up I do my best
Maybe I'll have better luck at nigh

Sometimes treacherous
Often elusive
A complete mystery
I know what love is
I just can't find it
Or maybe it just can't find me

I need a witness who will tell me the truth
I've heard too many alibi
I could write a book about my ex lovers
It would only make you cry

I'm just trying to keep it together
To keep my wits about me
How can I be three places at once
Just tell me where I got to be.

ALBUQUERQUE (Johnson) Instrumental

JUST THREE WORDS (Johnson/Barnard/Weeber)
There's so much written and said
I can't keep it all in my head
There are three words of simplicity
Good things come in threes

In just three words, I'll be there
To let you know that I'll always care
Count on me when things go wrong
In three words, I'll be strong

In just three words I will understand
I'll be there with a helping hand
When the sun ain't so bright
I will hold you though the night

Don't be afraid
This is our day

You can say it too
I love you

In just three words, baby it's true
The first time I saw you I said
These three words so true
Just three words, I love you

MESA
(Alone in This Crowd of Stars) (Merrily Weeber, Neville Johnson, John Barnard)
Alone in this crowd of stars
On this desert night
Driving down the highway
But I'm still full of fight

If you'd just listen to me
Please think this thru
I've got your back
I'm In this for you
In this for you

Alone in this crowd of stars
I race on and on
Further away from you
You got it all wrong

Love don't come easy, baby
Not every day
And I'm mystified
Why you pushed me away.
In this for you
In this for you

Meet me at the mesa
It will be all right
We can make it baby
Just meet me tonight

Solo...

Alone in this crowd of stars
On this desert night
Just give me a chance
I know I'm right,
I'm in this for you
In this for you

NO LOVE, NO HOPE (Johnson/Sokolow)
No is not what I want to hear
No, get me out of here
No love, no hope

No love, no hope
The future could be ours to own
Instead you're gone and I'm alone
No love, no hope
No love, no hope

Know that I'm scare
Scared of what I just saw
Scared enough to cry
Just plain scared and you know why

All I've got is the moon and the stars
In my jail, the one with no bars
No love, no hope

NEW MEXICO SUNRISE (Johnson) Instrumental

MY TRUE LOVE WILL SAVE THE DAY (Johnson/Sokolow)
What if I'm not good enough, I don't know what to do
It's tough enough just being me, now I've got you
And this situation, over which I have no control

It's the same all over
My true love will save the day
That's what I believe, that's what I pray
Danger may lurk, but true love is gonna save the day

So here I go to give it all I got
I'm here for you, keep that thought
You can trust me, I'm your friend
We're in this together until the end

BLUE SWANEE (Johnson/Easter)
Blue Swanee, blue, here and tonight with you
Dancing on the river, the perfect thing to do
I say blue, Swanee blue, in this breeze so soft and cool
Aren't we luck to be living in this world

They can see our silhouette as the orchestra lay
I'm about to steal kiss, maybe they'll be amazed

Blue, Swanee blue, drifts on by under the summer moon
And we're just cruising on this lovely night in June
Blue, Swanee blue, everyone's a winner so we cannot lose
And tonight I only have eyes for you

Here we are and there we go dancing so slow
Holding you, holding me, here we go 1,2, 3

Blue Swanee blue, we tried and now it's true
We're bound to be together, I like the sound of me and you

IT'S MORE THAN HEAVEN (Johnson/Easter)
It's more than heaven
More than I could wish
Just to be with you
And how about that kiss
That tells me that you love me
It's just me and you
Together for a lifetime
In ecstasy, so true

Gentle in the softest ways
Strong and resolute
Always got my back, you say
Yes indeed you do
Each day is so special
All our skies are blue
The best thing that ever happened
Is the day that I met you

It's what I believe in
Faith imbued with hope
All that I had dreamed of
It's simply beautiful
Savoring each moment
It's one long holiday
Giving my life meaning
Always in all ways

THERE WILL NEVER BE ANOTHER ONE (Johnson/Easter)
There will never be another one
There is only you
And for all that has ever been done
There is no greater fool

I love you til the end of time
You will always be mine
Listen girl
I need you in my life

Seems like only yesterday
You were always by my side
I was wrong, confused
Say goodbye to my foolish pride

The promises we made back then
They still ring true
Listen girl, I have one love
A true one for you

The days are getting longer now
They come in every shade of blue

Let me prove to you how I've changed
For the better, all because of you

Let's take it easy baby, take it slow
Easy does it as we let our love control
Listen girl, this time it's for sure

SHE DOESN'T KNOW HOW MUCH I LOVE HER (Johnson)

She doesn't know how much I love her
It's something that has to wait
She's all I have, there is no other
But such is life, such is fate

You know, you know when you've met the right one
This has happened to me
But she is betrothed to another
There is no hope, she wears his ring

All I can do is watch from a distance
All I can do is hope for luck
That somehow, some way, someday
She will see that I am the one

In this sad story there are no heroes, no villians
Just certain facts, cold reality
I am in love with a beautiful woman
Who does not that I so feel

HERE'S TO ALL WHO SING (Johnson/Tempchin)

Never been kissed, alone with her cat
All she wanted to do was sing
So she did, wherever she could
Whenever she could
She gave it her everything

Scorned and derided by some in her small town
Hers was the dream that just would not die
As luck would have it, she got her chance
The result brings tears to any eye
There on the stage for all to hear
Is the voice that rings true with joy
God has given her a gift she now shares with us
What can you say, but "Oh boy."
Now her future is assured

Susan gets what she wants
So do we all
Some respite from our daily lives
Some hope, some happiness
Some laughter, some beautiful noise

Here is to her
Here is to life
Here is to what can be
When we open our hearts
When we give it a try
Here is those who sing.

DOUBLE TROUBLE (Johnson,/Graham/Hunter) (Wilder Than Music BMI)
Now Mary Anne she don't know Linda Lou
Love in a circle that ain't nothing new
And I love she loves me like I love you
I'm a leaving with somebody
But don't know who

Poor little me. more than I need
One and one and one makes three

I got double trouble, double trouble
I got double trouble, double trouble
I got double trouble, double trouble
An embarrassment of riches
Leaves me way beyond my wishes

I can't account for what you do in your bed
Some like to party and some sleep instead
In walks jealousy and paints the room red
Somebody's sorry and somebody's upset

Poor little me, more than I need
One and one and one makes three

I got double trouble, double trouble
I got double trouble, double trouble
I got double trouble, double trouble
An embarrassment of riches
Leaves me way beyond my wishes

I know that some would say
I'm just a lucky guy
But I don't wanna play
To love two love's a lie

Poor little me. more than I need
One and one and one makes three

I got double trouble, double trouble
I got double trouble, double trouble
I got double trouble, double trouble
An embarrassment of riches
Leaves me way beyond my wishes